Dee Williams was born and brought up in Rotherhithe in East London, where her father worked as a stevedore in Surrey Docks. Dee left school at fourteen, met her husband at sixteen and was married at twenty. After living abroad for some years, Dee moved to Hampshire to be close to her family. She has written eighteen previous novels including *All That Jazz*, *After the Dance* and *Sunshine After Rain*.

By Dee Williams

Carrie of Culver Road
Polly of Penn's Place
Annie of Albert Mews
Hannah of Hope Street
Sally of Sefton Grove
Ellie of Elmleigh Square
Maggie's Market
Katie's Kitchen
Wishes and Tears
Sorrows and Smiles
Forgive and Forget
A Rare Ruby
Hopes and Dreams
Pride and Joy
Love and War
Sunshine After Rain
After the Dance
All That Jazz
This Time for Keeps

This Time for Keeps

Dee
WILLIAMS

headline

First published in 2009 by
HEADLINE PUBLISHING GROUP

First published in paperback in 2009 by
HEADLINE PUBLISHING GROUP

1

Cataloguing in Publication Data is available
from the British Library

ISBN 978 0 7553 3958 7

Typeset in Palatino by Avon DataSet Ltd,
Bidford-on-Avon, Warwickshire

Printed in the UK by CPI Mackays, Chatham, ME5 8TD

HEADLINE PUBLISHING GROUP
An Hachette UK Company
338 Euston Road
London NW1 3BH

www.headline.co.uk
www.hachette.co.uk

Acknowledgements

As I have now been with my publisher, Headline, for twenty years, I would like to thank and dedicate this book to those people who have helped me along the way.

First, a special thank you to Jane Morpeth who, back in 1988, looked at my very first manuscript and suggested I rewrite it, which I did on a portable typewriter. She then arranged for an agent to help me, and I also bought my first word processor.

Dot Lumley became my agent. I wish to thank her for all the help she gave me in that first year. In April 1989 she phoned me and told me that Headline wanted to publish *Carrie of Culver Road*. I was over the moon.

At that time I had Anne Williams (no relation) as my editor, followed by Marion Donaldson. I would like to thank them both for all they did for me. Now my editor is Sherise Hobbs, who I am very happy with.

My agent is now Caroline Sheldon, and we have a very good working relationship.

So twenty years and nineteen books on, I would like to say a big thank you to one and all. Including Mr Tim Hely-Hutchinson for starting Headline in the first place.

Chapter 1

BARBARA SCOTT LEANED on her hoe and stared out over the fields, blinking away the tears that filled her brown eyes. The sun was warm on her face and she tucked under her turban the wayward lock of her dark wavy hair that always managed to escape, no matter how hard she tried to keep it under control. She gave out a long, low sigh and brushed away her tears as she remembered what her mum had always said: 'You mustn't cry on your birthday, otherwise you'll cry all year round.' Her dear, dear mum. If only she was still here. Today, Thursday the twenty-sixth of August 1943, was Babs's twentieth birthday. Lydia, her friend and workmate, had told her that on Saturday night they were going to the local hop in the village hall to celebrate.

Babs liked Lydia. She always knew how to

cheer her up. They had known each other for over two years now, both having joined the Land Army on the same day. They met when they were sent to an agricultural college to do their training, then on to Sussex, and had worked on the same farm ever since. Babs and Lydia were lucky to be on a medium-sized farm that with its small herd of cattle and fields of cereal and vegetables gave them a good all-round training. The farm's owners, Mr Johnson and his wife Edna, were kind and understanding and took them under their wing after all their male workers had been called up. Babs had joined the Land Army in January 1941 because in December 1940 her home was bombed and both her parents killed. She could still remember the fear she'd felt when she turned the corner into Green Street and saw that her home had been reduced to a pile of rubble. She knew then that her dear mum and dad had died, and was devastated. She was an orphan and homeless. She felt that her world had collapsed around her.

Babs came from Rotherhithe, south London, and Lydia from a place called Woodford. Babs only knew it was somewhere north of the Thames, and thought it must have been very posh. Lydia, a tall, striking blonde with blue eyes and a ready smile, was an only child and had been to a grammar school. From the start Babs was told to call her Lydi; her father always called her that but her mother used her full name. Despite their different backgrounds, the two girls were very good friends, and Lydi had proved a shoulder to cry on whenever Babs thought back to her old, happy life before the war changed everything.

Babs had an elder sister. Joy was five years older than her and along with her twins, who were three last November, had lived a few streets away from her parents. So far their house had remained intact, apart from some ceilings down and broken windows. Joy, like so many young mothers with small children, had been evacuated out of London almost at the beginning of the war and had been living in South Wales ever since. At first she hated it and was very homesick, but since their parents' deaths, she appeared to be quite happy to keep her children away from the bombs. Joy's husband Stan was in the Merchant Navy and had been almost all of his life. Babs liked Stan; he was kind and had always made her welcome in their home. She hadn't seen Joy since their parents' funeral, Stan was away at the time, so it was just her and her sister and a few neighbours who had survived that land mine who stood at the graveside on that cold, damp

January afternoon. Babs shuddered as she remembered that sad, sad day nearly three years ago. Her life now couldn't be more different. Busy working on the land, she had gradually learned to accept her parents' deaths and, with the help of Mr Johnson and Edna and her friend Lydi, had even started to laugh again. She wiped her eyes with her hankie.

Today the sun was shining and Babs was looking forward to dressing up and going out dancing. Secretly she was also hoping to see a young airman, Andy, who was stationed at the airfield ten miles away. She had met him a few times at the dances that were held in the local village hall.

Babs worked her hoe into the parched ground. Today she and Lydi were clearing weeds in the field behind the house so that the winter cabbage could be planted. She looked up when she caught sight of her friend coming towards her. Babs knew that in her rucksack there would be a flask of tea and some sandwiches and perhaps even a piece of Edna's delicious home-made cake.

'The postman's been, and there's a birthday card from your sister.'

Babs smiled. 'And how do you know that? You been reading my mail?'

'Course not, but who else would know it's your birthday?'

Babs shrugged. 'You never know, I might have a secret admirer.'

Lydi sat down. 'I suppose the King or Churchill might know and send you a card.'

Babs laughed and sat down next to her.

'You don't seem to have done a lot while I've been getting food and sustenance for us.'

'No, sorry about that. This weeding is hard work; the ground's as hard as nails. I got a bit carried away day-dreaming. Besides, look at me blisters.'

'After two and a half years they should have hardened up by now. Spit on them, I always do.'

'You sound like some old farm hand.'

Lydi picked a blade of grass and put it in her mouth. 'Ooh aarh.'

Babs laughed. 'Mind you, it would be a help if Mr J could get a tractor round here.'

'That would mean driving through the hedges. Besides, we've only got this job till he can get hold of the machinery, then he can cut the wheat in the top field. Then it's all hands on deck as we stack the stoops and help with making the haystacks.'

'I know. I like doing that.'

'Well, we have a lot of laughs with the other farmers who come to help.'

'I love this time of the year when we go off and

help at the other farms,' said Babs.

'These locals certainly know how to enjoy themselves when they get together, even if they are working.'

Babs smiled. 'Pass me a sandwich. We're lucky to get so well fed. My mum used to tell me how she would queue for hours and not really know what she was queuing for half the time.'

'My mother is still cross that she can't have all her goods delivered.' Lydi laughed. 'Gosh, this tastes good,' she said, biting into the thick cheese doorstep.

'Edna certainly looks after us.'

They drank their tea and settled back.

'What you wearing on Sat'day?' asked Babs.

'Don't know. I might wear my black skirt and white blouse. What about you?'

'Well, let me see. It could be me blue frock, or me skirt and blouse – you know, the only one I've got and that wants mending – or I could wear me leggings and gaiters. That would go down a treat.'

Lydi sat up and looked at her. 'D'you know, I reckon that could drive the blokes mad. They do say that men love a woman in uniform.'

Babs laughed. 'I was even wondering about going into Horsham and seeing if I could get a new frock. I've got the money and the coupons.'

'Lucky old you. I get through my wages and my own and my father's clothing coupons almost before the ink's dry.'

'D'you know, we used to be able to go to Petticoat Lane and get stuff cheap. I bet now you could get gear without coupons if you paid the right price.'

'I daresay there are still plenty of those types about. If only we knew someone who knew someone.'

'I expect there are plenty around if you know where to look.'

Lydi stood up. 'Come on, this won't get the job done.'

'Slave driver. Remember, it's me birthday and I should be treated as such.'

'You'd better tell Hitler that, then he'd stop the war for the day.'

'If only,' said Babs wistfully.

After their evening meal, where they enjoyed a special cake Edna had made for Babs's birthday, the girls sat on the swing that was hanging in the large oak tree and watched Edna and Mr Johnson's grandchildren playing.

'It's a pity Mr J's son has his own farm, otherwise he could be helping here.'

'Then we wouldn't be here,' said Lydi.

'That's true.' Babs knew that Edna worried about her husband's health at times and wished her only son could help out more, but he had his own farm to run. Norman's wife Iris had inherited it from her father, and between them they had built up their herd of cattle. They had two lovely children, Grace and Robert, and fortunately their farm wasn't too far away and the children often came to see their grandparents on their way home from school.

'That was so nice of Edna to make me a sponge cake. She said she was a bit upset at not being able to ice it.'

'And don't forget the bottle of elderberry wine that Mr J took out of his storeroom.' Babs giggled. 'D'you know, I feel a bit tiddly.'

'Well let's face it, you're not used to drinking.'

Babs closed her eyes. 'I wish sunny days like this could go on for ever.'

'I do agree with you, but it's not very practical. We have to have rain.'

'Oh shut up. Let me dream.'

'I'm looking forward to Saturday. Let's hope some of the boys from the camp can get leave,' Lydi said.

Depending on the weather, sometimes the planes from the airfield would fly overhead, and as they watched them, Babs and Lydi often wondered how many of them went out and never returned.

'I think a few of the pilots have gone on a course,' said Lydi.

'I know. I only hope those that can dance have been left behind.' Babs didn't want to know if any of them were missing; after all, some of them were just boys.

They settled down into a comfortable silence, each lost in her own thoughts.

On Saturday evening, Babs felt good after curling her hair and putting on her make-up. Since she'd been working outside, her skin had a lovely healthy tan. This was so different from working behind a counter in a shop. She'd loved her job at Woolworth's and her life in London. She would wear make-up and do her hair in the latest styles. She'd been a great film fan and tried to follow the fashion of her favourite stars. How she would have loved legs like Betty Grable, hair like Veronica Lake and to be able to dance like Rita Hayworth. Could she ever go back to all that when this war was over?

'Right. Best foot forward,' said Lydi.

'I only hope some of the blokes remember which is their best foot.'

'As long as they hold us in their arms and don't smell, that's all I want.'

'You sound like a right old tart.'

'Could be. Now come on.' Lydi pushed her through the door.

The evening air was still and full of scent.

Babs took a long sniff. 'I love this time of evening,' she said as they cycled along the road.

'It certainly has a kind of magic. That's of course if you don't suffer from hay fever.'

'Trust you to say something to shatter my dreams.'

'I can't help being very practical.'

'I know.' Babs grinned.

When they walked into the church hall, the local band was playing a toe-tapping quickstep. Babs and Lydi made their way to a seat and waited for their evening to begin.

Chapter 2

AS THE EVENING wore on, Babs and Lydi were danced on and off their feet. They were on nodding terms with a few of the local boys, and some looked as if they had just come straight from school. For others this must have been their first dance, and they were prepared to try the dances without any thought to their partners or their feet. There were also some older men, who hadn't bothered to bath but who had changed their shirts and slicked down their hair, hoping that would give them the edge over the young lads with the ladies. Fortunately some of the boys from the nearby RAF camp had managed to get the evening off, but not Andy, Babs realised.

One young air force lad called Billy, who had been whirling Babs round the floor in a quickstep, said, 'I've seen you here before. You're the one what's going out with Andy Harper.'

'I'm not.'

'That's not what he says.'

'What's he been saying?'

'Just that he fancies the Land Army girl he dances with, he reckons you're a bit of all right and he'd like to take you out.'

Babs was taken aback. 'Well he ain't said nothing to me.'

'Just wait till he gets back off this course.'

Babs smiled. Andy had told his mates he liked a Land Girl, but what if it was someone else? After all, he was good-looking and danced with a few of the other girls.

As they cycled back to the farm, Babs was telling Lydi what the young airman Billy had said. 'So, d'you reckon it could be me he's been talking about?'

'Could be. But there's a few girls from the other farms that go to the dances, and don't forget some of them deliver stuff to the camp.'

'I know.'

'D'you like him?'

Babs nodded. 'Not that I know anything about him.'

'Well just see what happens next week. Will he be back by then?'

'According to Billy he should be.'

'Well remember, even if this is wartime, keep your knickers on on the first date.'

'Yes, Mum! But he's got to ask me out first.'

'Come on, let's get a move on. We've got an early start in the morning,' said Lydi, racing ahead.

'Oh for a lovely long lay in bed.'

'You'll have to wait till the end of the war for that.'

'I know.' As they continued, Babs thought about what Lydi had said. She so desperately wanted to be loved. To have someone's arms round her to make her feel safe. But she knew that might not happen for a very long time.

It was early September and Farmer Johnson had borrowed the cutting machine and binder. All weekend the girls and men from other farms had been stacking the corn and helping to make haystacks. Babs loved the atmosphere, as there was plenty of banter and laughter. Edna kept them well supplied with food and drinks. But they had to stop work when the light began to fade, and on Saturday they were too tired to go to the dance. When they sank into bed, they each had their own thoughts.

Lydi, who was twenty-one, was happy doing physical work; this was something she enjoyed.

She smiled to herself as she remembered the look on her mother's face when she told her parents she had joined the Land Army.

'But you're not used to working.'

'I know, Mother, and it's about time I did. There's a war on and everybody should do their bit.'

Lydi remembered the huge grin her father gave her.

'You could go into an office or something like that,' her mother had said.

'No, I'm sorry. Besides, it's too late. I'm just waiting for my papers.'

'Well I think it's all wrong.'

'So is war.'

Babs was thinking about Andy. Did he really like her? She knew she was a dreamer, but she didn't care. To her, life was too short and she longed to find that special someone. Slowly a tear ran from the corner of her eye, as she remembered her mum and dad's love for each other. Why had they had to die? They were both only in their forties. They had been honest, hard-working people who had only lived for their family. Her dad had been on the docks since he left school at fourteen, and her mother had been a cleaner since Joy and Babs had been old enough to go to school.

Babs sighed and turned over. Although she had been working hard all day and had gone to bed tired, sleep just wouldn't come.

Lydi listened to Babs tossing and turning. It would be lovely for her to find someone to love. Lydi was happy to go back home to her family when all this was over, but what did Babs have to go back to? Her sister would have her own life with her husband and children. Lydi gave a little sigh. What would she do if she lost her parents?

A week later, the girls were ready to go off to the local hop again, and to Babs's joy she saw Andy standing at the doorway. With his light brown wavy hair, dark eyes and air-force-blue battle dress unbuttoned, he looked handsome and relaxed.

'Hello,' she said shyly. 'Did you enjoy the course?'

'It was all right. Look, me and a few others are going to the pub in a bit. D'you fancy coming with us?'

'I don't know. I'll have to see what Lydi wants to do.'

'Why? She ain't your keeper, is she?'

'No. But we always like to do things together.'

'Well, go and ask her.'

'So how about it?' asked Babs after she'd told her friend about the pub.

'Why not? It'll make a change to do something a bit different.'

Later that evening, when the girls walked into the pub, all the old men looked up and stared at them. This was a local with regular old boys who didn't approve of young ladies going into pubs.

'Get a seat, girls,' said Andy as he and his mates went up to the bar.

Babs smiled at some of the older men, but they quickly turned away and began talking to their friends.

'Not very welcoming, are they?' said Lydi, looking round.

'Well, we are in the country, and some of these old boys look as if they've been sitting here since the year dot, while we're just a couple of girls out with four air-force blokes.'

'Yes, and I daresay they think we're just a couple of good-time girls.'

'Opportunity would be a nice thing,' joked Babs.

Lydi smiled. 'D'you know, young Barbara, you are getting to be very wayward.'

'Yes, Mum.'

'Got you two half a shandy, is that all right?' said Andy, putting the drinks on the table.

'That's fine,' said Lydi. 'How much do we owe you?'

'You can get the next round in,' said Andy.

Babs was secretly thrilled. Perhaps Andy did want to spend time with her.

As the evening wore on, she couldn't resist trying to find out more about him. 'So you come from London as well?'

'Yer. North of the river.'

'Got a wife hidden away somewhere, Andy?' asked Lydi.

'No, and I don't intend to get one. Seen too many marriages go on the rocks, so I don't wonner go down that road. Besides, I only want a good time. Love 'em and leave 'em is my motto.'

Babs felt deflated. She certainly didn't want to be one of his trophies.

After a few more drinks she was feeling very light-headed, and every joke sent her into loud peals of laughter.

'I think it's about time we went back,' Lydi said to her.

'Don't be such a spoilsport.'

'Babs, you are showing yourself up,' said Lydi softly. 'I suggest we leave now, while you are still able to walk.'

'I ain't that bad. Am I?'

Lydi nodded.

Babs struggled to her feet. 'I was having such

a good time,' she said as they made their way to the door.

'I know you were. But you're not used to drinking and I think all the excitement has gone to your head.'

'Where's Andy?' asked Babs when they were outside.

'Gone to the gents. Now come on.'

'I want to wait for Andy.'

'He goes in the other direction, and you don't want to hang about waiting for the likes of him.'

Babs looked round and shouted, 'Andy! Where are you?'

Lydi cringed as an elderly couple came out of the pub and looked at the girls. The woman tutted and said loudly, 'This war is certainly bringing some of the worst people into our village.'

'We're only here to do a job,' said Lydi.

The couple moved on quickly.

'Now come on, Babs, behave.'

'Yes, Mum,' she said with a huge grin on her face.

'Will you be all right on your bike?'

'Of course.' Babs collected her bike and, together with Lydi, began a very wobbly journey back to the place she now called home.

Chapter 3

BABS SLOWLY OPENED her eyes, then shut them again very quickly. The sunshine flooding their room was so bright.

'So you're awake, then,' said Lydi, who was standing over her.

'What time is it?'

'Seven.'

'Seven.' Babs sat up, and then fell back down again, holding her head. 'Me head feels as if it's gonner burst.'

'It's what's known as a hangover.'

She sat up again, but this time very slowly. 'Why didn't you wake me? The milking. What about the milking?'

'Don't worry, me and the boss saw to that. Now when you're ready, breakfast is on the table.'

'Don't think I fancy any.'

'We've got a long day in front of us, so come on, show a leg.'

Carefully Babs got out of bed and, going over to the washstand, poured some water from the fancy floral jug into the matching bowl and threw some over her face. After getting dressed as quickly as she could, she very gingerly made her way downstairs.

'Good morning, young lady,' said Mr Johnson. 'From what Lydi here tells me, you had a good time last night.'

Babs gave him a weak smile and gently nodded.

'Come on now, girls, sit yourselves down and I'll bring in the breakfast,' said Edna, bustling around them. She was round and always smiling and had a rosy glow like the farmers' wives in children's books.

'Not too much for me, thanks, Edna,' said Babs.

'Nonsense. A young girl like you needs all the nourishment she can get.'

Babs looked at Lydi, who only smiled.

After breakfast and as they left the kitchen, Mr Johnson said, 'When you turn the cows out, watch the gates up in that far field; make sure they're shut. Joss from up the road said those evacuee kids have been leaving them open again.'

'Will do,' said Lydi.

'I'm surprised those kids go anywhere near the cows,' said Babs as they made their way to the sheds. 'I remember when I first saw a cow, frightened the life out o' me. I couldn't believe how big they were. Trouble is, we don't see a lot of cows in Rotherhithe.'

Lydi laughed. 'Now you look after them like a mother hen.'

'Well, they are daft old things.'

It was with great effort that Babs got through the morning. 'I'm never, ever gonner drink again,' she said to Lydi when they were sitting quietly eating their lunch.

'I've heard a lot of people say that, including me when I got my first hangover.'

'I can't ever imagine you having a hangover. You always seem so self-controlled and in charge.'

'I have had my moments. At least you can still ride a bike when you're drunk.'

'I wasn't drunk, just a bit merry.'

'Yes, I could see that. Now come on, we've got a lot to do today.'

'You can be such a slave-driver.' Babs got to her feet.

*

As the weeks went on, the girls' lives consisted of working, going to the pictures and dancing on some Saturday nights. When Andy didn't come to the hop one night, Babs asked one of the lads from the camp if they knew where he was. She was told that a lot of the blokes had been posted. So that was it, he had gone from out of her life. At least she hadn't let herself get too serious about him.

It was at the end of September that the girls were laughing as they made their way back to the farm after a day in the top field, both looking forward to their dinner. Edna was a great cook, and often the smell of something delicious would greet them before they arrived. But when they got back to the farmhouse it looked deserted and unusually, it was all closed up.

'Edna!' called Lydi.

There was no reply.

Babs began looking around the yard. 'The lorry's gone.'

'They did say the children might be over this afternoon. Perhaps they've taken them home,' said Lydi, going through into the kitchen. 'There's a note for us.'

'What's it say?'

'Oh my God. They've gone to the hospital.'

'Why?'

'It seems Mr J has been taken ill.'

'Oh no. Does it say what's wrong?'

'No.'

'So how did they manage to take the lorry? Edna can't drive.'

'I don't know.'

'Do you think Norman knows?'

'I think we'd better go and find out. It won't take us long on our bikes.'

As they made their way to Norman's farm, they were both terribly worried about the dear old farmer who'd been so kind to them. What would happen if he was very ill? How would they manage to run the farm?

They threw their bikes to the ground and rushed round to the kitchen door. Iris, Norman's wife, was sitting at the table with the children. She jumped up as they walked in

'What's happened to Mr Johnson?' asked Lydi.

'Thank goodness you're here. Is Norman with you?'

'He must be with his dad. A note said they'd gone to the hospital.'

Iris put her hand to her mouth. 'Sidney collapsed when the children were there and they ran all the way here to get Norman.'

Babs looked at the children's tear-stained

faces. She went over and, sitting between them, put her arms round their shoulders. 'Don't worry. Grandpa will be all right. He's a big strong man.'

'So Edna must have gone as well,' said Iris.

Lydi nodded. 'Norman must have driven the lorry.'

'Grandpa looked ever so funny,' said Robert. He was six and was a lovable boy with tight dark curls, which he hated.

Babs ruffled his hair. 'I'm sure he'll be fine.'

'He won't die, will he?' asked Grace, a slim, thoughtful girl with straight dark hair and big brown eyes.

'No, course not,' said Lydi.

'I'll make a cup of tea,' said Iris. 'I wonder how long they'll be there? I hope Sidney is all right.'

'Me too,' said Lydi.

'I don't know what to do if Norman doesn't come home in time for milking.'

'We can manage for the moment with our cows. How many have you got now, Iris?' asked Lydi.

'Twenty.'

'That's a lot of milking.'

'I know.'

'Perhaps Norman will be home before long,' said Lydi.

'I hope so.' Iris put the teapot on the table.

Babs looked at Lydi. 'Look. What say we have a cuppa, then we'll be off and get ours milked, and if Norman's not home by then, we'll come back and give Iris a hand,' she said.

Iris gave them a weak smile. 'Thanks. I'd be very grateful.'

When the girls had finished the milking and there was still no sign of Norman and his mother, they set off once again to Norman's farm. It was much larger than Mr Johnson's, with a bigger dairy herd.

'Thank goodness you're here,' said Iris, peering round the backside of the cow she was milking. She stood up and stretched her back. 'Would you mind carrying on here so I can put the children to bed? They do have to go to school tomorrow.'

'You go ahead, we'll manage,' said Lydi.

Iris stopped at the door. 'Thank you so much.'

'That's all right,' said Lydi, giving her a beaming smile. 'Don't worry too much about Mr J, I'm sure he'll be fine.'

'I hope so.'

Babs always admired the way Lydi could put anyone at ease as she took over the situation.

'What d'you think's wrong with Mr J?' She asked.

'Wouldn't like to say.'

'I hope it's not too serious. We couldn't manage the farm on our own. Whoa, Polly, settle down now,' said Babs as she patted the cow she was milking.

'I know. We could get help from some of the other farmers, but most of them have got more than enough to do now the government wants more production. Let's hope everything will be fine and Norman will be here soon.'

There was still no sign of Norman when the girls left. It was dark as they cycled along the country lanes.

'That was a lot of cows.'

'I know,' said Babs. 'Me poor little fingers feel like sausages.'

'It was nice of Iris to give us a meal.'

'I don't think she wanted us to leave.'

'It would be wonderful if these people were on the telephone, then at least they would know what was happening.'

'Don't forget that some of the residents here only had electric just before the war.'

'In a town, you tend to forget how some people live. I tell you something, young Babs. Even with a war on, I'm glad I live in this century.'

'So am I. And I tell you something else. I won't need anyone to rock me to sleep tonight.'

'You never do. And don't snore.'

'I'll try not to.'

Chapter 4

EVEN THOUGH THEY were both exhausted, Babs and Lydi couldn't go to bed till they knew what had happened to Mr Johnson. They were quietly listening to the wireless and for once didn't speak at all. When they heard the lorry come into the yard, they both jumped up and ran to the door. They could see that only Norman and Edna were in the lorry.

'How is he?' asked Lydi.

'Not so good,' said Norman as he helped his mother down the vehicle's high step.

'The kettle's on, I'll make a cuppa,' said Babs as the sorry bunch made their way into the kitchen.

Edna, who looked lost and drawn, sat at the large deal table. The kitchen, the hub of the household, was always warm and friendly.

'He's had a stroke.' Edna looked from one to the other. 'How're we going to manage?'

Babs took hold of her hand. 'I am so sorry,' she said, fighting back the tears.

'We'll manage somehow,' said Lydi.

'But how?'

'Don't worry about it now. Is the tea ready, Babs?' Lydi asked.

Babs put the brown china teapot in the middle of the table and covered it with the brightly coloured knitted tea cosy.

'How bad is he, Norman?' asked Lydi.

'He's lost the use of his left arm and leg, but although his face is slightly one-sided, he can still talk after a fashion.'

'They said that with care and exercise he could recover completely, but it's going to be a long road and you know how impatient he can be.' Edna gave them a weak smile.

'Well I reckon between us we can sort that out,' said Babs, trying to sound cheerful and upbeat when really she was terribly worried. Mr J and Edna had taken her mum and dad's place, and to her they were family.

'Mum, I must go.' Norman stood up. 'I don't know how Iris will manage. She's got all those cows to milk.'

'Don't worry, Norman, we did it. After we

finished here we went and helped her while she put the little uns to bed.'

Norman patted Lydi's arm. 'Thanks. You two have certainly turned up trumps. I must admit, when Dad first told me he was having a couple of Land Girls, I had my doubts. But you've both proved me wrong. Thank you.'

'We're not bad for a couple of townies,' said Babs.

'I'll send one of my lads to take you to the hospital tomorrow, Ma.'

'Thanks, son.'

He kissed his mother's cheek and left.

'He's good lad,' said Edna as she watched him get on his bike and stood waving him goodbye.

The following morning Edna tapped on their bedroom door. They were lucky to have a front bedroom. It was sparsely furnished but practical, with a washstand and a wardrobe that had a full-length mirror on the inside, plus two single beds with colourful counterpanes. A small chest of drawers that was old and had been painted cream served as a dressing table with a set of three mirrors on top. Apart from a couple of old painted chairs, that was all the room possessed, though Mr Johnson had put up some shelves for their make-up. It was a bright room with a large window that overlooked the farm, and Edna kept it spotless.

'Do you want help with the milking this morning?' she asked, coming into the room. Her grey hair, which was normally neatly pulled into a bun on top of her head, was hanging down and they could see she hadn't had much sleep.

'No, that's all right, we can manage,' said Lydi, who was up and dressed.

Babs jumped out of bed.

'Well, I'll get breakfast for you when you've finished. There's a pot of tea already made. Got to start the day right with a cup of tea, so Sidney always says. I'll leave you to get dressed, Babs.'

Babs smiled at her.

'She don't look so good, does she?' she said after Edna left.

Lydi shook her head. 'And not had a lot of sleep by the look of it.'

'This is a big farm for just us to manage.' Babs sat on the bed and pulled on her woollen socks. 'What we gonner do?'

'I don't know. We'll just take one day at a time. I'm sure Norman will sort something out.'

'I hope so.'

They both knew they couldn't work this place on their own, so what would the outcome be?

*

In the cowshed they were busy with their heads against the cows they were milking when Lydi said, 'Do you know, I think I should learn to drive.'

'Whatever for?'

'Just think what an asset I'd be. I could take Edna to the hospital and collect any supplies that were needed.'

'I suppose it would be a good idea. But who could you get to teach you?'

Lydi shrugged. 'I'll ask Norman to make a few enquiries.'

As the morning wore on, Lydi was getting more and more excited about the thought of driving and had been talking about it all the time they were working. 'When we've finished milking tonight I'm going to go and ask Norman if he can help me, or at least tell me the right way to go about it.'

They waved Edna goodbye as she got into the lorry Norman had sent, and told her to tell Mr J not to worry.

'We've got it all under control,' said Babs.

'You're good girls,' said Edna as her eyes filled with tears.

'Right, Babs, get on your bike. We're going to see Norman,' said Lydi.

Although they were worried about Mr J, they

couldn't help laughing as they pedalled fast along the lanes. As they went round a corner, they suddenly came face to face with a big RAF lorry. The lorry braked sharply but Babs and Lydi went careering into a ditch.

When Lydi picked herself up, she yelled at the young man who was walking towards them.

'What the bloody hell do you think you're doing driving so fast? You shouldn't be let out, you're a danger to everyone.'

'Sorry, ladies,' he said.

Babs scrambled out of the ditch. 'You could have killed us.'

'Are you all right? You've not broken anything, have you?' he asked, helping her up.

'I ain't, but me bike looks a bit sad,' said Babs. 'Look at it. There's some spokes missing, and Lydi's back wheel's buckled.'

He picked up Babs's bike and examined it. 'It does look a bit sad. Can I give you both a lift somewhere?'

'No thank you,' said Lydi, rubbing her ankle.

'I'll put the bikes in the back of the lorry and then I'll take you home.'

'I said no thank you. We can walk.'

'Do you live far?'

'No. But what about our bikes?' said Babs. 'We can't push them, not the state they're in.'

'Don't worry, I'll get a mechanic on the camp to repair them and then I'll bring them back.'

'When?' asked Lydi.

'We can't do without them,' said Babs.

'I'll return them as soon as I can. By the way, my name's Pete.' He held out his hand.

'I'm Babs, and this is Lydi.' Babs shook his hand. 'We work at Johnson's farm.'

'I know it. I've passed it a couple of times. Didn't know a couple of good-looking ladies worked there. Now, do let me take you back home.'

'We can walk, thank you.' Lydi began to hobble away.

'Are you in pain?'

'No.'

'Look, please hop up.'

'Come on, Lydi.'

Her ankle was hurting so she gave in, but Lydi was very angry with this arrogant man. As she climbed up into the lorry, she could see that Babs had a wicked gleam in her eye as she watched the handsome airman put their bikes in the back.

'I'm so annoyed with that bloke,' said Lydi after he had dropped them off at the farm. 'He stopped me from going to see Norman. Now I'll have to wait till he brings our bikes back.'

'We could have walked.'

'I know. But I was too angry to think straight. Besides, I thought I'd done myself some damage.'

'Is it all right now?'

'Yes thanks. I limped to make sure he felt really sorry for what he'd done.'

'Well let's hope it's not too long before we get 'em back. I feel as if our lifeline has been cut.'

'I'd like to cut *his* lifeline,' said Lydi.

Babs laughed. 'But you must admit he was rather good-looking.'

'I don't know. I was too angry to take any notice.'

Babs grinned. 'Look, we can go tomorrow to see Norman.'

'I suppose so.'

The following evening Lydia and Babs went to see Norman and Iris.

They were sitting in the kitchen, and after talking about Mr J and the farm, Lydi told them about wanting to drive. 'So, what d'you think? Could you give me the name of someone who could teach me?'

'I'll make a few enquires. I think it would be a good idea. Did you come on your bikes?'

'No,' said Lydi angrily. 'Some idiot drove us

off the road last night and ruined our bikes.'

'No,' said Iris. 'Did he stop?'

'Yes. He comes from the RAF camp.'

'So what happened to the bikes?'

'He's taken 'em to get 'em repaired,' said Babs. 'We walked here.'

'When you going to get them back?' asked Iris.

'Don't know. We feel lost without them.'

'I expect you do,' said Norman. 'Now leave this driving thing with me. I'll sort something out.'

'Thanks, Norman. Come on, Babs, we had better make our way home. Don't want Edna to get back to an empty house.'

'I'll drop you off. That way I can find out how Dad is.'

Lydi and Babs stood up and kissed Iris's cheek. They knew they were part of this family now.

At the end of the week, Babs pushed the cows out of the milking shed and returned to help Lydi wash down the stalls. They were singing at the tops of their voices when an RAF lorry came into the yard and Pete jumped out.

Lydi looked up. She was holding the hose and it took her all her self-control not to turn it on him. She went and turned the water off.

'I'm glad you did that. I thought I might get a shower.' Pete was grinning.

'Well you certainly deserve one.'

'How's your ankle?'

'I'll live.'

'I was worried about you both.'

'I bet.'

Babs came out of the cowshed. 'Hello,' she said sweetly. 'Have you brought our bikes back?'

'I certainly have.' He climbed into the back of the truck. 'Catch hold of these.' He handed their bikes down to them.

'Wow,' said Babs. 'They look as good as new.' She put them on their side stands and stood looking over them. They had been painted black, the chrome was shining and the tyres had also been painted. All in all, they looked great.

'The lads back at camp have made a good job of them.'

'They certainly have,' said Babs.

'What about you?' he asked Lydi. 'Aren't you impressed?'

'With the work your servants have done, yes, but not with you.'

'Look, I'm really sorry. Please let me take you both out one evening,' he said, looking long and hard at Babs.

'That would—' Babs didn't get a chance to finish as Lydi interrupted.

'No thank you.'

Babs looked at her with daggers.

'In that case, ladies, I'll say goodbye.' He turned and walked away.

'How could you?' said Babs. 'We was going to have a night out.'

Lydi also walked away, leaving Babs fuming.

Babs turned and walked up to the lorry. 'Pete,' she called out.

He opened the door. 'I seem to have upset your friend.'

'Look. We would love to come out with you.'

'Are you sure?' He looked excited.

Babs glanced at the door Lydi had gone through. 'Yes.'

Pete smiled, showing even white teeth against his slightly tanned skin. 'That's great. I'll pick you up about eight tomorrow, is that all right?'

'That'll be fine. Do we need to dress up?'

'Why not. I'll take you both to a restaurant in Horsham. Perhaps that will help to heal the rift.'

'We going in this?' She pointed to the lorry.

'No. I'll collect you in my car.'

'Good. See you tomorrow.' She closed the lorry's door and watched him drive away. Now she had to face Lydi.

*

'What!'

'I said we would go out with him tomorrow.'

'Well I'm not going.'

'Oh Lydi. Don't be mean. He's taking us in his car to a restaurant in Horsham. What could be better than that?'

'Him *not* taking us out.'

'He is trying to put things right.'

'You can go.'

'You know I won't go without you. He is so good-looking *and* he's a machine-gunner. Did you see his badge?'

'I did notice.'

'What, that he was good-looking?'

'No. That he was a machine-gunner.'

'Oh come on, it'll be fun, and I'm sure Edna and Mr J would want us to. Besides, he might have a posh car.'

'I suppose we could do with a night out, especially if he's paying.'

Babs threw her arms round her friend. 'Good.'

'So you've got over Andy, then?'

'That wasn't serious. He was all right for a dance and a drink, but I didn't want to be another notch on his bedpost. Now Pete does look rather nice.'

'Miss Scott, you are a downright hussy.'

'I know, and just in case you hadn't noticed,

there is a war on and they do say that all's fair in love and war.'

'Babs, don't get too fond of him. He might be posted soon and then where would you be?'

'Yes, Mum,' said Babs, laughing and walking away. But deep down she wasn't laughing. She knew you shouldn't get too fond of anyone during this war. They could suddenly be taken from you.

Chapter 5

EDNA WAS REALLY pleased when she heard the girls were going out. 'And with a lad from the camp. You said he's taking you for a meal?'

'Yes, so there's no need for you to cook tonight,' said Babs.

'It'll do you good. Sidney's very worried about you. When Norman visits him on Sunday he's going to ask him about getting you some help.'

'Thank goodness the haymaking is finished,' said Babs, draining her welcome cuppa.

'I asked Norman if he knows anyone who could teach me to drive a car,' said Lydi. 'We both know how to drive a tractor, but I think a car might be a bit different, and besides, you have to have a licence.'

'I'm sure Norman will be able to help you. Are you going to buy a car?'

'Not yet, but I would like to one day.'

'I think the petrol rationing might be a bit of a problem.'

'Could be. Still, I'll wait and see what Norman says.'

It was a warm October evening, and while Edna and Norman were at the hospital, Babs and Lydi were patiently waiting for their date.

'I don't think he's coming,' said Lydi, throwing her handbag on the kitchen table.

'He must be held up.' Babs was anxiously looking out of the back door. Surely Pete wouldn't let them down?

'Perhaps he's been caught siphoning petrol from an officer's car.'

'Lydi, what's wrong with you? I've never heard you be so down on someone before.'

'I don't know. Time of month, worried about Mr Johnson. Babs, what if he has to sell the farm and we get moved away? We may not be together.'

'Don't say that.' Fear took hold of Babs. 'You're more like a sister to me. I'd hate it if we wasn't together.'

'Sorry. Didn't mean to upset you. Where *is* that bloke?'

'You don't think he's been flying?'

Lydi suddenly looked guilty. 'I'm sorry. I didn't give that a thought.'

'That's not like you.'

'I wasn't thinking. I'm sure he's fine, just decided to stand us up, the sod.'

'So, what shall we do instead?'

'Can you ride your bike in that skirt?'

'I can always hitch it up, why?'

'Let's go to the village pub. I feel like getting drunk.'

Babs giggled. 'Now that sounds like a very good idea, but I mustn't drink too much. Remember, there are some cows that have to be milked in the morning.'

They got out their bikes and made their way to the village.

The next morning, when they were doing the milking, Lydi was going over what Babs had said when that airman hadn't turned up. What if he had been on a mission? What if he had been shot down? Everybody knew that being a machine-gunner was one of the most dangerous jobs in the RAF.

'You're very quiet this morning,' said Babs, poking her head round a cow's bottom. 'Didn't think you had that much to drink.'

'No, I didn't.'

'Well let's face it, those old boys and the landlord didn't make us feel all that welcome.'

'No, and that didn't help my bad mood.'

'Are you in a better mood this morning?'

'Yes thank you.'

'So why are you so quiet?'

'I've been thinking over what you said last night. What if Pete has been shot down?'

'What?' Babs jumped up and knocked her stool over. Her cow started to moo and move about. 'Sorry, old girl,' she said, patting its rump.

'I should have been a little more polite to him.'

'Yes, you should.'

'But he was still a road hog.'

Babs grinned. 'And still good-looking.'

'That's as maybe.'

'Well let's hope he comes and tells us he was sorry he let us down.'

'We shall see.' Lydi wasn't sorry he hadn't turned up, but she didn't want Babs to be upset.

It was late on Sunday afternoon when Norman brought Edna back to the farm.

'How's Mr J?' asked Babs as she poured out four cups of tea.

'I think there is a slight improvement since I saw him last,' said Norman. 'But only slight.'

After all the usual chat about the farm and

things in general, Lydi asked Norman if he'd found anyone to teach her to drive.

'There's plenty that would, but it's getting hold of the petrol that could be the problem.'

'What if Mr J let me use the lorry? We get the pink petrol for that.'

Everybody knew that farmers were allowed petrol but it was coloured pink so that ordinary folk couldn't use it. If they were caught with it they could be heavily fined and even sent to prison if they were selling it on.

'That's true. I'll try and find out more. After all, it would be a priority with Dad being laid up.

Lydi smiled. 'Thanks.'

At the end of the following week, an RAF lorry pulled into the farm. Edna walked over to it wiping her floury hands on the bottom of her overall. 'Are you the young man that took the girls out to dinner?'

'I'm afraid I let them down.'

'They didn't tell me that. I was in bed by the time they got home. They are in the top field. Would you like to come in for a cup of tea?'

'That would be very nice, thank you.'

When they were inside, Pete said, 'I don't think I made a very good impression with Lydi when I knocked them off their bikes, and now

I've let her and Babs down. Do you think they'll forgive me?'

Edna smiled. 'They are good girls and work very hard. I'm sure when they see you here they'll forgive you.'

'How long will they be?'

'Quite a while, I'm afraid. They're ploughing the top field.'

'Could I go up there?'

'You'll have to walk and it's a bit of a trek. Finish your tea first.'

'Thanks.'

Lydi was looking behind her, making sure the furrows were reasonably straight. Babs was clearing the undergrowth when Lydi stopped.

'Got a problem?' yelled Babs.

'No. Look.' She pointed towards the end of the field at Pete, who was making his way towards them.

Babs smiled and called out, 'Hi there, Pete.'

He waved.

'What does he want, coming all the way up here?' asked Lydi.

'I don't know, but please try and be polite.'

'Of course I will, look at my great big smile.' She put on a very false smile.

'Hello, girls,' he said, coming up to them. 'It's

quite a trek up here.' He looked very hot in his uniform and ran his finger round the inside of his collar.

'So, how are you?' asked Babs. 'And what are you doing up here?'

'I've come to apologise for letting you down last week. I'm afraid something came up.'

'That's all right,' said Lydi. 'We went to the pub.'

'I couldn't let you know.'

'That's all right,' repeated Babs. 'Did you have to go on a mission? Or perhaps I shouldn't ask that.'

'That's a big thing for a girl to drive,' he said, changing the subject.

'In the Land Army we have to tackle anything and everything,' said Lydi. 'Now if you don't mind, we have to finish this field.'

'Of course. I was just talking to Edna.'

'Edna?' said Lydi.

'Yes. She was telling me what an asset you both are, and more so now that her husband's in hospital.'

'Yes, it is very sad, but we just have to get on with the job.' Lydi started the engine and began to move on.

'Don't mind her,' said Babs. 'She can be a bit stroppy sometimes.'

'Anyway, I've got to get going. Perhaps we could go out sometime?'

'That would be lovely.'

'I promise I won't let you down again.'

Babs knew her smile was wide. 'How will you get in touch?'

'I'll drop by. It might have to be at short notice.'

Babs smiled. 'That's all right, we don't have a very full social calendar.'

He grinned. 'Now I must go. Bye for now.' He walked away, and turned and waved to them.

Lydi stopped again and waited for Babs to catch her up. 'I know I shouldn't say anything, but he really makes me annoyed. Do that sort always think women are going to throw themselves at them just because they are wearing a uniform?'

'He said he'd take us out. He'll come and let us know when.'

'And pigs might fly.'

Babs was deep in thought as she carried on with her job. Pete was rather nice and she longed for a boyfriend, but that was probably all wishful thinking. She'd wait and see if he got in touch first.

Chapter 6

THE FOLLOWING WEEK, Lydi and Babs had just finished the milking and were rolling the heavy churns out on to the roadside to be collected by the company that took the milk when Pete pulled up in the RAF lorry.

'I'm so pleased I've caught you,' he said, jumping out. 'Is there any chance you'll both come out with me on Saturday night as a sort of apology?'

Babs looked at Lydi, waiting for her to answer.

'I promise I'll pick you up. I shall be at camp all day. What do you say?'

'That's fine by me,' said Babs. 'What about you, Lydi?'

'OK.'

'How about if I bring a friend along to make it a foursome?'

'That'd be nice,' said Babs.

'Good, I'm really looking forward it. See you about seven.'

'That's fine.'

'Must go. Bye.' He gave Babs a warm smile and got back in his lorry and drove off.

'That was quick,' said Babs, beaming.

'Look, if you want to be alone with Mr Road Hog, I can always say I've got a headache.'

Babs was leaning on a milk churn. 'Oh no you don't. You're coming as well. Besides, he said he'd bring a friend.'

'Suppose that would be better. I don't want to spoil your chances.'

'No, we'll go together. His friend might turn out to be rather nice.' Babs winked at her.

'All right. You win. Now let's get back and wash out the stalls, then we can go and have breakfast.'

On Saturday night, Babs was ready and waiting, while Lydi was still hovering around upstairs.

When Lydi finally walked into the kitchen, Babs was really surprised at how lovely she looked. Her blonde hair was gently curled and resting on her shoulders.

'Are my seams straight?' She turned for Babs to check.

'They're fine. I love that frock. I ain't seen you in it before.'

'No. Not really had a chance to wear it. Not the sort of thing to wear when we go on our bikes or in a lorry to the local hop.'

'It's such a pretty blue.' Babs suddenly felt very frumpy in her only frock. She knew it was about time she treated herself to something new, but like Lydi she hadn't really felt the need. Till now. 'I wish you'd told me you was dressing up, then I would have gone to Horsham and got something new.'

'I'm sorry, Babs.' Lydi felt guilty. She shouldn't have bothered to make such an effort, but she was hoping that Mr Road Hog would keep his word and bring along a friend. It would be nice if he was good-looking and intelligent, not like some of the RAF blokes that went to the local dances.

Pete's little Morris pulled into the yard and they could see he had a friend with him.

He got out, and so did the friend. 'Babs, Lydi, this is Frank. He helps fly the plane while I sit and point a gun.'

Frank was tall, dark and very handsome. Babs felt her heart flip as she looked at Lydi, who she could see was smiling widely.

'Hello,' said Frank. 'Pete told me he'd knocked a couple of smashers off their bikes, and by Jove, he was right.' He smiled, showing even white teeth.

Babs giggled.

'Right, girls. Hop in,' said Pete.

The girls got in the back and Babs could see that Lydi was relaxed. At first they just stared at the heads of the men in front. Pete had a shock of light brown wavy hair, and Babs wondered how he managed to keep a forage cap on. Perhaps he wore a peaked cap. Frank had straight dark hair slicked down with Brylcreem. Then the journey to Horsham soon became full of chatter. The two men wanted to know where the girls came from, and what had made them choose the Land Army.

'Should have gone in the WAAFs,' said Pete, talking to them through the rear-view mirror. 'It seems the girls on our camp have got a cushy number; they're not up in the middle of the night milking cows and driving tractors.'

'We happen to like milking cows and driving tractors,' said Lydi.

'Sorry,' said Pete.

'Don't mind her,' said Babs. 'So where are you from?'

'Here and there,' said Pete. 'Could say we're of no fixed abode.'

'I meant before the war,' said Babs.

'I'm from Surrey,' said Frank.

'That's nice,' said Lydi. 'Whereabouts in Surrey?'

'Purley.'

'I've heard it's very nice there.'

'Yes, it is.'

'What about you, Pete?' Babs asked.

'Essex.'

Babs smiled to herself. This could be a great evening.

They arrived at a very exclusive restaurant and were shown to their table.

'The usual, sir?' said the waiter.

'Of course.'

Babs looked round. 'This is very nice. It looks like you come here often.'

'Not as often as I would like. The food's much better here than on camp, even in the officers' mess.'

'So how many girls have you brought here?' asked Lydi.

'A few. Does that bother you?'

'It's no business of mine what you do.'

Pete smiled. 'Now this wine is good,' he said, pointing to the wine list.

'I can't believe there's a war on when we can sit and eat and drink like this,' said Babs.

'It does help if you have the cash to spend,' said Frank, studying the menu.

The wine arrived and they settled down to a lovely evening. Babs relaxed and watched Lydi, who appeared to be getting on very well with Frank. She desperately hoped so, as she would love the four of them to do this again.

At the end of the evening they made their way back to the car, and Babs could see Frank and Lydi were deep in conversation.

'Have you got a car, Frank?' asked Lydi.

'Yes, but it's up on blocks for the duration. Can't get the petrol.'

'Pete seems to be able to.'

'Well he's often sent to other places, so he gets a small allowance.'

'That's a pity,' she said.

'Why, because he gets an allowance?'

'No, because you don't.'

'Have you got a car?' asked Frank.

'No. I can't drive, only tractors. I would dearly love to learn, then I could use the lorry, especially now that Mr J's in hospital.'

'I wish I could be around to teach you,' said Frank.

'Oh, are you being moved on?'

'Yes, unfortunately.'

'Anywhere exciting? Sorry. I shouldn't ask.'

'I think I can trust you. We're off to Canada to teach some of the youngsters over there.'

Lydi felt sad. This was the kind of man she would love to get to know better.

When they were settled back in the car, Frank said, 'Pete, how about between ops you teach Lydi here to drive?'

'I thought you could already drive,' he said.

'Only tractors.'

'Could do, I suppose. You'd have to get a licence.'

'I know.'

'Let me know when you've got one and I'd be more than willing to take you out.'

'I'll do that.' As much as he annoyed her, she was desperate to learn to drive. 'Thanks, that would be great. So you're not going with Frank, then?'

'No such luck. It seems those Canadian boys already know how to fire a machine gun.'

Lydi sat back. 'Just make sure you don't let me down.'

'Can't promise, I won't get called up to go on a raid.'

Babs caught her breath. In these past wonderful hours she had almost forgotten what dangerous lives these brave men led.

*

When Frank and Pete dropped the girls off, they kissed them long and lingering. When Babs came up for breath, she knew she wanted to see Pete again.

'It's a shame Frank's leaving,' said Babs as they sat in the kitchen drinking their cocoa.

'Yes. He was rather nice.'

'And if Pete's gonner teach you to drive, you'll have to be nice to him.'

Lydi got up to wash the cups. 'I suppose I will. After all, he doesn't seem a bad chap.'

Babs was grinning. 'That's good.'

'Oh no. You've not fallen for him?'

'Just say I'd like to get to know him better.'

'Babs, I don't want to sound like an old woman, but . . .'

Babs held up her hand. 'Look, I know you think I'm daft, always daydreaming about romance. But I can't help it. You see, all I want is to love someone and be loved back.'

'Oh Babs.' Lydi went and held her friend. 'I'm sorry. I know that one day you will meet Mr Right. But please, don't marry the first one that comes along.'

'I won't.'

'Promise?'

'I promise. But I do like Pete a lot.'

'Well, try and find out more about him.'

'You might be able to do that when you're out together.'

'I will, and don't worry, I won't steal him away,' promised Lydi.

Babs grinned. 'You had better not.'

Chapter 7

IT HAD BEEN A mild October, and at the end of the month Norman came into the field that the girls were working in. They were lifting the potatoes after they had been turned over with the machine. It was hard work putting them into sacks; they weren't as mechanised as some of the larger farms round here. For the past four weeks they had just about managed. Sometimes Norman sent his foreman to give the girls a hand, and some of the other farmers would help out too. But both girls knew that some of the maintenance jobs were being neglected.

'That's a back-breaking job,' said Norman, coming up to them.

'We know,' said Lydi, slowly straightening up. 'What are you doing up here at this time of day? It's not your dad, is it?'

'No. I've come to tell you some good news.'

'Your dad's coming home?' said Babs eagerly.

'No, not yet. But I've got you some help.'

'That's good,' said Lydi. 'Has he got experience running a farm?'

'I've actually got two blokes coming.'

'That's even better,' said Babs. 'Will they stay when we have to pick the sprouts?'

'Hopefully.'

'That'll be great,' said Lydi. 'I hate picking sprouts, especially when they're covered with snow and ice.'

Norman looked a little uncomfortable. 'They're Italian prisoners of war, and they are allowed out to work on farms.'

Babs looked at him. 'Thanks all the same, but we can manage without them,' she said, returning to picking up the potatoes.

'I know how you must feel after what happened to your family,' said Norman. 'Mum's not overjoyed either, but you need help.'

'But not them. Not the enemy.'

'That's all we can get at the moment.' Norman was definitely very uneasy. 'Besides, Italy has signed an armistice.'

'That's as may be, but they still killed our boys.'

'I know.' Norman thrust his hands into his

pockets and kicked the ground. 'Please, Babs, give them a chance.'

'Why should we?'

'Dad's worried about you and knows you need help.'

'But not the likes of them.'

'Look, as I said, it's all we can get at the moment. They'll only be here for a while, so at least let them come and give you a hand. This is a big field, and soon the weather will start to close in and you'll need all the help you can get. Besides, I've heard they can be bloody good workers.'

Babs stopped feverishly picking up the potatoes. 'It ain't my farm and it ain't my place to say anything.'

'When can we expect them?' asked Lydi.

'They should be here tomorrow. They get dropped off in the mornings and picked up again at night. Quite a few of the farms round here use them. After all, it's cheap labour.'

'Are they farmers?' asked Lydi.

'No. You'll have to teach them the ropes.'

'What's their English like?' she asked.

'Don't know, but don't let them have any tools that can be used as weapons.'

'That's a daft thing to say. Everything on a farm is dangerous and can be used as a weapon,' said Lydi.

'Oh thanks,' said Babs. 'So we could be raped and murdered in the field up here and no one would know.'

'They have all been vetted and have been working out of the camp for a while. Besides, it'll give Dad a bit of peace of mind. He's really worried about you, you know.'

Babs felt guilty at her outburst, but she couldn't help her feelings. She didn't want Mr J to worry about them, so she returned to picking up the potatoes.

'I'll call in tomorrow and see how things are working out.' Norman turned and left the field.

'We could certainly do with the help,' said Lydi as she watched him walk away. 'And if this is all he can get, then we'd better get used to it.'

'I know that, but bloody prisoners of war. I bet our lads don't get let out to enjoy a bit of freedom.'

'We don't know that.'

'We know the Eyeties and the Germans fly over our cities and kill innocent civilians.'

'And our boys do the same. Babs, this is war.'

'You don't have to tell me, remember.' She angrily carried on grabbing the potatoes and throwing them into the sack.

Lydi knew there wasn't any point in continuing with the conversation, so she got back to work.

*

When it was milking time, they made their way home to the farm.

'Don't have a go at Edna about these prisoners. She's got enough to worry about with Mr J, so she doesn't need you upsetting her,' Lydi snapped.

Babs looked at her with surprise. Lydi had never spoken to her like that before.

Then Lydi added. 'Sorry if I sound a bit harsh, but we've all got to pull together to keep this farm going.'

'Suppose so,' said Babs.

As usual Edna welcomed them with a cup of tea. 'Norman said you wasn't very pleased about the Italians coming here, Babs.'

'I was very surprised,' she said, trying to force a smile.

'I must admit, I'm not that keen on it, but you need some help.'

'I know.'

'Let's hope they don't burst into Italian opera too often,' said Lydi, trying hard to lighten the situation. 'They might spook the cows.'

'You'll be glad of them in the winter when you're picking the sprouts.'

'D'you know, Edna,' said Lydi, 'that's the one job I really hate. Especially when they're frozen.'

'It must be quite hard for some of them to be here in the winter,' said Edna. 'So very different from the sunshine they get in their own country.'

Babs wanted to scream out, 'They are prisoners! They were fighting against us and killing our boys.' But she knew she had to keep her thoughts to herself.

For the rest of the evening Edna and Lydi talked about the prisoners and what they could do. Babs went to bed early. She was angry, but as Lydi had pointed out to her, this wasn't her farm and they did need the help.

The following morning, it was very early and still dark when a lorry pulled into the yard. The driver got out and banged on the side of the lorry, and two men scrambled out of the back.

Lydi, who was on her way to the milking shed, went over to meet them. Edna had come out to see who had arrived and closely followed her.

'This is Gino and Demetrio,' said the driver as the two men stepped forward, quickly snatching off their caps. 'They have been working on a few farms round here.'

'Do they speak English?' asked Lydi.

'We understand you very well, madam,' said a smiling Demetrio. He appeared to be the older of the two. The younger man looked shy but also smiled.

'That's good,' said Lydi. 'It'll make our job a lot easier.'

The driver went to move away. 'We pick them up at seven for now, but if you ever want them to stay later, that can be arranged.'

'Thank you,' said Edna.

They watched the lorry leave.

'Would you like a cup of tea?' asked Edna, very slowly and deliberately.

'Yes thank you,' said the smiling Demetrio.

They exchanged names and Lydi also smiled.

They were all sitting at the kitchen table when Babs walked in. Both men quickly jumped to their feet and gave her a slight bow.

'It didn't take them long to get their feet under the table,' said Babs.

'This is Babs,' said Lydi.

'Don't suppose they can understand a word you're saying.'

'They speak English,' said Lydi, talking as if they weren't there.

'Oh that's great. So they could be spies as well.'

'Babs, come on, give them a chance.'

'Why should we?' She picked up her cup of tea and walked out.

'You must forgive Babs. Her parents were killed in an air raid.'

'I can understand how she must feel,' said Demetrio.

When they'd finished their tea, Lydi took them round the yard and showed them what they would be doing this morning, and after giving them their instructions, she and Babs got on with the milking. The men cleaned the stalls and fed the cows, and then took the heavy churns to the side of the road. All the while Babs was watching them very carefully. She didn't like it when they started talking to each other in Italian.

'I wonder what they're saying about us,' she said to Lydi as they watched the men washing their hands in the yard.

'Wouldn't know. We'll have to learn Italian.'

'Ha ha. Very funny.'

'Oh come on, Babs, where's your sense of humour? Try to be a little more civil.'

'I can't. I'm gonner see to the chickens.'

'You could show Gino where the food is and he could do that.'

'It's my job.'

Lydi watched Babs walk away. It worried her to see her so upset.

Gino came over to her. 'Your friend doesn't like us,' he said, also watching Babs walk away.

Lydi smiled. 'I'm sorry about that.'

'You must not be. Even though our war is over, we are still your prisoners. But we will work hard and help you.'

'Thank you.' In some ways Lydi felt sorry for these men, who were so far away from home and their loved ones. If only she could make Babs feel the same way.

After they had finished their breakfast, they all went to the potato field and continued the picking.

'At this rate we should get this finished before nightfall,' said Lydi, watching both the men getting down to it.

'I hope so,' said Babs. 'By the way, did Pete say when he was coming to teach you to drive?'

Lydi shrugged. 'No, that's if he bothers to turn up, I suppose.'

'You've not got a lot of faith in him, have you?'

'No. Not really. But time will tell.'

Chapter 8

IT WAS TWO WEEKS later and a cold, wet and windy morning when Pete drove into the yard just as Lydi was going into breakfast. She had her head bent against the wind and rain.

'I can take you out tomorrow morning, is that all right?' he yelled, not bothering to get out of the car.

'That's fine, but it depends on what time,' she said, walking over to him. She had almost given up on him keeping his promise, and although this man annoyed her, she knew she had to be nice to him if she wanted him to teach her to drive. And as tomorrow was Sunday, when they tried to keep the jobs down to a minimum, she wouldn't have to worry too much about leaving Babs to do the work.

'About nine?' he called out.

'I'll be ready. I've got my L-plates and provisional licence.' She had been to Horsham with Norman and got that sorted.

'Good. See you tomorrow then,' he shouted as he left the yard.

'Was that Pete?' asked Babs, coming out of the chicken coop just as he drove off. They hurried to the kitchen out of the rain.

'Yes. He's taking me for my first lesson in the morning.'

Babs looked disappointed. 'He didn't say he'd take us both out again?'

'No. In fact he didn't even bother to get out of the car. Can't say I blame him in this weather.'

'Thought he might have popped in to say hello to me.'

'He'll probably do that tomorrow.'

'Yes,' said Babs, wishing it was her that Pete was taking out driving.

The next morning the rain had eased and at nine o'clock, Lydi stood waiting with her L-plates. She looked at her watch. If Pete was going to be late again, she would forget the whole idea. As it was she didn't want him teaching her, but what else could she do? She desperately wanted to learn to drive. She was just beginning to walk away when he turned into the yard.

'I'm not late,' he said, getting out of the car.

'Just as well,' said Lydi.

'Give me your L-plates and I'll tie them on.'

'I'd rather wait till we're away from the farm.'

'Why's that? Frightened of making a fool of yourself?'

Lydi held her tongue; she didn't want to antagonise him if he was her only means of learning to drive. 'Yes,' she said defiantly.

'Good luck!' shouted Babs as she watched her friend climb into Pete's car and drive off. She still wished it was her.

She and Edna walked back to the kitchen.

'I hope she gets on all right with Pete,' said Babs.

'So do I. It'll be such a blessing when she can drive,' said Edna.

For the next hour or so Babs busied herself round the farm, but all the while she was on the lookout for Lydi. She wanted to know how she had got on with Pete and whether he'd talked about her at all.

Babs was still cleaning out the chickens so she wasn't around when Lydi returned an hour later.

'Well,' said Babs when Lydi eventually found her. 'Where's Pete?'

'He couldn't stay.'

'How did you get on?'

'OK. He reckons after a few more lessons I should put in for my test. We're taking the lorry out next time, that's if it's all right with Edna. That way I don't have to use his petrol. He says driving a tractor has been good practice for me.'

'That's good,' said Babs.

'How about me and you going out tonight to sort of celebrate?'

'If you like. When are you going out driving with Pete again?'

'I don't know. It depends on his ops.'

Over the next couple of weeks Lydi went out driving with Pete twice, and although to Babs they seemed to be getting on OK, he hadn't asked them both out for the evening again. Babs asked Lydi to find out why, and was upset when he told her friend that a lot of nights the men had lectures. Babs wanted to yell, 'But he's not too busy to take you out driving!' She wondered if he liked her at all, or was it just her imagination again?

It was the end of November, and after they had finished the milking, the girls were looking forward to their breakfast. While they were washing their hands, Edna asked, 'Is everything working out all right with those two foreign lads?'

'They certainly seem to want to work,' said Lydi.

'That's good,' said Edna as she placed plates of scrambled eggs in front of them. The men hadn't come in for breakfast yet.

'This looks good,' said Babs, ignoring the comments about the Italians.

'So what's to be done this morning?' asked Edna.

'While it's dry and we've got Gino and Demetrio here I thought we'd try and sort out the fence round the top field,' said Lydi. 'A few of the poles are down and the cows could get through the hedge, so I've sent them on ahead with some poles and wire.'

'D'you know,' Edna sat down, 'I can't tell you how much Sidney and me really appreciate all that you do for us. He was very worried when he first saw you both. His first words were, "How can two townie slips of girls look after animals and work the land?" Well you've certainly proved him and everybody else wrong.'

'It would be nice if we could all get in the lorry and go and see him,' said Lydi.

Edna looked uneasy. 'As I said before, I don't think he would like that. He's embarrassed about how he looks just now.'

Babs smiled. 'Well you tell him from us that

he's been laying around for far too long. He's got to come back and look after us.'

Edna brushed a tear away. 'If only it was that easy.' She went over to her large butler sink and, staring out of the window at the fields in front of her, dabbed at her eyes with the bottom of her overall.

Lydi went and held her close. 'Give him our love and tell him we miss him.'

'I will.'

'Come, Miss Scott, to work,' said Lydi.

'That woman's such a slave-driver,' said Babs, going to Edna and giving her a hug. 'See you later.'

As they made their way across the fields, Babs said, 'I wonder how long it will be before Mr J gets back.'

'Don't know. Don't know a lot about strokes.'

'He must be very frustrated.'

'Miss Lydi, Miss Lydi.'

Lydi stopped and looked up when she heard her name being called.

Gino was hurrying towards them. He sounded very agitated.

'What the hell's wrong with him?' said Babs. 'Can't trust them to do a thing on their own.' Although she knew this was wrong and they were good workers, she wouldn't admit it.

'What is it, Gino?' asked Lydi when he caught up with them.

'The cows, they've escaped.'

'Great,' said Babs.

'How did that happen?' asked Lydi.

He looked very worried and, waving his arms, danced in front of them. 'Please come, quick now.'

Lydi and Babs raced along to the field the men had been working in. It was hard running on the wet ground, and even though she was wearing her heavy boots, Babs worried she might fall and twist her ankle.

When they went into the muddy field they could see that some of the cows had wandered through the fence into the next field, and some were in the road.

'How did those get out?' yelled Lydi, gesturing at those that were in the road.

Gino pointed to the gate. 'It was open.'

'Where's Demetrio?'

'He was here.'

Lydi and Babs began to run across the field, shouting, 'Demetrio, where are you?'

'I hope the bugger ain't run off,' said Babs. She turned on Gino. 'How the hell did this happen?'

He stopped running and looked at Babs, his deep brown eyes full of worry and distress. 'I'm sorry,' he panted. 'When we arrived we found it like this. Demetrio would not run off. He's here somewhere.' He waved his arms around. 'I don't know what happened.' Even in his excitable state his English was still impeccable.

Babs began screaming at him. 'Is this your way of getting at us?'

'Babs, calm down.'

'Why? Look what he's done.'

Lydi grabbed her arm. 'Let's get those cows off the road before a car comes round the bend and causes an accident. Besides, we don't know he's done anything.'

'That's right, stick up for him. Edna don't need any more problems on this farm.' Babs was very angry.

'I'm sorry, Gino,' said Lydi. 'But where is Demetrio?

He looked at her. 'I don't know. He was here when I left to get you.'

They reached the road and began shooing the cows back into the field.

'Demetrio!' shouted Lydi.

'I'm here,' came his voice from further up the road.

Babs and Lydi ran over to him. He was in a ditch, kneeling next to Poppy, Babs's favourite cow.

'Oh my God,' said Lydi. 'What's happened?'

He looked up at her. 'I think she has broken her leg.' He was gently stroking Poppy's head.

Babs jumped down beside him and began to cradle the animal's head. Poppy looked at her through her long eyelashes and blinked. Babs was trying hard to suppress her tears.

'We'll get this lot off the road, then someone will have to go for the vet,' said Lydi, taking charge of the situation.

Demetrio looked at Babs. 'I am so very sorry. I know you are very fond of this one.'

Babs moved slightly as the water began seeping through her dungarees. She noted that Demetrio was also sitting in the muddy, smelly ditchwater. This was the first time she had really looked at him. He looked an old man with worry etched on his face. The war was over for him. He had been a fighter. Had he lost some of his family, like her? Babs felt guilty at the way she had acted towards him and Gino. 'You go and give them a hand,' she said, moving her position as she watched Lydi and Gino getting the cows back into the field. 'There, there, Poppy,' she said. 'Everything will be all right soon.' Although she knew it wouldn't be, as a cow with a broken leg would have to be put down. A tear trickled slowly down her cheek. She brushed it aside.

Who would have thought that she, a girl from Rotherhithe, would get upset over a cow?

'Right, that's all of them back in the field,' said Lydi, bending down to talk to Babs. 'Why don't you come out of there and go and get the vet?'

'What about Poppy?'

'Gino will stay with her.'

Reluctantly Babs left Poppy and ran to the farmhouse. She hated to see any animal in distress. She burst into the kitchen and told Edna what had happened. 'I'll just get me bike and go. Let's hope Bill's in his surgery.'

'I'll go up and see if I can help,' said Edna.

Babs was pedalling as fast as her legs would go, and she shivered as the cold got through her wet clothes.

She was thankful that Bill was in his surgery. In his car, he made it back to the farm before Babs, and by the time she arrived, Poppy had mercifully been put down.

'I'll get the carcass removed later,' the vet said, climbing into his car.

'So who left the gate open?' Babs glared at Gino.

'Leave it for now, Babs. It was probably one of the evacuee kids again,' said Lydi, who could see that Edna was very distressed. 'I'm sorry Edna;

we should have repaired that fence between the fields weeks ago,' she added as the three women slowly made their way back to the farm.

'You can't be expected to do everything at once. That fence has been all right for a good many weeks. Now come on back, and Babs, you can get out of those wet things.'

Babs looked over at Demetrio. He too was wet through, and she almost felt sorry for him, as he had to work the rest of the day in wet clothes.

Edna must have been thinking the same, as she said, 'Demetrio, I can find you some dry clothes.'

'No thank you. I will be all right.'

'You can't spend the rest of the day wet through. We don't want you to catch a cold.'

'Thank you, Mrs J. You are very kind.'

'Go in the barn and I'll bring them over.'

Babs looked at Edna and felt guilty at her outburst, but that didn't alter her feelings towards the two men. They were the enemy, after all.

Chapter 9

It was late afternoon and the light was rapidly beginning to fade when the two girls finally finished repairing the fence.

The men had gone back to camp and Edna had gone to the hospital. Babs and Lydi were exhausted, and after finishing their meal they were both looking forward to a long hot bath when they heard a car come into the yard.

'Oh no, who can that be at this time of night?' asked Lydi.

They went outside to see Pete getting out of his car.

'Hi, girls. I thought I'd come and see if I could take you both out.' He was smiling at Babs.

Babs and Lydi, who were in their dressing gowns, stood and looked at him standing there in his uniform and all scrubbed up.

'You're not going to bed already, are you?' He looked at his watch. 'It's only nine o'clock, and a Friday night as well, so we still have plenty of drinking time left.'

'We've had a very busy day,' said Lydi.

'Well, can I come in?'

'We'd rather you didn't,' said Lydi.

Ignoring Lydi, he looked at Babs. 'What about you, Babs? You look as if you could do with a drink.'

Babs looked at Lydi. She desperately wanted to go out with him.

He came up to her and put his arm round her waist. Her heart gave a little leap.

'Come on. Go and put some clothes on and come out with me. I need cheering up, and female company tonight.'

'All right.' Babs ran inside, not wanting to hear what Lydi was about to say. She needed cheering up; losing Poppy had really upset her.

She was back down in a few moments. 'Right, I'm ready.'

Lydi stood to one side as she watched Babs get into the car. She knew Babs wanted to find love, but to throw herself at this fellow? She didn't want her friend to get hurt.

Babs waved as they drove out of the yard, and then settled back against the leather upholstery. 'I didn't think you wanted to see us again.'

'I have been very busy, though that's no excuse. I've had to run one of the higher-up bods about; he's trying to get his family down here and he's been looking for a house. I won't be able to get petrol when he finds something.'

'That'll be a shame.'

'I'll have to get my bike out next time I want to see you.'

Babs felt a little tingle. He *did* want to see her again. 'When are you taking Lydi out again?'

'Whenever I can.'

'Well I think that's very nice of you.'

He laughed. 'Let's hope it's worth it.'

'What d'you mean?'

'Let's hope she passes her test first time. I don't want to waste too much time with her.'

'So why are you doing it?'

'I'm a nice guy. Besides, I promised Frank.'

'Does he like Lydi, then?'

'Think so.'

'But he's not here.'

'He'll be back. Good pilots like him don't stay in Canada for long. They get restless.'

Babs smiled to herself. This could really work out rather well.

They spent the rest of the evening sitting quietly in the pub just talking about their lives and families. Babs felt the stresses and strains of the day melt away.

He told her he was twenty-three and had lived with his widowed mother in Essex. He also had a younger brother, Tony, who wanted to go to sea.

He pushed back some of his unruly brown hair. 'Mum's dead against it, but as I pointed out to her, if this war lasts for much longer, he'll have to go. That didn't go down too well.'

When Babs told him about her parents, he looked concerned.

'So you are all alone, then?'

'I do have a sister, but she's married and lives in Wales now.'

He squeezed her hand, and again she felt tingles run up her spine. 'So why did you need cheering up?' she asked.

'One of our planes didn't come back. That makes you feel very vulnerable.'

'Oh Pete. I'm so sorry.'

'Let's change the subject.' He stood up. 'I'll get us another drink.'

As the evening wore on, they talked about life in general, and while Pete was at the bar getting another drink, Babs felt her eyes closing. Although she didn't want to, she knew it was time to go. 'I'm sorry, it's been a long day,' she said when he came back to the table.

'Drink up, then it's time for bed.'

That statement quickly woke her up.

He laughed. 'Don't worry. I meant you in your bed on your own.'

When they arrived back at the farm, he turned off the engine and, putting his arm round her shoulders, drew her to him and gently kissed her lips. Babs didn't want him to stop.

'I'm glad Lydi didn't want to come out tonight.'

'Why? You seem to like her.'

'I do, but I've wanted to be alone with you ever since I first saw you. I could get very fond of you,' he said, running his fingers through her hair.

'And so could I.'

He pulled away and laughed. 'What? You could get very fond of yourself?'

Babs also laughed. 'No, silly. I meant I could get fond of you.'

'It wouldn't do, though, would it?'

'What do you mean?'

'Not the sort of job I do. It wouldn't be fair to ask you to wait for me and see if I come out of this lot alive, not after what you've been through.'

Babs was taken aback. 'I'd be more than happy to wait for you.'

He kissed her again with so much passion she thought she would explode. 'Oh Pete,' she murmured.

He gently pushed her away. 'Come on. You've got to get up early in the morning to see to your precious cows, so out you get before I do something I'll regret.'

'OK. I'll go. When will I see you again?'

'I don't know. Never know when we're on ops.'

'Please take care.'

'I will. Now go on.'

She kissed his cheek and got out of the car. She waved as he drove away. She had never felt happier.

It was late when Babs crept into the house. She was surprised to see Lydi was still up.

'You look as if you've had a nice time,' Lydi said, looking up before closing her book.

'Yes, I have, thank you.' Babs giggled. She wasn't going to tell her friend too much about this evening. 'And before you ask, I kept me knickers on.'

'What you do is your own affair.'

Babs walked over to the sink. 'Do you want a cup of cocoa?'

'No thank you. I'm off to bed. Don't wake

Edna when you stomp up the stairs.'

'I don't stomp. By the way, Pete said he's looking forward to taking you out driving again when he can.'

'That's good.'

'See you at five.'

Babs plonked herself in a chair and waited for the kettle to boil. She went over the few hours she had been with Pete.

In the pub, Babs had told him about her day.

'So you got upset over a cow?'

She had nodded. 'I know it sounds daft, but when you've been milking 'em day and night, you get really attached to them.'

'Suppose you do. A bit like us with a plane.'

'You get attached to a plane?'

'Yep. Sometimes when we're on ops, we spend more time in them than in camp.'

The fact that Pete did such a dangerous job reminded Babs that life was very frail. You had to grab each opportunity for happiness, as you never knew what tomorrow could hold.

Everybody was very happy when the following week Edna announced that Mr Johnson was coming home.

'I'm so pleased that he'll be home for Christmas. He would have been most upset to be away from his family,' said Edna when she broke the news.

'That's wonderful,' said Babs. 'We'll have to cut down a tree and put up the decorations again.' Every Christmas since they had been on the farm had been special for Babs.

'Are you going home, Lydi?' asked Edna.

'No, not this year. I wrote and told my parents that with Mr J in hospital I was needed here and couldn't be with them.' She grinned.

'Thank you. But won't your mother object?'

'Dad'll sort it out. As I said in my letter, there is a war on.'

'But it's such a pity you won't be with your family.'

'I don't mind. Besides, we have more fun with the children here.'

'Yes, I told Norman that they must spend the day with us. Robert and Grace are longing to see their grandpa again.'

'We're all longing to see him again,' said Lydi. 'How are you bringing him home?'

'Norman is going to arrange it.'

'If I'd passed my test, I could have got him,' said Lydi.

'I think he might have a job climbing up into the lorry.'

'Yes, he might.'

'I wonder what those Italian boys will be doing for Christmas,' said Edna.

Babs looked at her, horrified.

'Staying at camp, I shouldn't wonder,' said Lydi.

'That's a shame. I'm going to make them both a pair of gloves. I've got plenty of old wool left over from when I make the children jumpers, and I'm sure they won't mind if they're odd colours. Did you see their poor fingers the other day? They were all cracked and bleeding,' said Edna.

'I know,' said Lydi. 'I did offer them a pair of Mr J's old ones, but they were much too big for them, so they put them aside.'

Babs was not going to join in this conversation.

'I thought Babs and myself could pop into Horsham one afternoon to do a bit of shopping, if that's all right with you,' said Lydi. 'We must try and get the children something, but heaven only knows what we can find.'

'Yes, it is very hard.'

For the rest of the evening the conversation was about Christmas. Babs was worried that Edna might invite the Italians to share it with them. She sat thinking about Pete. He had only been round once to take Lydi out driving since he had kissed Babs, and then he'd said he couldn't stay. Did he regret telling her his feelings for her?

He did say he was getting some leave at Christmas and that he would be going home. She desperately wanted to be with him again.

It was lovely to see Mr J again, and both Babs and Lydi put him in the picture about all that was happening round the farm.

'So how's the driving going, Lydi?' asked Mr J when they were having tea.

'Great. Driving a tractor has helped. Pete said I should put in for my test.'

'Is that the young air-force lad who's teaching you?'

'Yes.'

'Brave boys, those air-force lads. A few of them that were in the hospital used to count the planes as they flew over on a mission. It was always so sad when they came back and we were told that some of 'em were missing. We used to hope they had landed somewhere else, especially now they are going over and bombing Berlin.'

Babs looked at her watch. 'We must go and do the milking.' She didn't want to be reminded of what a dangerous job Pete did. She was very fond of him and he was always in her thoughts.

'Yes, of course. So how are the Italians settling down?' asked Mr J. 'Edna and Norman said they don't mind a bit of hard work.'

'No, they don't, and they never complain,' replied Lydi.

'I should think not,' said Babs. 'Not the way Edna here feeds them.'

'I only give them a sandwich and a cup of tea.'

Babs wanted to add, 'What about the hot soup and cake?' but she knew she had to hold her tongue. They all knew how she felt about the Italians. But even she had to admit that they were always polite and worked hard.

'I'd like to meet 'em.'

Babs looked at Edna.

'Lydi, can you send 'em over?' asked Mr J.

So while Babs and Lydi got on with the milking, Edna invited the Italians to come and meet her husband. After removing their boots and hats, they both stood very upright.

'What are you doing for Christmas?' asked Edna.

'We will be at the camp. The soldiers have arranged for us to have an English Christmas dinner,' said Demetrio.

'And we are having a Christmas pudding,' said Gino, smiling. 'I am looking forward to that.'

'What about your families?' she asked.

'My wife will miss me,' said Demetrio, looking down and twisting his hat round and round.

'Do you have any children?'

'Yes, two. A boy, Marco, who is now ten, and a girl, Rosa, who will be six.'

'You must miss them.'

He looked sad. 'Yes, I do. When we come again I will bring a picture to show you.'

'I'd like that.'

'What about you?' Mr J asked Gino.

'My father was in the army and killed in Albania. My mother died in a road accident at the beginning of the war.' He looked down. 'So I have no one,' he said softly.

Edna thought what a pity it was that Babs wasn't here to see how these men had also suffered.

'Please, excuse us, but we must get back and help Miss Lydi and Miss Babs,' said Demetrio.

'Of course,' said Mr Johnson. 'And thank you, boys, for all your help.'

'We like being here,' said Gino.

'That's good.'

'They seem a nice couple of lads,' said Mr Johnson after they left.

'Yes, they are. I only wish that Babs could see that.'

'She'll come round.'

'I hope so. I wanted to ask them here for Christmas, but I didn't want to upset her.'

'Don't worry about it, love. You've got me to look after now.'

Edna gave him a warm smile and patted his shoulder. 'I'll make you another cup of tea.'

Chapter 10

On Christmas Day, it was almost one o'clock when Norman and his family finally arrived. When they all sat down to eat, everybody was chattering and happy. There was much laughter when Babs produced the paper hats that she and Lydi had made from newspapers.

'Well we can't get crackers, so these will have to do,' she said, plonking one on Edna's head.

'And they look very grand as well,' said Edna, straightening her hat

The children kept looking at their grandpa's arm, which just sat on his lap. They were intrigued and kept asking why he couldn't move it.

'I will one day,' he said, giving them a lopsided grin.

After they had cleared the dinner things away,

it was time to give out the presents, and it was those from Gino and Demetrio that brought forth the loudest gasps. Edna, Lydi and Babs all had brooches in the shape of butterflies that they had made from thin metal strips and painted in bright colours. They were beautiful and delicate. Grace had a rag doll and Robert a toy car that they had also made. They had said they didn't know what to give Mr J, so they gave him some cigarettes. Everything had been wrapped in hand-printed paper.

'These are so lovely,' said Lydi, turning her brooch over. 'It must have taken them hours to make them.'

'Those lads are very clever,' said Norman.

'I expect they have a lot of time on their hands,' said Iris, admiring her daughter's doll.

'I am so glad I made them the gloves,' said Edna.

Lydi and Babs were both pleased that they had given the Italians the socks that Edna had made for them.

'It makes my newspaper hats look very sad,' said Babs.

'But they are good,' said Mr J, laughing.

After the presents, Norman said that he and his family had to go.

'Do we have to?' asked Grace.

'Cows don't know it's Christmas Day and still need to be milked.'

'Can't we stay here with Nan and Grandpa?' asked Robert.

'No, I'm sorry, but I won't feel like coming out again. Not in this weather.' It had been raining hard all day.

As Babs helped Grace put on her coat, the little girl said, 'I wish I could stay with you.'

'We've got to go and milk our cows as well.'

'I know. But we could stay and talk to Grandpa.'

'Some other time,' said their mother. 'Don't spoil a good day.'

Grace pouted.

'And don't pull that face, young lady,' said Norman.

Babs kissed the little girl's cheek. 'You can play with your new doll and do a lot of skipping now that you've got a new skipping rope.'

Grace gave her a smile. 'Thank you.'

Robert was standing at the door hiding his cardboard fort under his mac; his car was in his mother's bag.

Babs remembered the lovely doll she'd had one Christmas, but that had gone, like so many of her possessions. Last week when she and Lydi had scoured the shops for something for the children, all they could get was the skipping rope and the cardboard fort, and the shopkeeper had told them they were lucky to get those.

They stood at the door waving goodbye and then returned to change their clothes ready for the evening milking.

That evening in the warm cowshed, Babs rested her head against Rosie the cow and thought about Pete. She knew he was on leave and had gone home for a few days. Would he take her out again when he came back? She desperately hoped so; after all, he had told her that he could get very fond of her. She also thought about what Edna had told her about Gino and Demetrio. They had given them such lovely presents. Tomorrow she would thank them. After all, they must miss home and their families. From now on she would be a little more compassionate and a little more understanding.

The following morning when the Italian men arrived, Edna called them into the kitchen. Babs and Lydi were sitting at the table drinking their tea.

'Thank you so much for our presents,' said Edna.

'Those brooches were really lovely. Did you make them?' asked Lydi.

Demetrio smiled and nodded. 'We are so happy you like them.'

'And the children loved their toys,' said Edna.

'You are very clever,' said Babs.

'We have got a lot of time,' replied Gino.

'Thank you for our gloves and socks,' said Demetrio.

'You'll need them when Lydi sends you out working in the cold,' said Babs, smiling.

'Well come on, everybody, this won't do,' said Lydi.

'She's such a slave-driver,' said Babs.

They all made their way out of the cosy warm kitchen.

Babs was overjoyed to see Pete when he arrived at the end of the week.

He had come on his bike, and before he went into the kitchen he stood in the porch and banged the water off his wet greatcoat. 'I was going to suggest we went to the pub, but it's a bit wet out here.'

'I can see that. We could go in the barn,' said Babs, looking at the kitchen door.

It was then that Edna came out. 'I thought it was you, Pete. Come on in.'

Babs looked embarrassed. 'Edna, would you mind if we went in the barn?'

'Course not. I expect you've got a lot to talk about.' She smiled. 'But I'm sure the front room would be much more comfortable.'

'Thank you.'

Pete nodded his thanks as Babs opened the door.

'I really don't think it will be,' she whispered, closing the door. It was a cold, uninviting room and was hardly ever used except at Christmas. There was no fire, so it would be chilly, but Babs wanted to be alone with Pete.

'Did you have a nice Christmas?' she asked, snuggling close to him on the hard sofa.

'Very quiet. I would rather have been with you.'

'I did miss you,' she said, looking up at him.

'Babs, I've never felt this way about anyone before. I always said I wouldn't get involved, not with the times we live in and the life I lead, but with you it's different. You are always in my thoughts and I want to be with you. I love you.'

That statement took her breath away. He kissed her and she felt wonderful.

'When I get another pass, would you come away with me?'

'I don't know.'

'Please say yes.' He covered her face with kisses. 'I do love you.'

'I'll have to arrange it with Lydi and Mr J.'

'I'm sure they wouldn't begrudge you some time with me.'

'No.' At this moment she would have gone to the ends of the earth with him. He loved her.

He took her in his arms and kissed her again, and she let his hand wander under her jumper. She almost moaned with ecstasy as he gently fondled her breasts.

'My God, I want you so much,' he said, burying his face in her neck.

The knock on the door sent them apart. 'I've just brought you a cup of tea,' said Edna, placing the tray on the small table. 'Sorry there isn't any cake left.'

'That's all right,' said Babs, trying to act normal.

'This is very kind of you,' said Pete.

'It's no bother.' Edna closed the door.

Babs wanted to laugh. 'She's like a mother hen to me and Lydi.'

'Well she certainly knows how to cool my ardour,' said Pete, smiling and kissing her cheek.

'All this red tape,' said Mr J one afternoon when he and Edna were going over the books.

'I'm afraid that's what the government wants. The girls have been very good keeping everything up to date while you've been in hospital.'

'I know.' He sat back and put his pencil on the table, grateful that he was right-handed. 'I'm really worried about young Babs,' he said out of the blue.

'Whatever for?'

'That young man of hers.'

'She seems to be very happy when he's around.'

'I know. That's what worries me. What if anything happened to him? How's she going to cope?'

'Please don't even think about that.'

'I can't help it. He leads such a dangerous life and I look on her as the daughter we never had.'

Edna smiled. 'And she looks on you as a father figure. She's very fond of you, you know.'

He also smiled. 'Always said I could charm the girls.'

'You'd better start to charm these papers if we're going to get any more food for the chickens.'

'Slave-driver.'

Edna thought about what her husband had said. The times Babs had brought Pete in to see them, Edna and Sidney had made him welcome. He was a very likeable lad and they could see that a romance was beginning. Lydi had also voiced her fears to them, but that was natural. Everybody lived in fear during war.

The new year came in very harsh, and the cold, wet weather made life on the farm hard work.

One cold, windy day, Gino, who had been picking sprouts, was banging his hands against his sides when Babs, with her scarf wound round her head, came up to help him take the basket away. She looked at his hands, which were blue.

'Where's the gloves Edna made you?'

He smiled. 'They are too nice to wear here.'

'That's what she made them for.'

Over these past few weeks, since Mr J had been home, he'd told them he thought the men were doing a good job. He'd also made it clear to both Babs and Lydi that without their help, things could be very bad. Both girls had been concerned that he might sell, then where would they finish up? They loved it here.

After they'd hoisted the basket on to the trailer, Babs went over to Demetrio. 'I was talking to Gino. His hands are blue. I told him to wear his gloves. Where are they?'

Demetrio smiled. 'He says they are, how do you say, too good.'

She smiled back at him. 'He's very silly.'

Demetrio shuffled. 'I am so pleased, Miss Babs, that you are now talking to us.'

She looked away, embarrassed. 'Lydi will be up soon, so shall we put this load on the trailer ready for her to take away?'

'I hope Lydi passes her driving test next week.'

'She should do, she's got a good teacher.'

'He's a very nice young man.'

'Yes, he is.' Babs began thinking about Pete and the night he'd told her that he loved her. She couldn't believe she could feel so happy.

Looking up, she saw Lydi making her way towards them. She could see that she was carrying a flask and guessed it would be full of hot soup. Edna certainly tried to look after them.

'Why don't we go in the barn out of this cold wind?' said Lydi when she was within shouting distance.

'Come on,' said Babs to the men. 'We deserve a break.'

They made their way to the barn and sat themselves on bales of straw.

'This is better,' said Babs, unravelling her scarf. 'Put your hands round the cup, Gino, It'll help to warm your fingers up.'

'Thank you, Miss Babs.'

Lydi smiled. She never thought she would

hear Babs being polite to the Italians. But since Christmas she had been very different. 'There's some thick bread in that bag,' she said, handing it over.

'We are very lucky,' said Demetrio. 'Some of the men don't get anything to eat all day.'

'That's dreadful,' said Lydi. 'I would have thought that it was in the farmers' interests to feed them.'

'As I said, we are very lucky.'

At the end of the month, Norman took Lydi for her driving test, and everybody was pleased to hear that she had passed.

Also at the end of January, the war seemed to be stepping up. It was reported that British and American troops had invaded Italy.

'Is that anywhere near where you live?' Babs asked Gino when they heard the news.

'No. I live in Milano, Demetrio lives near Lake Como. That is a very beautiful place.'

'I expect you'll go back one day.'

He didn't reply.

When the news came over the wireless that the Allies were bombing Berlin, Babs worried till she saw Pete come to the farm. Lately he seemed to be able to get away less and less.

It was early on a Tuesday morning when Pete,

who was on his bike, came bursting into the yard, scattering the chickens, just as Babs was going into breakfast.

'I've got my twenty-four-hour pass for this weekend,' he said, throwing his bike on the ground and running up to her. 'Those ten miles seem endless,' he added, trying to get his breath, 'but it's worth it to see you.' He grabbed her and swung her off the ground. He smothered her face with kisses. 'Is there any chance you could get away?'

'I don't know,' she said.

'We could go to Worthing for the day, and perhaps stay in a hotel, just for the night.'

Babs grinned. 'That sounds very naughty.'

'I hope it will be.'

'I can only ask Lydi and Mr J.'

He took hold of her hand. 'Come on. Let's go and ask them now.'

Lydi and Mr J were seated at the table.

'Hello, Pete,' said Edna. 'Would you like a cup of tea?'

'Yes please.'

'Have you had breakfast?'

'Yes thank you.'

'And to what do we owe this early-morning call?' asked Mr J as Edna began putting marmalade on his toast.

Lydi could sense this wasn't a social call, not at this time of the morning. 'Is everything all right?' she asked.

'Yes.' Pete looked at Babs and grinned. 'You see, I've got a twenty-four-hour weekend pass and I was hoping that you could spare Babs and we could go to Worthing.'

'I'd do the milking before I went,' said Babs hurriedly.

'Would you be back in time for the evening milking?' asked Lydi.

Babs looked at Pete, who said, 'Well, no. You see, we were hoping to stay the night.'

Edna looked away. What could she say? In her eyes this was wrong, but these were very different times.

'It will make it very hard for Lydi,' said Mr J.

'So you wouldn't be here for Sunday morning's milking either?' Lydi said.

'No. Perhaps Gino or Demetrio would be able to help out.'

'Can they come out on a Sunday?' asked Mr J.

'I don't know.' Suddenly Babs felt all her euphoria leaving her. She desperately wanted to be with Pete, but the way they were looking at her was making her feel cheap and dirty.

'Even if they could, how would they get here?' asked Edna.

'I don't know,' said Babs in a soft voice.

Pete finished his tea and stood up. 'Look, I'm sorry, but I do have to get back. I'll come over when I can get away and you can tell me what's going to happen, but with these night flights it's always a bit difficult.'

Babs went to the door with him. Outside she said, 'You rode all this way just to ask me out?'

'It's worth it just to see you.'

'What we gonner do?'

He held her tight. 'Don't worry. I'm sure something will get sorted.'

'I hope so. I do want to be with you.'

'I know.' He kissed her long and passionately. 'Roll on Saturday.'

She watched him get on his bike and ride off into the dark morning. She loved him and wanted to be with him. Now she had to go back in and face everybody. There could be no secrets on a farm like this.

That evening, when Babs and Lydi were getting ready for bed, Lydi said, 'Tomorrow I'll ask Demetrio if they are able to come here on Sunday morning.'

Babs stopped brushing her hair and looked at her. 'But how would they get here?'

'Now I've passed my test I can go and get

them. It means getting up about four, but it's not every weekend that you jump ship, is it?'

'You would do that for me?'

'Yes. Well, you are like a sister.'

Babs went and held Lydi tight. 'Thanks. Do you think Mr J will approve?'

'What, of you having a dirty weekend?'

'No. Demetrio milking his cows.'

'Well he has done it a couple of times before.'

'Yes, he has. Thanks, Lydi.'

'Thank me when it happens, and Babs, don't get pregnant. I couldn't bear it if you left.'

'I promise I won't.'

Chapter 11

'GOOD MORNING,' DEMETRIO called out as they came into the cowshed and right away began collecting the buckets of milk.

'It's snowing,' said Gino, jumping about. 'I love the snow. We have to go up into the mountains to see snow.'

Babs laughed. 'You won't say that when Lydi sends you out to the top field.'

'I wouldn't be so wicked,' said Lydi. 'I can find jobs for you round here this morning. Mr J said he thought the cowshed wanted a lick of whitewash, so you could get on with that.'

'Thank you,' said Demetrio.

'When I've finished breakfast I'd like a word with you.'

'What have we done wrong?'

'Nothing.' Lydi smiled but Demetrio looked

very worried. 'Honestly, nothing's wrong.'

Babs didn't say a word. She just hoped that everything would work out fine for her, as she desperately wanted to be with Pete.

When the girls had finished their breakfast, they hurried back into the warmth of the cowshed.

'Demetrio,' called Lydi.

'Yes, Miss Lydi.' He put down the brush he'd been painting the walls with. He looked very down.

'If I collect you on Sunday morning, would you be able to come here?'

His weather-beaten face lit up. 'Yes, of course.'

'You see, Babs is going away and I shall need help with the milking.'

'Will she be gone for ever?' he asked.

'No, just for the weekend, and if you could help on Saturday evening as well, that would be wonderful. I can take you back to camp.'

'Do you need Gino as well?'

'If he wants.'

Gino, who was standing close by, said quickly, 'Please. Yes. I can come.'

'That's settled then.' Lydi looked at Babs, who grinned.

As Lydi walked past her, she said softly, 'Let's hope you-know-who doesn't let you down.'

Babs bristled and followed her out. 'Why don't you like him? After all, he taught you to drive.'

'I'll always be grateful to him for that, but . . .'

'D'you know, sometimes you can be a right snotty so-and-so.'

Lydi stopped and looked shocked. They had never fallen out all the time they'd known each other. 'Babs, I don't want to argue over Pete. He's a nice guy and I really do like him, but I'm more worried about you. I don't want to see you hurt.'

'I won't be.'

'I don't want you to build your hopes up over him.'

'I won't.' Babs walked away. She didn't care if Lydi liked Pete or not. She was going to be with him for a whole weekend. Although it would only be for twenty-four hours, he could have used his pass to go and see his mother, but instead he had chosen to spend the weekend with her. She loved him so much.

Lydi watched Babs walk away. How could she tell her her real fears? Pete was a nice guy and she did like him, but he did a very dangerous job and she couldn't bear it if anything happened to him and her friend had her heart broken.

*

'Thank you for going to collect Demetrio and Gino on Saturday and Sunday,' said Babs. She was sitting up in bed with her cardigan round her shoulders, watching Lydi go through her night-time cleansing routine.

'I think they're glad to get out of the camp.'

'I wished you liked Pete.'

'Babs, I've said over and over that I do like him,' Lydi said, rubbing cold cream into her hands. 'But I like you more and I'm worried that you might be building up your hopes for a wedding or something and he'll disappoint you.'

'I'm not doing anything like that. I'm only living for the moment.'

'That's good.' Lydi tried to shake off her fears. The bedroom was very cold so she took off her greatcoat and placed it over the eiderdown. Jumping into bed, she moved the hot-water bottle further down. They were grateful that Edna was so thoughtful.

'I am worried about one thing, though,' said Babs.

Lydi poked her nose over the bedclothes. 'And what's that?'

'Tomorrow I'll have to wear me Land Army greatcoat.'

'What's wrong with that? I expect Pete will be in uniform.'

'I know, but it ain't very glamorous, is it?'

'I suppose not.'

After a long silence, Lydi laughed.

'What's so funny?'

'You tottering along on your high heels with your skirt flapping round your blue legs.'

'Thanks. Do you know, you can be very cruel at times. Besides, I won't be wearing me skirt to travel in. I shall wear my trousers; those trains can be very cold.' Pete had told her that he wouldn't have any petrol so they had to go by train. Not that she cared; she would have gone on her bike if it meant being with him.

Lydi sat up. 'Sorry. I tell you what, you can borrow my top coat and my blue dress, and please, have a great time.'

'That lovely blue dress?'

'If you want. I don't get a lot of chances to wear it, and besides, you need to look glamorous tomorrow night.'

'Are you sure?'

'It's there if you want.'

Babs jumped out of bed and, hugging Lydi, said over and over again, 'Thank you. Thank you. I promise I won't spill anything on it.'

Lydi slid back down. 'Now come on, let's get some sleep. You've got a busy day tomorrow.'

Babs knew that Lydi was a true friend and was

just concerned about her. She turned over, but knew sleep wouldn't come easy tonight. Her head was too full of what was going to happen tomorrow.

It was almost lunchtime when Pete arrived in an RAF lorry. He took his bike from the back of the lorry and propped it up against the wall. Babs knew he would need it to get back to camp on Sunday. She kissed everybody goodbye and climbed into the lorry. She snuggled against Pete as the driver turned the lorry round and they headed for the station.

The train was crowded with the colourful uniforms of service personnel, and Babs was offered a seat but Pete had to stand. When they got to Worthing, they took a taxi to a hotel that Pete knew. It did worry her a bit, as he seemed to know his way around. He had booked them a room in the name of Mr and Mrs Rice.

Babs had kept her gloves on while they were being booked in; she wasn't wearing a wedding ring. 'Why did you choose the name Rice?'

'Because that's my name. Peter Rice at your service, ma'am.'

Babs giggled. 'Sounds like a pudding.'

'Cheeky. Come here.' He pulled her to him and kissed her long and hard. 'I do love you,

Babs. You're the best thing that's ever happened to me.'

Although she enjoyed his kisses, she pulled nervously away and casually asked, 'Have you been here before?'

'Once, and no, before you ask, it wasn't with a lady. One of the lads got married and his aircrew stayed here. Now come here.'

'I must hang up me frock.'

'You can do that later. Come here.'

Once again she was in his arms, but this time she didn't resist. It felt good and she knew that time was too short for any preamble.

He kissed her gently at first, then passionately. It wasn't long before they had their clothes off and were in each other's arms.

'I do love you Babs,' he said between kisses.

'And I love you.' She felt a wonderful sensation when he ran his hands over her body. She knew she was ready for love and gave herself to him completely.

All too soon it was over and they lay together contented. He continued kissing her cheek.

'Did I hurt you?'

'No.' She blushed and snuggled up to him. She wanted to say that it was worth that first moment of pain but couldn't. She wasn't sure if it had been his first time; girls didn't ask that sort of thing.

Pete looked at his watch. 'Are you ready to go out, or shall we stay here and make love again?'

She giggled. 'I don't mind.'

He rolled on top of her. 'We can eat after.'

Later, as she was standing in her camiknickers and about to put on Lydi's dress, he said, 'That looks nice.'

'Lydi said I could wear it tonight.' She held it against her. 'Good job we're the same size.'

'And I'm sure you're going to look lovely, but you looked even lovelier without your clothes.'

'I bet you say that to all your girls.'

He laughed. 'If you must know, young lady, there haven't been many girls. And before you say anything, in a barracks with a lot of hairy blokes you learn a lot of things. Including how to please a lady.'

She gently kissed him. 'I believe you, though thousands wouldn't.'

He gently slapped her bottom. 'Cheeky. Now come on, get dressed, otherwise we shall be here all night. Not that I mind, but I'm hungry and they don't do room service.'

Babs was so happy she thought she would burst.

They went downstairs to the restaurant, and when they'd finished their meal, Babs said she'd like to go for a walk, so hand in hand they made their way along the wet and windy sea front.

'We must be mad walking along like this,' Pete said.

'I don't care,' said Babs. 'This is wonderful, you can even forget that there's a war on.'

'Well, not really, with all the rolls of barbed wire strewn along the beach.'

'I'm not looking at that.'

'You are such a romantic.'

'I know.'

Pete stopped at a bus shelter and pulled her in. He took her into his arms and kissed her.

When they broke apart she laughed.

'What's so funny?'

'Us. We look like a couple of drowned rats.'

'Well I reckon it's time we went back and got these wet things off.'

'Then what?'

He kissed her again. 'What do you think?'

Babs was fast asleep and Pete's shouting made her sit bolt upright. For a moment or two she wasn't quite sure where she was.

'Pete, Pete.' She gently shook him.

He too looked bewildered when he sat up. 'What's wrong? What is it? Is it a raid?'

'No. You were shouting.'

'Sorry about that. Normally I get a boot thrown at me.'

'You must have been dreaming.'

'I guess so. Don't worry about it.' He pulled her close. 'Now come on, let's get some sleep.'

She nestled in his arms, and soon he was asleep and making a comforting snuffling sound. Her heart was so full of love and she didn't want this moment to end. She smiled to herself as she went over the day. This was something she would remember for the rest of her days. If they were lucky enough in the future to get married and have children, she would tell them all about today . . . well, perhaps not every detail.

All too soon it was morning. She couldn't believe it was seven o'clock and she was still in bed.

Pete was awake and looking at her. 'Hello, sleepy head.'

Babs quickly tried to straighten her hair. 'I must look a mess.'

'A lovely mess. Let me mess you up some more.'

And once again they made love.

Chapter 12

On Sunday afternoon everything was back to normal. Pete had left to get back to camp before his pass was up, and Babs was in the bedroom, changing ready for work. Everybody wanted to know if she had had a nice time. She smiled and said yes, although she guessed Edna and Mr J disapproved. But she didn't care. She and Pete loved each other, and that was all that mattered.

'So did you manage all right with Gino and Demetrio?' she asked Lydi as she was hanging up Lydi's clothes.

'Yes. That camp looked a very dreary place. No wonder they were pleased to come here.'

'They've never said.'

'Well, it might be all right inside.' Lydi was waiting for Babs to say what did they expect? After all, they were prisoners of war.

'I didn't spill anything on your frock, look.' Babs held it up.

'I trust you. Did it suit you?'

'It was smashing. I felt like a million dollars when we went in to dinner.'

'Was it a nice hotel?'

'I thought so, but then again, I've never stayed in a hotel before. It's just been bed-and-breakfast places for me.'

'I have missed you and I'm pleased you had a great time.'

'So am I. Lydi, I do love Pete.'

'I know you do.' Lydi didn't want to air her fears, as Babs had suffered enough. 'And Babs, I like Pete, he's a nice guy.'

Babs smiled. 'I think so as well.'

Some weeks later they were sitting quietly listening to the news. Babs was darning her socks and Lydi was reading the newspaper. The announcer was telling them that there was fierce fighting at Monte Cassino.

'Is that in Italy?' asked Edna.

'Shh, and yes,' said her husband impatiently.

'Is it anywhere near where Gino and Demetrio live?' Edna asked Lydi in a very soft voice.

'I don't think so,' whispered Lydi, looking up from her paper.

Edna was still keeping her voice down. 'I feel really sorry for those two lads so far away from home,' she said.

'Well at least their war is over,' said Mr J as the music started again.

'I know,' said Lydi. She folded her newspaper and put it on the floor. 'When I was taking him back to camp, Gino said that when this is all over he doesn't want to go back to Italy. It seems that he's got no one to go back to.'

'He's not got anybody here either, has he?' asked Babs.

'I don't think so,' said Edna.

'I think that's very sad,' said Lydi.

'Would he be allowed to stay here?'

'I wouldn't have thought so,' said Mr J, banging his pipe out into the fireplace.

'When this war's over, there's gonner be a lot like that with nowhere to go,' said Babs. 'At least I've got me sister, though I don't know how long she'll put up with me. In her letters she always says she can't wait to come home to her own house.'

'I shall miss this life,' said Lydi.

'So will I. Can't say I like the idea of standing behind a counter again.'

'So many lives have been turned upside down,' said Edna.

Everyone knew the war could be coming to an end. The raids on Germany had intensified and Burma was about to be taken, and everybody was waiting for the second front.

'Now come on, old girl, stop getting so melancholy. Things are getting better. I fancy a cup of tea. How about you two girls?'

'That's a good idea,' said Babs, jumping up. 'I'll make it.' She wanted to be on her own, to think about Pete. He had told her not to worry if he couldn't get to see her for a few days. They were busy, and if he'd been on night flights he had to catch up on his sleep. She understood this, but it didn't stop her from worrying about him. 'Please God, look after him,' she whispered to herself as the kettle began to whistle.

Spring was just around the corner and everybody felt an air of expectancy. The raids over Germany were filling the pages of the newspapers, and Babs seemed to live her life just waiting for Pete to appear.

When she saw him ride into the yard on his trusty old bike – his car was now up on blocks through lack of petrol – she ran to meet him and they were locked in each other's arms for a few moments. Sometimes they went to the pub, but other times they were quite content to go in the barn and settle on the hay. They always made sure the door was closed and put a pitchfork against it so that they wouldn't be disturbed. They would spend as much time together as possible. If it was during the day, Pete would seek her out and would help with any job she was doing. She loved him so much.

In the quiet, still night that was only broken by the occasional hoot of a nearby owl or foxes barking as they roamed around the chicken coop, Babs would lie in bed and listen to the far-off drone of the planes as they left the airfield to fly to Germany, and pray that Pete would come back safe to her.

It was May; everyone knew the second front was imminent.

One warm evening the kitchen door was wide open and Babs and Lydi were singing along with the wireless as they helped Edna bottle some fruit. An RAF lorry pulled into the yard. Babs, who hadn't seen Pete for almost a week, ran into the yard smiling hugely, but when an airman she hadn't seen before got out of the lorry, she felt her legs turn to jelly.

'Does a Miss Babs Scott live here?' he asked her.

Her face drained of any colour. 'Yes. I'm Babs Scott.'

Lydi and Edna were at her side.

'What is it?' asked Lydi, taking hold of Babs's hand.

'I'm afraid I've got some bad news.'

For Babs suddenly the world began to spin and she felt Lydi's arms around her.

'You'd better come inside,' Edna said to the airman as she and Lydi began to manoeuvre Babs into the kitchen and sat her in a chair.

Lydi quickly turned off the wireless and, sitting next to Babs, held on to her hand.

'I'm all right,' Babs whispered.

Edna went to the sink and filled a glass with water. 'Here, drink this.'

Babs took a sip.

'Is it Pete?' she asked the young airman, who looked very uncomfortable.

'I'm afraid so.'

Babs gave a sob. 'Is he in hospital?' she asked, full of hope.

The airman folded his forage cap again and again.

Babs looked at Lydi, her face ashen. 'I knew it. I knew I should have gone to the camp to find out if he was safe.'

'Babs, it's ten miles away,' said Lydi.

'I could have gone on me bike.' Tears were streaming down her face. 'I should have gone to the camp,' she said softly.

'Do you know what happened?' Lydi asked the young man.

'Only what some of the other guys who were up there with him have told us.'

'Please, take a seat,' said Edna, pulling a chair out for him.

'Thank you. I hate this part of my job.'

Babs was just staring at him, her silent tears still running down her face. 'Is there any chance he may get back?' she asked quietly.

Pete had told her that sometimes when a plane was damaged, the pilot somehow managed to get it back over the coast or ditch the crew in the sea before it went down. So there was always hope.

The young man shook his head. 'Those that were in that formation saw the tail of the plane blown off. The pilot might have been lucky, but I'm afraid no one else stood a chance.'

Lydi asked, 'How did you know about Babs being . . .'

He gave her a weak smile. 'Pete was always talking about her. Everyone knew she was his girl and where she worked, and someone said she should be told.'

Babs gave a long, deep, heart-rending sob. 'Thank you.'

'Would you like a cup of tea?' asked Edna, for something to say.

'No. Thanks all the same. I must get back.'

'Of course,' said Lydi. 'I'll walk out with you.'

Babs looked up. 'Is it possible I could get his mother's address?'

'I would think so. Goodbye.'

Outside, Lydi thanked him and watched him drive off. She wanted to get away from Babs because she wanted to shout and yell at the sky. Why did people have wars? What good did they do? And why had Babs been made to suffer all over again? She sat on the ground and cried. 'It's not fair!' she screamed out.

'My dear girl, whatever is the matter?' asked Mr J, coming into the yard leaning heavily on his stick. He had been for his evening walk. When the weather was fine, he liked to wander round his farm; he felt this was something he should do.

Lydi looked up, her face red and tear-stained.

'Whatever it is I'm sure it will all be better soon.'

Lydi shook her head. 'It can never get better.'

He looked alarmed. 'What on earth is it?'

'It's Pete. He's been killed.'

'Oh my dear. Does Babs know?'

Lydi nodded. 'She and Edna are in the kitchen.'

'Come along, let's go and see if we can help.'

'Nobody can help Babs now,' said Lydi. 'And now she'll always have the fear of loving.'

They walked back into the kitchen together, each with Babs in their thoughts. How would she cope with this?

Chapter 13

For weeks Babs seemed to be in a dream as she went about her jobs. She had written to Pete's mother and had received a lovely letter back. Mrs Rice had said that she knew all about Babs and that she had been very pleased to hear from her. She had also kindly sent her a photo of Pete, which Babs kept beside her bed.

Gino and Demetrio had liked Pete. He'd always spoken to them when he was around and they were very upset when they heard what had happened.

One day when Gino and Lydi, who were working together in the top field, stopped for lunch, Gino said, 'I hope Miss Babs doesn't hold us . . . how do you say? I don't know the right word. That it was us who killed Mr Pete.'

'Responsible.' Lydi sat on the ground next to

him. 'No, of course she doesn't.'

'We were just beginning to be friends.'

'Yes, I know you were. It was the Germans who shot him down. Besides, you are on our side now.'

'But we are still prisoners. Will Miss Babs go back to her family now?'

'No. She only has a sister and she's in Wales till the end of the war. Then if her sister still has a home to come home to, Babs will go and live with her.'

'She will miss this life.'

'Yes, she will.'

'Will you go back to your family, Miss Lydi?'

'Yes, but I shall also really miss this life, and Babs, and you and Demetrio. What about you?'

'I have to go back to Italy, but what have I got to go back to? I have no brother or sister, and my parents are dead.'

'But your English is excellent. Where did you learn it?'

'I went to college. I had a very good education.'

'And you end up working on a farm. I would have thought with your knowledge of English they could have found you a job at the camp.'

'I don't like the camp. I'm afraid some of the prisoners are fascists and always looking for a fight. Deme and I like to keep ourselves to ourselves.'

Lydi began to pack the flask away. 'Don't you miss the lovely Italian sunshine and the wonderful buildings?'

He smiled. 'Yes, I do, but how many of the buildings will be left?'

'I don't know.'

'My life has been good here, very different but good. Perhaps I will be able to come back one day.'

'I'll give you my address, then if you ever do manage to come back, you can come and see me. And who knows, I might even get to Milano one day.'

'We did have some very beautiful buildings.'

'Let's hope they have been saved.'

'Rome is wonderful.' He smiled and his face lit up, then he kissed his fingertips. '*Magnifico*.'

Lydi also smiled. 'It will be nice when this is all over. But it's Babs I worry about.'

'I was very sorry when I heard about Mr Pete.'

'Yes, it was very sad.'

'Miss Babs has lost her sparkle.'

'Yes, she has.'

'She doesn't smile now.'

Lydi smiled. 'I hope she will one day.'

*

A week later, when Gino saw Babs on her own, he gave her a small parcel.

'This is for you.'

'For me? Why?'

'I hope it will bring your smile back.'

She swallowed hard and on opening the packet saw it was a necklace. 'Thank you, Gino. This is lovely. Did you make it?' She turned over the delicate metal flower that was in the middle of the chain.

He nodded. 'I hope it will help to, how do you say, cheer you up.'

'Thank you.' She didn't know what else to say. 'Did you make the chain as well?'

He blushed and moved from one foot to the other. 'No. I was telling Mrs Edna what I was making and she said she had a broken chain that I could have.'

'But it's not broken now.'

'No. I repaired it. I don't like to see you so unhappy.'

Babs looked at him and tears ran down her face. 'Thank you.' She turned and quickly walked away.

'Babs, are you all right?' said Lydi as her friend brushed past her. She was worried. It was still early days and everybody was walking on eggshells as far as Babs was concerned. She had seen Gino talking to her, and the thought that went quickly through her mind was, if he's upset her, I'll give him what for. She followed Babs into the house.

Edna had her arm round Babs's shoulders.

'Is she all right?' Lydi mouthed.

Edna shook her head.

'Babs, what did Gino say to upset you like this?'

'Nothing.' Babs looked up at her friend. 'He is so kind. Look, he has made me this.' She held out the necklace. 'But when will I be able to wear it?' Once again the tears fell.

Lydi took the gift. 'This is lovely.'

'I know.' Babs blew her nose. 'I'm sorry. I wish I was stronger.'

'Now don't you worry,' said Edna.

'I was ready to blast him,' said Lydi. 'Good job I came in here first. He is so kind.'

'Yes, he is.' Babs wiped her eyes. 'And what makes it worse for me is the way I treated him and Demetrio when they first came here.'

'They don't hold any grudges,' said Edna. 'They knew the situation. Now, I must get on with the lunch. Will you be around, Lydi?'

'I think so. Mr J was going to tell me what he wants doing.'

'It's so nice to see him pottering around again,'

said Babs, knowing she had to stop feeling sorry for herself.

'Yes, and I can tell you, I'm more than pleased that he gets out from under my feet,' said Edna.

It was June, and everybody was excited when they heard the news that Allied forces had landed on the beaches of France. The invasion had started and there was talk of the war coming to an end very soon.

One evening Babs and Lydi were sitting on the garden swing discussing their futures.

'So, your sister's coming back home.'

'That's what her letter said. She's gonner wait till the school holidays; that way she won't upset the kids too much.' Babs smiled. 'I can't imagine them with a Welsh accent. Lydi, what's gonner happen to us?'

'I don't know. We've got all the summer to get through yet.'

'How's Mr J gonner manage when we're demobbed?'

'Will they call it demobbed?'

'Dunno.'

'I was wondering about that. He can't manage the farm at all now, and he wouldn't be able to afford farm labourers,' said Lydi.

'I reckon he'll have to sell it.'

'I don't know if he owns it or just rents it.'

'So they could be homeless as well?'

'Could be.'

'That must be very worrying for Edna.'

'Yes, but she always looks cheerful.'

At that very moment, Edna and Sidney were having roughly the same sort of conversation.

'So what shall we do, old girl?'

'I don't know.'

'I know I'm getting stronger, but when this is all over, the girls and Gino and Demetrio will have to go and we won't be able to afford help.'

'Norman would help out if he didn't have such a big spread,' said Edna.

'He couldn't manage this as well.'

'I know.'

They settled back into a comfortable silence, each with their own thoughts and fears for their future.

Johnson's farm was in a relatively safe area, and they only had the occasional plane come over. Although the airfield where Pete had been stationed was only ten miles away, occasionally they heard the bombs exploding. Pete had told Babs that they always managed to get the planes in the air before the enemy bombers came over.

The farm and village had been saved from the bombing, although when an unexploded bomb dropped in a field a few miles away, it was the talk of the pub for days.

The new menace that everybody was talking about now was the doodlebug.

'Hitler's certainly trying to get us,' said Mr J one morning when he was looking at his newspaper.

'It sounds frightening,' said Edna. 'No pilot, so it can fall anywhere.'

'It's London that he's aiming them at again,' said Babs.

'There won't be much left of the capital at this rate,' said Mr J.

'Your sister won't come back just yet, will she?' asked Lydi.

'I hope not.' Babs was worried about her sister and the twins. 'She'll be mad if she comes back now,' she said, airing her thoughts out loud.

Lydi looked at her. 'She must read the papers. Surely she wouldn't bring the twins back, not till it was really safe.'

Babs shrugged. 'I hope not,' she repeated.

Two weeks later, as Lydi, Babs, Gino and Demetrio were busy cutting back hedges, they looked up when they heard what they thought was a plane in trouble.

'He sounds low,' said Lydi, shielding her eyes from the sun. 'Quick!' she yelled. 'Everybody down.'

They did as they were told and covered their heads with their hands as the putt-putt of the engine went over their heads.

Slowly they sat up and watched the flame behind the doodlebug move away.

'So that's what they look and sound like,' said Lydi.

Gino had his head in his hands and was trembling.

Babs went and squatted beside him. 'It's all right,' she said softly, patting his hand. 'It's gone.'

'I'm sorry.' He wiped his eyes, then stood up and quickly continued cutting the hedge.

It was then that they heard an explosion in the distance.

'Some poor devil got that one,' said Lydi.

'I'm glad it wasn't us.'

Babs looked at Gino, whose eyes were focused on the hedge. What had he been through during his war?

Babs was pleased when at breakfast on the twenty-fifth of August she received a birthday card from her sister with a letter telling her that they were going to stay in Wales a little longer.

The letter said that Joy had read that they were evacuating children again from London, so she might as well stay where she was.

'Your birthday's not till tomorrow,' said Lydi, looking at the card.

'I know. Perhaps she thought the post could be all over the place.'

'So, you're going to be twenty-one,' said Edna. 'Have you got anything special planned?'

'No.' Babs's thoughts went to Pete. She knew that he would have taken her out somewhere very special.

'Twenty-one! Now you can have the key of the door.' Mr J smiled.

'It would be nice if I had a door, let alone a key.'

'You will one day.'

'I think we should celebrate it anyway,' said Lydi, trying to lift the atmosphere. 'How about the pictures?'

'I could do a nice tea after,' said Edna.

'Sounds good,' said Babs. They didn't go to the local hop very much at all now. She knew she didn't want to see young men in air-force blue, dancing and laughing. She knew she would never get over losing Pete.

'So the pictures it is,' said Lydi, breaking into her thoughts.

This was all Babs could hope for now; perhaps next year things would be better. She stood the card on the dresser. Although things on the war front appeared to be getting better – the Allied armies had now reached Paris and everybody was overjoyed – when would it all end? And what would happen to them all?

Chapter 14

IT WAS THE BEGINNING of September, and hay-making time again. They were all pleased that it was going to be fine on the weekend when they would hire the equipment, and everybody who could would come to help, even the children.

'Daddy said you and Lydi might be going home one day.' Grace was helping Babs stack the heavy bundles.

'We will when the war is over,' said Babs.

'Do you want to go home?'

'No. I love it here.'

'So why don't you stay?'

'I won't be in the Land Army any more and your grandpa can't afford to keep us here. I wouldn't want to work for any other farmer.'

Grace's young face took on a worried expression. 'Will Lydi go as well?'

'I'm afraid so.'

'I shall miss you and Lydi.'

'And we shall miss you.'

'Daddy said that Gino and Demetrio will go back to Italy. He showed me and Robert on the atlas where that was. It's a long way away.'

'Yes, it is.'

Grace looked thoughtful. 'Would you stay if my daddy paid you?'

Laughing, Babs stood upright and held the little girl close. 'I don't think he would be able to.'

'I'll ask him.'

Babs watched Grace, who was wearing red shorts and a white blouse and a big floppy sunhat, skip across the field. Babs swallowed hard. She would miss all this. She had been so happy here. It had been a wonderful life, hard work with a lot of tears, and now with the end of the war in sight, it was time to start again.

Although it was Saturday, Gino and Demetrio were here helping. They were spending more and more time at the farm, and even Babs found it interesting when they sat and talked. She was learning about Italy, their life and culture.

Gino came running across the field.

'You look happy,' said Babs.

'Yes, I am,' he said breathlessly. 'Mrs Edna said that Demetrio and myself can stay here for the night so that we can help first thing in the morning and it will save Miss Lydi coming to get us.'

'That's good news. We can certainly do with your help. You won't get into any trouble with the camp, will you?'

'No. A lot of the men stay at the farms now.'

Gino looked up when he heard his name being called. 'I have to go and help make the haystack.'

Babs smiled and watched him run off. He was such a nice man and so eager to please.

It was late evening and getting dark. They were all sitting round the kitchen table, chatting and going over their day, and everybody was happy in the relaxed atmosphere and enjoying Edna's cooking.

'Now, the four of you go and sit outside,' said Edna, clearing away the empty plates.

'Let's help with the washing-up first,' said Babs, jumping up.

'No. Shoo. You've all been working hard, so go and sit with your feet up for a while.'

'And you can take one, and I mean only one, of my bottles of home-made wine. I want you all bright-eyed and wide awake in the morning,' said Mr J.

Lydi went and kissed his cheek. 'Thank you.'

'Go on, be off with you.'

They went out and the girls sat on the swing.

'Today has been so good,' said Demetrio, sitting on the chair next to them.

'Yes, it has,' said Lydi. 'Are you sure you two will be all right in the barn?'

'It will be fine. The smell of the straw is good for you.'

'Not if you've got hay fever,' said Babs.

'What is this hay fever?' asked Gino.

'It makes you sneeze.'

Edna came out with the bottle and glasses.

'Thanks, Edna. We could have got that,' said Lydi.

Edna nodded towards the house. 'He wants to make sure you only have the one bottle,' she said, grinning.

'As if we'd take more than one,' said Lydi, laughing.

'It'd be more than we'd dare do,' said Babs.

'I'll bring you boys some blankets later on.'

'Thank you, Mrs Edna.'

As she walked away, she was still smiling at the way they called her Mrs Edna. She'd said they could call her Mrs J or Edna, as the girls did, but they'd decided it would be more polite to combine the two as long as she didn't mind. She'd said she didn't.

Lydi reflected on the day. It had been good,

and it was lovely to see Babs relaxing and laughing and talking to the boys at last.

The following morning Babs went along to the barn to wake Gino and Demetrio. She slowly pushed open the door, and to her surprise they were still both fast asleep. They looked so peaceful and relaxed she didn't have the heart to tell them to wake up. She stood for a few moments looking down on their sun-tanned faces. Gino was a very good-looking young man. She smiled at his straight black hair sticking up in the air. Her opinion of him had changed so much. She'd realised he was very kind and would make a lovely husband for someone one day. Demetrio began to move.

'Miss Babs.' He scrambled to his feet. 'I am so sorry.' He grabbed the battered old hat that he always wore, then kicked Gino and shouted something in Italian.

Babs laughed when Gino also scrambled to his feet. 'Sorry. Sorry,' he said quickly, smoothing down his hair.

'There's nothing to be sorry for. Now go and have some breakfast while me and Lydi milk the cows, then you can put the milk out while we have our brekkers.'

'What is this brekkers?' asked Gino.

'Breakfast. I can see I'll have to teach you proper English. Now go along.'

'Thank you,' they both said together as they hurried from the barn.

Hitler was now sending over rockets. These wicked things just fell out of the sky with no warning. Babs was glad her sister was still in Wales. In one of her letters Joy had written and said that she was worried the house might not be standing when they returned to Rotherhithe.

'Would you like to go and see if it's still there?' asked Lydi one morning when Babs was reading out loud her sister's latest letter with the same theme.

'It would put her mind at rest if it is, after all the work Stan did on making the place look nice.'

'She must be worried about her husband. We hear of so many merchant ships being sunk.'

'Yes, she is. What d'you think, could I go one Sunday? If I could tell her that her house is still intact, that would help settle some of her fears.'

'I don't see why not, not now Gino and Demetrio stay here at weekends.'

'I'll ask Mr J.'

'I'm sure he won't mind.'

*

It was all settled, and the following Sunday Babs went off to the Smoke.

As she looked out of the train window as they got closer to home, the devastation almost took her breath away. Roofs with tarpaulins draped over them, windows boarded up, piles of rubble where once houses had stood all made her feel very sad. Would her sister's house still be there?

'London's looking a bit battered now,' said a young woman sitting opposite her. She was wearing a WAAF's uniform.

'Yes, it is.'

'Not been around for a while, then?'

'No.' Babs was still looking on the desolate scene.

'I hope everything is still there for you,' said the young girl as the train pulled into the station.

'So do I.'

As she made her way to Rotherhithe, Babs felt sick. Whole roads had disappeared and she didn't know where she was. At last she turned into Packhurst Place. To her great relief, Joy's house was still standing. It looked a little sad and war-torn, but it was still there. As she stood looking up at the windows, which were covered with plywood, she felt tears trickle down her cheeks. This was her sister's house. This had once been Joy and Stan's pride and joy.

'You all right, love?' The woman next door came out and looked at Babs curiously.

Babs quickly wiped her eyes and gave her a weak smile. 'Yes thanks.'

'That house ain't fer rent. The young couple what live there 'ave been evacuated and they should be back when this is all over.'

'I know. Joy is me sister and she's worried that it might have been blown away.'

'Yer sister, yer say? 'Ere, you ain't young Babs?'

'Yes.'

'Well I'll be buggered. Didn't recognise yer in yer uniform. You use ter live round in Green Street, didn't yer? I was sorry to hear about your parents.'

'Yes, I did.' Babs didn't want to say too much, as it still upset her.

'I've got a key if you want to see inside yer sister's place.'

'Yes please.'

'It's a bit of a mess, but it can be cleaned up all right.'

Babs waited for the neighbour to waddle back, then followed her as she opened the front door. She was right: it *was* a bit of a mess, and very dark. 'Who boarded up the windows?'

'Bill Cross organised it. He's our local air raid

warden; he's a good bloke. Every morning after a raid he comes round to check we're all still alive. He knew yer sister was away, and after the bomb dropped up the road, he saw to getting the windows boarded up.'

They scrunched over bits of ceiling and broken glass as they made their way down the dismal passage and into the kitchen. Joy had packed away all her ornaments and crockery, so everywhere looked sad and unlived in.

'We're lucky we ain't had no real damage in this road.'

All these terraced houses were much the same. Three bedrooms, a front room, kitchen and scullery. There was only a postage-stamp-size yard, but Joy and Stan had been happy here. Babs walked into the scullery. Stan had knocked out the old copper and in its place stood a modern gas one. Joy was always proud of that, not having to get up at the crack of dawn to light the fire under the boiler and wait till the water boiled; now all it took was to light the gas.

Babs walked back to the kitchen with Joy's neighbour.

'Mind you, it'll take a bit of cleaning up,' the woman said, looking around.

'I'll be able to do that when I leave the Land Army.'

'Will it be long before yer gets out?'

'I don't know. I'll hang on as long as I can.'

''Ere, come on in fer a cuppa.'

'Thanks all the same, but I do have to get back.'

'That's a pity. Would be nice to talk over old times. Ain't many old 'uns left round 'ere now. I remember when you used to pop round to see yer sister and her babies. I bet they've grown up a bit now.'

'Yes, they have. I haven't seen them, only in photos, and I only saw Joy at Mum and Dad's funeral, but I expect the twins have grown.'

'My Terry used ter be quite sweet on you, yer know.'

'Terry? I remember him. What's he doing now?'

'Prisoner of war.'

'Oh, I'm sorry.' Babs looked at her watch. 'I'm sorry, but I do have to get back to help with the milking.'

'But it's Sunday.'

'*I* know that but the cows don't.' She smiled. 'I really would love to come in and have a chat and a cuppa, but the trains are all over the place.'

'I understand, love. Give yer sister me love when you write.'

'I will.' Babs turned and walked away. She

knew she should have gone and sat with the woman, but it would have opened up so many sad memories. Part of her had wanted to go and see her old house, but she wasn't ready for that just yet.

Autumn gave way to winter, and every day the papers and the news were full of the war and the advancing army. Everybody knew that it must end soon.

All too soon it was sprout-picking time again.

'Just think,' said Lydi, sitting back on her hunkers, 'we won't have to do this next year. D'you know, I think I'll probably even miss it.'

'I wonder where we'll be,' said Babs.

'I expect I shall be in an office,' said Lydi. 'What about you, Babs?'

'Dunno. Behind a counter, I expect. What about you, boys?'

Demetrio smiled. 'I shall be with my wife and children. I expect they have grown.'

'What about a job?' asked Lydi.

'I hope to go back to working in my hotel.'

'You've got an hotel?' said Babs. 'You've kept that very quiet.'

'It's only a very small one.'

'Who knows, perhaps one day we can visit you,' said Lydi.

'You will be very welcome. I only hope the Germans haven't destroyed it.'

'What about you, Gino?' asked Babs.

He gave them a weak smile. 'I might have to go and stay with Demetrio; he might even offer me a job.'

Demetrio gave them one of his rare smiles. 'I might be able to find you work.'

'Perhaps you'll find yourself a nice girl when you get back home, Gino,' said Babs.

'I don't know. I wish I could stay in England. I love it here.'

'What, even picking sprouts?' asked Lydi.

He smiled. 'Yes, even picking the sprouts.' He looked at Babs, and she was sure there was a tear in those large brown eyes, or was it just the cold making them water?

'It would be lovely if in years to come we could all meet up again,' said Lydi. She had never had true friends before and the thought of them all going their separate ways distressed her.

Babs looked at Gino, who was busy picking sprouts. He was like her, one of the many homeless. At least she did have a sister to turn to, but for how long would she be welcome in their small house?

Christmas was almost on them again and Mr J was managing to do a few small jobs, but they all knew he would never be able to run the farm on his own. What was to become of him and Edna?

Chapter 15

FOR WEEKS NOW Gino and Demetrio had lived in at the farm. They had been made reasonably comfortable in one of the disused stables. There had been plenty of laughter and good feelings as Babs and Lydi helped them to move in. They had very few possessions and only needed beds, and they managed to borrow those from the local pub, which used to do bed and breakfast before the war. Everybody knew the end of the war was in sight and that the men would be going home soon, and so people were more than willing to help Mr Johnson out.

'Miss Babs,' said Gino one day when she was helping him put on the clean pillowcases Edna had sent over. 'I want to say thank you.'

'You don't have to thank me, Gino. These pillowcases belong to Mrs Edna.'

'I don't mean these.' He picked up a clean pillowcase. 'I think you are very nice.'

Babs blushed. 'I'm only doing a job.'

'I know you didn't like us when we first arrived, but now you are very nice to us.'

Babs sat on the bed. 'Well, yes. I was horrible, but now you've made me see how wrong I was.'

'Like me, you have lost dear ones.'

'Yes, I have.'

'When this war is all over, I would like you to come to Italy.'

'I expect travel will be very hard.'

'Could I write to you?'

'Yes, why not? Mind you, I don't know how long I shall be living with my sister.'

'I have Miss Lydi's address, she said she will write.'

'I'll let you know Joy's address.'

'Thank you.'

Babs jumped up. 'Right, come on, we must get these dirty bedclothes over to Edna. She's doing the wash today.'

'Thank you.' He tenderly touched her hand and smiled.

Babs looked at Gino. He was a very kind person and she was always filled with guilt at the way she had treated the two Italians when they first came to the farm. She was so pleased they were now all friends.

It was the twenty-fifth of December, and very early on a cold, dark, drizzly morning everybody had been busy seeing to the cows. After breakfast they helped Edna prepare the meal. They all had mixed feelings over what could be their last Christmas together.

When Norman, Iris and the children arrived, the house was full of laughter and happiness. After a wonderful dinner, it was present time. Gino and Demetrio had made gifts for them all: another brooch for Edna, Lydi and Babs, another doll for Grace that was better dressed than last year's, and a car for Robert that was made from a can. It had been painted red and was very streamlined.

All too soon it was time for Norman and his family to leave.

After the goodbyes and the chores for the day were finished, they were all sitting in the front room before a roaring fire. Mr J had nodded off, Edna was busy sewing and Lydi was doing a crossword.

'I'm just going outside,' whispered Babs. She wanted to be alone. She wanted to think about Pete.

She pulled her greatcoat round her shoulders and hurried to the barn. Although it was dark, the cows were all standing quietly and they made the place feel warm. 'I'm gonner miss you,' she said, gently patting one or two backsides. She knew the time was coming soon for her to go back to London. She and Lydi had been talking about it for weeks. But what did she have to go back to? She couldn't call it home any more, and it had looked so depressing when she'd gone to check on Joy's house. She sat on a stool and began to cry. If only Pete was here, her life would be full of love and happiness. 'Why did you have to die?' she said out loud.

A sudden noise made her stand up. 'Who's there?' she asked.

'I'm sorry, Miss Babs. I didn't mean to frighten you.'

Babs could see in the gloom that it was Gino. She quickly wiped her eyes. 'Gino, what is it?'

'I just came to see if you were all right.'

'I'm fine, thank you.'

'Do you want to be alone? I can go.'

'No, please stay.'

'Would you like me to sit with you?'

'If you want to.'

He sat on another stool. 'You are very sad. I

expect you are sad about Pete. He was a nice man.'

'Yes, he was.'

'And you are a nice lady.'

Babs let a weak smile lift her sad face.

'I am very sad that we will have to go back to Italy soon. I have liked it here in England,' said Gino.

'And we have liked having you here. But you must be eager to see your country again – all that lovely sunshine.' She tapped the back of his hand.

At first he didn't reply and they sat in silence.

'Miss Babs, if I can stay in England, would you show me London? I've always wanted to see London with its wonderful buildings.'

'Do you think you will be allowed to stay here?'

'I don't know. I have no family to go back to.'

'If you can stay, I would be more than pleased to show you London. What's left of it.'

'Thank you. Thank you very much. You are very kind and I like you very much.'

'And I like you. Now come on, we'd better get back inside, otherwise they'll wonder what we're up to.'

'Up to?' he asked in a puzzled voice.

She only smiled, and they went back to the house.

*

It was towards the end of January, and Edna was looking very down. When one evening Norman came to the farm, he too looked worried.

'Could I have a word with you two?' he asked in a hushed tone.

Both Lydi and Babs could sense something was wrong as they made their way into the front room.

Babs shivered. 'You can't believe how warm and inviting this room was a few weeks ago, can you?' she said to lighten the atmosphere.

Norman sat on the sofa. 'Dad didn't want to say anything before, but you know he won't be able to keep this farm on?'

They both nodded.

'What's he going to do?' asked Lydi.

'He's only a tenant farmer, like a lot of them round here, and he's told the landowner that he wants to give up the farm.'

'Where will they live?' asked Babs.

'I've applied for permission to build on to my place. So as soon as this last crop of sprouts have been picked, and before spring planting, they will give it all up and move in with us till their place is ready.'

Lydi tried to smile. 'I knew we wouldn't be let off picking those damn sprouts.'

Babs could feel the tears begin to slowly run down her cheeks.

'I'm so sorry,' said Norman. 'Dad didn't have the heart to tell you himself. He thinks of you two as daughters.'

'And I think of Mr J as more than a boss,' said Lydi with a catch in her voice. 'But we knew this had to happen one day.'

'What will happen to Gino and Demetrio?' asked Babs.

'They will have to go back to camp till they are sent home.'

'It's gonner be hard for Gino. At least Demetrio has got his family to go back to,' said Lydi.

Babs shivered.

'Come on,' said Norman. 'It's chilly in here. Let's go and see Mum and Dad.'

Babs stood up and hugged him. 'I shall miss you and Iris and the children.'

'And they will miss you.' Norman moved away.

Both Lydi and Babs knew this was going to be hard. Their lives were about to change again for ever.

Chapter 16

BABS FELT VERY sad as the train took her back to London. It was March 1945, and nearly six years of war was behind them. Everybody knew it would soon be announced that it was all over at long last. So many lives had been lost, and for those who had survived, things would never be the same again. War had changed everything.

It was a bright, sunny day and everybody was full of hope. As Babs looked around at the happy faces of the servicemen and women, she knew that many of them were going home. But as she stared out of the train's dirty window, she knew she couldn't call Joy's house home. Her thoughts were full of her mum and dad and her real home, but that had gone. How different everybody's lives would have been if there hadn't been a war. She let a weak smile banish her sad expression for a moment. If it hadn't been for the war, she would never have known Pete. He was the most wonderful person she had ever met, and she knew she would never forget him and would love him for ever.

It was a sad day when she and Lydi left the farm, and there had been many hugs, kisses and tears. Gino and Demetrio had gone back to the camp a week earlier to be ready for the day they would be sent back to Italy, and although everybody had promised to write, they all knew they had to get on with their new lives.

For the past two weeks Babs had been staying with Lydi at her parents' home. They had made her very welcome, but she had felt out of place.

Her sister had told her she could go to the house in Packhurst Place any time she wanted. Joy was going to wait till the end of the school term before bringing the children back from Wales. Babs hadn't told Joy too much about the mess her home was in, and thought it would keep her occupied to go and try and clean the place up before her sister returned with the children.

As the train came to a shuddering, noisy stop, Babs got out and stood on the platform for a moment or two. Then, picking up her case, she walked out into the early spring sunshine to begin a new life. The old one now had to be left behind.

At last it happened. On the eighth of May 1945, the wireless told them that the war was officially over at last and there was to be two days' holiday. People rushed into the streets and hugged and kissed complete strangers. The feeling of joy was indescribable.

Babs rushed outside when Mrs Bolton from next door banged on her door.

'It's over!' she screamed, grabbing Babs and twirling her round and round.

Although everybody knew it, it was still a thrill being told by Mr Churchill himself.

'Me boy will be home soon,' said Mrs Bolton with tears streaming down her face. 'And yer sister will be back now.'

'Yes, she will,' said Babs, coming up for breath after being hugged by her buxom neighbour.

They sat on the concrete coping that ran round the bay window, surveying all the excitement in the street. Kids were running around screaming and people who didn't know one another were kissing and hugging. It was a happy, carefree sight.

'After all these years,' said Mrs Bolton. 'I shall be seeing me Terry after all this time.' She dabbed at her eyes with the bottom of her washed-out floral overall. 'I expect he's lorst a lot of weight. I hope they give us some extra rations to fill 'em up.'

Babs smiled. This was indeed a great day. One that would go down in the history books.

'Winnie said we could all 'ave a holiday.'

'As I ain't got a job yet, I feel as if I'm already on holiday.'

'Well let's face it, love, you was working for years and all hours.'

'Yes, I was.'

Babs sat back and reflected on these past six years. There had been a lot of good times amongst the bad.

'You gonner look for a job now yer sister's coming home?' asked her neighbour, interrupting her thoughts.

'Yes. I'll have to go and see if Woolies will take me back.'

'I expect they will. So you gonner stay with yer sister, then?'

'I'll have to. I ain't got anywhere else to live. Would you like a cup of tea?' Babs changed the subject. She really didn't want to worry too much about the future just yet.

'I would that, love. Mind you, if yer got anyfing stronger, that would be even better.'

'No, sorry.'

'Well that'll have to do for terday. There's been talk about having a street party.'

'That should be fun.'

'Old Bill Cross who was the warden says that he's gonner give everybody a job to do. You any good at making bunting?'

'No. But I can help put it up if he wants.'

'I fink he's coming round ternight.'

'I'll talk to him then. Come on, let's have this cuppa.'

'Good idea, love.'

Mrs Bolton followed Babs as fast as her bunioned feet would allow, along the passage and into the kitchen.

'You've done a good job with all the clearing up. Looks like a proper little palace now and no mistake,' said Mrs Bolton, looking round the neat kitchen before she plonked herself in one of the two armchairs next to the fireplace that Babs had black-leaded. She had found Joy's stock of cleaning materials; her sister had always been very fussy. The crockery was now displayed on the large dresser that lined the wall next to the fireplace

'Young Joy will be very happy when she sees what you've done.'

'Just as well she didn't see the state it was in

before. I shall be glad when they put the upstairs windows in; it makes it ever so dark with that boarding.'

'Bill Cross reckons we should be next. Knows everyfing, does that bloke.'

'Let's hope he's right.'

'They look nice,' said Mrs Bolton, looking at the flowers that Babs had arranged in a vase sitting on a runner in the middle of the table; she had bought them at the market yesterday. She felt she needed something to remind her of the wonderful countryside that she missed so much.

'So when do you think Terry will be home?' Babs asked.

'Gawd only knows. Poor little bugger.'

Babs put a tray on the table with matching cups and saucers. 'I was queuing up at the greengrocer's yesterday for some potatoes. Only let me have a couple of pounds. I don't know how women with families get on.'

'I hope things get back to normal soon. We're all fed up with this rationing.'

'I've not had to worry about it before, and things don't go far when there's only one set as rations.'

'I know that. It's been bloody hard.'

Babs put the teapot on the cork tablemat. That too matched the crockery. Her sister always liked nice things.'Help yourself to sugar and milk.'

'Can you spare the sugar?'

Babs nodded. 'I don't take sugar so there'll be a bit in the cupboard for when Joy gets back. I expect the twins have sugar with everything.'

'I expect they do.'

On Thursday afternoon everyone was busy preparing for Saturday's street party when Babs saw Joy and the twins turning into Packhurst Place, struggling with their bags and cases. She dropped the bunting she was holding and ran to meet her sister. They clutched each other and tears were mixed with kisses.

'Why didn't you tell me you was coming home?' said Babs as she bent down to hug the children.

'Only made up me mind yesterday. I want to be here when Stan gets home.'

'Is he on his way back then?'

'Dunno. Ain't heard from him for weeks and weeks.' Joy brushed away a tear.

'And look at you two.' Babs stood back and looked at the twins. 'Well, you've both certainly grown. You're nearly as tall as me now, John,' she joked, ruffling his dark hair.

'Are you my Auntie Babs?' asked Ann.

'Yes, I am.'

'What are you doing with all those flags?' the little girl asked, looking up at her with her large brown eyes.

Babs crouched down to her level. 'I'm helping these people to put them up because we're going to have a street party to mark the end of the war.' She stood up and said to her sister, 'I love her accent.'

'I expect she'll lose it as soon as she starts playing with the kids round here.'

'I don't know why we're standing here. Come on, let's take you home. And I expect you're dying for a cuppa,' said Babs, picking up her sister's suitcase.

'I should say so.'

As they approached the house, Mrs Bolton rushed as fast as her feet would allow to meet them. 'It's lovely to see yer again, Joy,' she said throwing her arms round her. 'And look at these two. Ain't they grown?' She bent down and hugged the children to her ample bosom.

Babs smiled at the look of horror on young John's face. When Mrs Bolton released them, Ann went and buried her head in her mother's skirt.

Inside, the children ran around in excitement.

'Why have we got wood up at the windows?' asked Ann.

'We're waiting for a man to come and put the

glass back in,' said Babs, filling the kettle.

'Who broke them?' asked John.

'The Germans.'

'Let's go and look at upstairs while we're waiting for the kettle to boil,' said Joy.

Joy followed by Babs went from room to room looking at her home.

'I managed to get most of the ceiling plaster from off the mattresses. It was a bit of a mess when I got here,' Babs said.

'I expect it was. Thanks, Babs.'

They stood in the gloomy bedroom. 'They should be putting the glass in the windows next week.'

Joy ran her hand over her dressing table. 'It's a pity about all the scratches on this. It was me pride and joy. Used to polish it till you could see your face in it.'

'At least you've still got one. There's a lot of folks who've only finished up with what they stand up in.'

'I know. I was a bit worried that the looters might have been in and helped themselves.'

'I think they would have had to get past Mrs Bolton first.'

Joy smiled. 'She's a good 'un. She used to write to me, you know. Got a heart of gold, that one. She was heartbroken when her Terry got captured. Thinks the world of him, she does. I pity the poor girl that marries him; she'll have to be very special to pass Mrs Bolton's requirements.'

'I have managed to wash and air all the bedclothes, so you'll be able to sleep in your beds tonight.'

'What about you, where are you gonner sleep?'

'Me and Mrs B have talked about that. I can go and sleep in there if I want, but I'd rather be in here with you. I was wondering about the sofa in the front room.'

'You can't sleep on that. It was bloody uncomfortable to sit on, let alone sleep. No, we'll get you a bed in Ann's room, that's if you don't mind sharing with her.'

Babs threw her arms round her sister. 'That would be great. It's really good to be together again.'

'I know. Pity Mum and Dad didn't make it.'

Babs swallowed hard.

'I was very sorry to hear about your feller,' said Joy. 'Sounds as if he was very special.'

'Yes, he was. You would have liked him.'

'Mum! Mum!' Ann came running in. 'Tell John that's my bedroom.'

'Come on, let's go and sort these two out. Are

you sure you want to stay with us? It's gonner be very noisy.'

Babs smiled. She knew that this was just what she needed: a house full of laughter, chatter and noise. 'Come on, let's have that cuppa, then we can see about making up your beds.'

Joy plonked a big kiss on her sister's cheek.

'What was that for?' said Babs, gently touching her cheek.

'Just for being my sister.'

Chapter 17

THE FOLLOWING MORNING when Babs was hanging out the washing, Mrs Bolton came out of her lavatory and up to the wire that divided the two back yards.

'Joy and the kids settling in all right, then, love?' she asked, adjusting her floral wrap-round overall.

Babs took the pegs from out of her mouth. 'Yes thank you. I'm going to get a bed and sleep in Ann's room. We know we have to go to the town hall for these docket things. Don't know how long I'll have to wait till I get a bed; someone said I might have to put me name down for one.'

'Don't worry too much about that. I know someone who might be able to get you a second-hand one for the time being.'

'That would be great. Thanks. It's got to be

better than sleeping on Joy's sofa.'

'Leave it with me.' With that, Mrs Bolton toddled off indoors.

Babs had told Joy about her conversation with Mrs Bolton, and that afternoon, to the girls' astonishment, two men arrived at the front door holding between them a bedstead; the wooden top and bottom were leaning against the wall.

'Where did that come from?' Joy asked the older man.

'Nell next door said you wanted a bed, and I just happened to 'ave one. That'll be five bob.'

Babs rushed to the kitchen and got her purse in case they changed their mind and took it away.

Nell Bolton came to her front door. 'Thought I 'eard young Billy's voice. All right then, me lad?'

Billy, who was about as old as Nell, said, 'Yes thanks, Nell. You did say they didn't want a mattress?'

Babs and Joy looked at each other.

'Yer, that's right.'

Babs went to speak, but Nell put her hand up to silence her.

'See yer around, Nell,' said Billy as he and the younger man pushed their empty barrow up the road. 'Let us know if there's anyfink else I can 'elp yer wiv,' he shouted over his shoulder.

'Will do, Billy.'

'Mrs Bolton, we did need a mattress,' said Babs.

'I know, love, but you didn't want one orf Billy. Could be full of bed bugs, and they're a bloody job ter git rid of once they get in.'

Babs shuddered. 'You don't think there could be some in the bed, do you?'

'Dunno. You'd better give the springs a good brush and wash, just ter be on the safe side. You can borrow Terry's mattress till he gets back; by then you'll 'ave found out all about this docket thing.'

The look on Joy's face when Mrs Bolton was talking about bed bugs was a picture of disgust. 'Come on, let's get that bed out in the yard and give it a good scrub.'

Between them they carried the springs through the hall and kitchen and out through the back door into the yard, then followed with the foot and headboards. These back-to-back houses didn't have back ways; everything had to come through the house, including coal, which went under the stairs, making a very dusty mess.

'I'll get a bucket of hot water and a scrubbing brush,' said Babs.

Joy looked at the pieces of bed. 'You don't think Nell's mattress might have bugs, do you?'

Babs laughed. 'Shouldn't think so, not by the

look on her face when she was telling us about them.'

'Well, let's hope we can sort out these dockets before too long.'

'I heard when I was queuing that you might be entitled to some for new curtains and bed linen.'

Joy's face lit up. 'That would be wonderful, seeing as how most of mine are in ribbons now.'

'Well, we can go and find out. But let's get this bed sorted out first.'

They set to and began to scrub the springs.

After helping Joy and the children settle back into their home, on Friday Babs decided to call in to Woolworths and see about a job.

She was shown to the manager's office.

Mr Carter was a thin-faced man with slicked-down black hair. 'Sit yourself down. So,' he said, leaning back in his chair, 'you worked here before?'

'Yes, I was on the cosmetics counter.'

'Bit short of cosmetics at the moment, but I daresay one day things will be better.'

'I hope so.'

'You've been in the Land Army, then?'

'Yes.' Babs didn't want to elaborate; there was something about this smarmy-looking bloke that she didn't like.

'We haven't got anything at the moment, but I'll take your name and address, and as you've worked here before you stand a good chance. A lot of the married women want to stay at home now the breadwinners are back from the war. But if you ask me, a lot of 'em will soon get tired of being shut up indoors all day and no extra money coming in.'

Babs kept quiet. She guessed that a lot of wives would miss being independent and not having wages of their own.

As Mr Carter stood up, so did Babs. 'I'll let you know if anything comes up.' He opened the door and Babs walked away disappointed. She'd been hoping to start work as soon as possible.

On Saturday the street party was quickly in full swing. Everybody had contributed food they could spare, including tinned stuff that had been hidden away for years, and somehow the table was full of cakes and sandwiches. It was surprising what came from under the counter from some of the local shops, and there was always someone who knew someone who could get something or other. Marge, salmon, tinned fruit and even icing sugar that had been stored away for heaven only knows how long suddenly saw the light of day. The kids had lemonade, and there was beer for the grown-ups; even the odd bottle of whisky came out, as well as port. The trestle tables and chairs came from the mission hall and were covered with sheets that were a little thin now. Bill Cross had certainly worked hard to make today a huge success. A piano was brought out into the street, and in the evening the sing-song and dancing was enjoyed by everyone. This was the day they had waited almost six long, hard years for. They forgot the boarded-up windows and the tiles missing from the roofs, and ignored the piles of rubble that were once somebody's home. Today they were going to enjoy themselves. The war in Europe was over; now only Japan had to be defeated.

Mrs Bolton was sitting on a chair in the street, watching all the merry-making, when Joy sat down next to her.

'All right then, Mrs B?'

'I should say so. Look at those kids dancing, and your Babs is enjoying herself.'

'Yes, she is. I'm so pleased. She's had a rotten war: first we lost Mum and Dad, then her young man got killed.'

'I didn't know that, the poor love. Was he in the forces?'

'Yes, he was a machine-gunner. Babs was very fond of him.'

'That's a shame.'

'What about Terry, any news yet?'

'No, but every day I'm hoping to hear something.'

Babs plonked herself next to Joy. 'All this dancing's wearing me out.'

'Go on with yer, you're only a young 'un. I wish me feet would let me jump up with 'em.'

One by one the children gradually went to bed, and there were only a few of the drunks and hardy ones left.

'Fancy a cuppa?' Mrs Bolton asked Joy and Babs.

'Why not?' they said together.

'I'll make it,' said Babs, jumping up and going inside.

'She's a good 'un,' said Mrs Bolton.

'I know,' said Joy. 'I just hope she meets Mr Right one day.'

'She will, she's young and very pretty.'

Joy smiled and nodded.

On Monday morning, Babs was very surprised to get a letter from Woolworths asking her if she could start work the following Monday. She was over the moon: she had a job and would be getting a wage.

'I shall miss you queuing up for me,' said Joy.

'Sorry about that, but at least I shall be able to pay my way.'

Joy was busy giving the twins their breakfast and Babs was sitting at the kitchen table.

'Auntie Babs, will you still stay with us when Daddy comes home?' asked Ann.

'Of course she will,' answered Joy quickly.

'I would like to,' said Babs.

'When will Daddy be home?' asked John.

'I don't know, but let's hope it'll be soon.'

Babs fingered the spoon in her saucer. It would be very crowded in Joy and Stan's small house when he came home. And would he want her around? Although they had always got on all right, it would be very different all living together. Once she got settled at work, perhaps she should think about moving to a place of her own.

'You look miles away, Babs. Everything all right? Not worried about this job, are you?'

'A bit,' she lied. 'It'll be different, and as for being stuck indoors all day, I just hope I can put up with it.'

'Go on. You'll be all right. You've always been adaptable.'

Babs smiled. 'I suppose I have.' Once again her thoughts went to Pete. If only he was still here, but it wasn't to be, and now like so many people she had to get on with her life.

*

Babs soon got into things at work. Although the counters were very bare, they tried to spread everything out to make them appear fuller. One day they had a few Tangee lipsticks come in and word spread like wildfire. The queue went right down the road. Babs was pleased that Mr Carter let the staff have one each; he said it was to stop any pilfering.

'I've got a present for you,' said Babs to Joy when she got home that evening.

'Me? But it ain't me birthday.'

'I know.'

'Have you got a present for me and John?' asked Ann.

'No, sorry, love.' Babs handed her sister the lipstick.

'A lipstick. A whole new lipstick.' Joy pulled Babs to her and kissed her. 'Thank you. Thank you. D'you know, I'm fed up with melting down all me old bits. It's so messy. Mind you, you never know what colour you're gonner finish up with.'

Babs laughed. 'I thought I was in luck today. Someone told us that Dolcis was having some shoes in, and as I had some coupons, I went and stood in a queue all me lunch hour. I got really excited when I got near the door, only to be told when I was inside that they only had size threes left.'

'What were they like?'

'Black suede with a high heel, just what I wanted. All me lunch hour I stood in that queue. What a waste of time.'

'It's things like that that make my blood boil. I bet the toffs manage to get everything they want.'

'And I bet they don't have to queue for 'em or give up coupons.'

'Still, it must get better one day.'

'Yes, but how long will it be?'

'Dunno. At least I've got the dockets for your mattress.'

'So it's my lucky day as well.'

Joy laughed.

'What's so funny?' asked Babs.

'Us getting excited over a mattress. And I've got the dockets for some linen and curtains, then on top of that I've got a new lipstick. Life just gets better. All I want now is for Stan to walk through that door, then my life will be complete.'

'That will be the icing on the cake.'

Joy grinned. 'I should say so.'

Chapter 18

THE RATTLE OF the letterbox sent the children scurrying to the front door to pick up the post.

'There's ever such a lot,' yelled John.

'Let me have some,' shouted Ann.

'Stop quarrelling, you two, and bring them in here,' called Joy from the kitchen.

Between them the children put them on the table.

'There's one for you, Babs, and look: I've got four from Stan.' Joy's face was flushed with excitement.

'Is Daddy coming home?' asked John.

'I hope so,' she said, her eyes shining.

'Look, why don't you two go and play in the yard and let Mummy read her letters, then she'll be able to tell you when your daddy's coming home.'

They rushed outside.

'So, who's your letter from?'

'Lydi.' Since coming home, Babs had had a few letters from her friend. She opened the letter. 'You'll never guess,' she said as she scanned down the page. 'Frank has come back to see her.'

'Hmm,' said Joy as she too read her letters, not a bit interested in what Babs was saying.

Babs sat quietly reading her letter. Frank had come back from Canada and gone to the farm to see Lydi, but of course she had gone. He'd managed to find Edna and Mr Johnson, who'd given him her address. Frank had written to her and asked to meet up with her. Babs smiled. It would be wonderful if they got together. She would love to see her friend happily married. She looked up when Joy gave out a little yelp.

'He's coming home.' She really did have stars in her eyes.

'When?' asked Babs.

'He was in America when this last letter was sent, so it could be any day now. John, Ann, come in here.'

They must have been just outside the door, as they were inside in a flash.

'It's Daddy. He's coming home.'

'When?' asked John.

'Very soon. So, John, you'll have to have a

haircut, and Ann, let's see if we can get you a new frock, and I've got to sort something out for myself.'

Babs began to laugh.

'What's so funny?' Joy asked her sister.

'You. Do you honestly think he's gonner be worried if John's hair needs cutting, or Ann is wearing a new frock?'

Joy looked hurt. 'He might not be worried, but I will. I want his homecoming to be very special.'

Babs went and hugged her sister. 'I'm sorry. Of course you do, and as tomorrow's Sunday, why don't we all go along to Brick Lane and see what we can get. We might be lucky and not have to part with any coupons.'

'Thanks.'

Babs put her letter in her handbag. 'Now I must be off. See you all tonight.'

'Don't work too hard,' said Joy.

'I won't.'

Two days later Joy had another letter from Stan, telling her he hoped to be with them on Saturday.

When Babs got up on Saturday morning, she could hear everybody bustling about. She knew that today was going to be very special; this was the day her sister had waited a long while for.

Joy was already pacing up and down and

going to the front door and looking up the road. The children couldn't wait to go outside and wait for their daddy to come home.

'Joy, why don't you go and get yourself ready?'

'I don't want to get dressed up too soon. Do you think that frock I got looks all right?'

'Of course it does, you'll look smashing.'

'I hope so.'

'Now go and get ready.'

'No, I'll wait. I don't want to end up looking a mess. I wonder what time he'll be home.'

'Will he know us?' asked Ann, standing next to Babs, who was putting on her make-up ready for work in front of the only mirror in the house that was still intact.

'Of course he will,' said Babs, putting a dab of lipstick on Ann's nose.

'I don't really remember him,' she said, rubbing her nose. 'Mummy shows us his photo and so I expect I'll see him first, then I'll tell him who I am.' Ann was a very clever little girl.

'I hope he likes us,' said John.

'How could anybody not like you two?' Babs held them both close.

But had Stan changed? He had been round the world many times. It was three years since he'd last seen them; he had had just a week with them when his ship docked at Cardiff. His children had been just babies at the time, so Joy had made sure since then that they would never forget him.

All day while Babs was at work, she was thinking of her sister and wondering if Stan was home. She was worried that she would be in the way and tried to think of ways to stay out. It was during her lunch hour that she decided to phone Lydi that evening. She was so pleased Lydi's parents had installed one. She knew her friend had gone back to work at the office she had been at before she went into the Land Army, and hoped she would be at home tonight.

On the way home, Babs stopped at the phone box.

'Lydi, it's me, Babs.'

'Babs!' screamed Lydi. 'It's lovely to hear you again. I've really missed you.'

'Me too. How's Frank?'

'Gorgeous. I can't tell you how thrilled I was to see him again. I never thought he would come looking for me. So how's Rotherhithe?'

'Still looking very sad. I told you I was back at Woolies, and guess what? Stan, Joy's husband, is coming home today, so I thought I'd hang around a bit before I go home. Don't want to be in the way.'

'I shouldn't think they would think that. Look, why don't you come and stay with us one weekend?'

'I'd love to, but I have to work on Saturdays.'

'So come just for the Sunday. I would really love to see you again.'

'I would like that. I miss the life we used to have.'

'So do I. It was hard work but it was still great.'

'Yes, it was.' The bleeps started. 'Oh, I'll have to go. Me money's running out and I ain't got any more change. I'll phone again tomorrow and we can make—' She couldn't finish her sentence as the line went dead.

Ann and John rushed to meet her when they saw her turn the corner.

Babs bent down and hugged them. 'So, is your daddy home?'

'No. Mummy told us to keep looking for him. She said he should be home soon,' said John, who looked sad and was kicking the ground.

Ann held Babs's hand very tight and asked her, 'Does he know where we live?'

'Will he go to Wales?' asked John.

'No. He used to live here with you and Mummy before the war started.'

As Babs walked in, she could see the worried look on her sister's face. 'You don't think anything's happened to him?' Joy asked.

'No, of course not. Remember, the trains are all over the place.'

'It would just be his bloody luck to go all through the war then get himself run over coming home.'

'Joy, don't talk daft. Besides, you'll upset the kids. Now go and sit yourself down and I'll make a cup of tea.' Babs got to the scullery door and, turning, said, 'Please don't upset yourself. He'll be here as soon as he can.'

'Yes, I know he will.'

It wasn't till ten o'clock that there was a knock on the front door. Although the children were in bed, as soon as they heard their mother open the door they were halfway down the stairs. When they saw the man standing in the passageway, they stopped.

Babs, who was right behind her sister, glanced up the stairs at the looks on their faces. To them this wasn't the man in the photos; he had been laughing and smart. This man looked tired and scruffy, with stubble on his face.

He threw his kitbag on the floor and, grabbing Joy, held her tight and kissed her hard and long.

When they broke apart, still holding on to his wife Stan said, 'Hello, kids. All right then, Babs?' he added over Joy's shoulder.

Joy let him go and wiped her eyes. Stan came and, hugging Babs tight, kissed her. Then he looked up the stairs. 'You two gonner come down here and give me a big kiss and a cuddle?'

Slowly they came down the stairs and Stan rushed to them and hugged them both together. Babs could see he had tears in his eyes.

'At times I never thought I'd see this day,' he said with a catch in his voice.

Joy went to him, and as they all stood holding each other, Babs could see they were a close, tight-knit family, and she felt very much on her own.

'I'll put the kettle on,' she said, going into the scullery. 'I expect you'll be needing a cuppa.'

'Yes please.'

She stood looking out of the window on to the yard. She was thrilled that Joy had Stan back, but she couldn't help worrying about her own future. She couldn't stay here for ever. She had to find somewhere to live, but where? Everybody was coming back to London, and any empty rooms or houses were quickly snapped up. The girls at work had told her it was all a question of knowing somebody and giving them key money. Who did she know who could help her? The kettle began to whistle and Babs made the tea. Joy had even somehow managed to get some cake. She had put it in the cake tin and dared anybody to touch it.

Babs took the tea and cake into the kitchen.

Joy's face was wreathed in smiles. 'Stan's coming out of the merchant navy and going to get a job here,' she said as her sister put the tray on the table.

'That'll be smashing. The kids will love having you around. Do you still take sugar, Stan?'

'Yes please. Can you spare it? I know how bad things have been here. I've got me ration card and a few bits in me kitbag. Could you two bring it in here?'

The twins scampered into the hall.

'It's ever so heavy,' said Ann, as between them they dragged it into the kitchen.

Stan laughed. 'Looks like we'll have to toughen you up.'

There was a look of horror on John's face. 'I'm already tough,' he said defiantly. 'She's not, though.'

'Yes I am,' said Ann, determined to have her say.

'Yes, that's all right,' said Joy. She didn't want

them quarrelling. She didn't want anything to spoil this wonderful night.

The excitement when the contents of the kitbag were revealed was wonderful. There were nylons for Joy and Babs. A beautiful china doll for Ann, with real hair, and eyes that opened and closed. For once the little girl was speechless at such a wonderful present. John had a wind-up American police car with flashing lights and a siren that sent him scurrying down the passage as he protested that everybody's legs were in the way.

Tins of butter, fruit and salmon were placed on the table, and when Stan brought out a beautiful box wrapped in lovely paper with ribbons and bows round it, everyone waited to see what was inside.

'I've never seen anything so lovely. I don't want to unwrap it,' said Joy, turning it over and over.

'The Yanks certainly know how to make a present look good,' said Stan.

Slowly and very carefully Joy opened her gift. She almost squealed when she held up a beautiful peach-coloured nightdress.

'The girls in the department store told me the other thing's called a negligee,' said Stan.

'It's the most beautiful thing I've ever seen,'

said Joy, tears running down her face as she held it up. 'It's so delicate. It's too good to wear.'

'Don't worry about that,' said Stan with a twinkle in his eye. 'Remember, it's been three years.'

Joy blushed as she wiped her tears away. 'Shh, not in front of the children.'

Babs also had tears in her eyes. She was so happy for her sister.

After a while, Babs could see the children were having a job keeping their eyes open. 'Come on, you two. I'll take you up. You've got forever to play with your toys and see your dad.' Turning to Joy, she added, 'I'll put them to bed.'

'Thanks, Babs.'

'I could be about an hour reading 'em a story. Will that be all right?'

'Should be,' said Stan, grinning.

Joy didn't answer as she was looking longingly at Stan.

As Babs lay in bed that night, she tried hard not to listen to what was going on in the next room. Joy and Stan deserved all their happiness. They had waited a long while to be in each other's arms. She turned over. Would she ever fall in love again? Would someone ever hold her tight and whisper nice things? Could she ever love someone like she had loved Pete? Only time would tell.

Once again she turned over and tried to let other thoughts fill her mind. Next Sunday she would go and see Lydi. That at least was something to look forward to.

Chapter 19

As soon as she opened the front door, weary after being on her feet all day, it gladdened Babs's heart to hear the children screaming with excitement and Stan laughing as he played with them. This was a sound she had feared she might never hear again during the dark days when ships were going down every day. But Babs and Joy also worried as they knew this euphoria couldn't last for ever. Soon Stan would have to start looking for work. Without a trade and with so many servicemen coming home, jobs could be hard to find.

On Saturday evening Ann was in bed watching Babs put a few bits in her handbag to take to Lydi's. She was going off first thing in the morning.

'You will come back?' asked Ann, propping herself up on her elbow.

'Of course I will. I shall be back tomorrow night, so don't worry. Besides, I expect your mum and dad will take you somewhere nice and you won't even know I've gone.'

Ann sat up. 'I will, Auntie Babs, I will.'

'I bet you love having your daddy home, taking you to see things.'

'There's ever such a lot of bombed buildings.'

'Yes, I know.'

'I'm glad we wasn't here then. I would have been very frightened.'

Babs went and sat on the little girl's bed. 'I'm glad you wasn't here as well. And yes, it was very frightening. But it's all over now. And there won't be any more wars in your lifetime.'

'We went to see Granny and Grandad Scott's house.'

Babs took a sharp intake of breath. 'Mummy didn't say you'd been there.'

'Well there ain't really a house there now, just a lot of old bricks, and Mummy started to cry.'

'Well it was our house and we did have a lot of nice memories.'

'Then we went to see the grave Mummy said your mum and dad were in. I didn't like that. It was very scary.'

'There's nothing to be scared of. They loved you.'

'I don't remember them.'

'No, you were just little babies when the war started and your mummy took you to Wales to be safe and away from the bombs. Your granny and grandad would have loved to have seen what little smashers you've grown into. Now come on, settle down.' Babs kissed Ann's forehead. Yes, her parents would certainly have been proud of the twins and would have spoiled them if they'd been given the chance.

Downstairs Joy and Stan were quietly listening to the wireless.

'You all ready for tomorrow?' asked Joy when Babs walked into the kitchen. It was lovely to see Stan stretched out in his armchair next to the fireplace.

'Yes.'

'Joy was telling me that your friend's boyfriend's been in Canada.'

'Yes, he has.'

'Lucky bugger. Being over there and missing all the trouble.'

Babs didn't say anything. Yes, Frank had been lucky.

'Joy said he was teaching the Canadians to fly.'

'Yes,' was all Babs could say. She didn't want to think about those days before Frank had left and they had all gone out together. Although

Pete often filled her thoughts, she didn't want to talk about him as it still upset her.

'Canada's a smashing place. So clean. I wouldn't mind going over there to live.'

Joy quickly looked up from her knitting. 'What?'

'Well let's face it, girl, there ain't much to keep us here.'

'But we live here. We was born here.'

'That don't mean ter say we have to stay here. There's a great big world out there. Besides, the kids would love it. Plenty of open space for 'em to run around.'

Joy put her knitting on the floor. 'I ain't going nowhere. I've just come back from being stuck in the country, and you can keep all that quiet and peaceful stuff, I like a bit more life and the shop just round the corner.'

'All right. Keep yer hair on. I was just saying, that's all.' He went back to his newspaper.

Babs looked at Joy. She could see she was worried. What if Stan did decide to take them away? She couldn't bear it if her sister left; she would be all alone again and in a dead-end job. Being in the Land Army had given her a whole new life, and she missed it. Suddenly she felt very sorry for herself.

Stan looked over his newspaper and grinned.

'Don't worry. We ain't going nowhere. I've been away far too long; besides, I'd miss me pint at the local. They don't have pubs in the States or Canada.'

'You got me worried there, Stan,' said Joy, smiling as she picked up her knitting again.

'Don't worry, love, it was just something that went through me mind.'

Babs picked up her book as the click, click, click of Joy's knitting needles disturbed the quiet. But was it something Stan was serious about?

As the bus made its way to Woodford, Babs felt very happy at the thought of seeing her friend again. Although she had stayed with Lydi and her family briefly after they had left the Land Army, she still felt slightly ill at ease. Lydi's house was lovely and her parents made her feel at home, but she was from London and spoke very differently from them.

When Babs got off the bus, she was thrilled to see Lydi waiting for her. They fell into each other's arms and hugged.

'It's so good to see you again,' said Lydi.

'You too.'

They walked along, laughing and chattering nineteen to the dozen. They talked about old times and the things that had happened.

'So Frank has got in touch again?'

'Yes. He's been here,' Lydi said, pushing open the gate.

'He has?' Babs was surprised at that answer.

'I'd almost forgotten what he looked like.'

'Why didn't he write when he was in Canada?'

'He said it was because he wasn't sure when he would be home and he didn't want to stop my chances of meeting someone else.'

Lydi opened the front door and Babs was hugged again, this time by Mr and Mrs Webb.

'The kettle is on and I expect you're dying for a cup of tea,' said Mrs Webb.

'Yes please.'

'You'll have to tell us all about your family now that you are all together.'

'Later, Mother. Babs and I have a lot to catch up on,' said Lydi.

'Of course, dear.'

'Let's take our tea in the garden, then we can make as much noise as we like,' said Lydi, picking up the tray.

Sitting on the hammock, Babs said, 'So tell me all about Frank. Did he meet someone while he was over there?'

'I don't know. I haven't asked.'

'I hope he's not seeking you out after being dumped by someone else.'

'I don't think so.'

'Well be careful.'

Lydi laughed.

'What's so funny?'

'You. I can remember when I was giving you advice.'

'Yes. That seems a lifetime ago.'

'Do you think you could ever love again?'

'I don't know. It could never be like I felt for Pete.' Babs let a slight smile lift her face. 'He was very special.'

'I know. Now come on, let's go for a walk. Unless you'd rather go to church with my mother and father.'

'No. A walk will be fine.'

'And guess what?' Lydi was laughing as she walked along.

'I don't know.'

'I've also had a letter from Demetrio.'

'No! How are he and Gino?'

'Demetrio's fine. He says he hasn't seen his wife or children yet; it's taking a while for them to get back to his hotel. Gino's finding life a bit strange and finding it hard to come to terms with going back.'

'Has Demetrio heard from his wife and children?'

'They're meeting soon. But he says he'll soon

get them all working to fix up the hotel and that will bring them together.'

'The old slave-driver!'

'He sounds full of hope of opening the hotel one day, and when he does, we are invited to be his special guests.'

'That would be lovely. How old are his kids?'

'I don't know. Anyway, I've given him your address to pass on to Gino. Do you mind?'

'No. What's his English like when he writes?'

'Not that great. But then again, neither is yours.'

Babs laughed. 'You cheeky what-name.'

'It's so good to see you again,' said Lydi, getting serious. 'I really miss our old way of life.'

'So do I. Standing behind a counter in Woolies is certainly not the be all and end all. I often go off in me own little world.'

'You want to be stuck in an office all day typing up some silly reports. I could throw the typewriter at times. In some ways I wish the war had gone on.'

'Don't you let your mother hear you say that.'

'I know. It is a wicked thing to say. But we did have a great time, didn't we?'

'Yes. We certainly did.'

They talked about the time they'd worked together. Then Lydi said, 'We must go and see the Johnsons one of these days.'

'I'd like that.'

'How about coming here and stopping over on Bank Holiday Monday, then I can drive us down?'

'Sounds great. As it's only a month away, I can survive till then.'

For the rest of the day they reminisced about the good and the sad times, then it was time for Babs to leave.

'You will write?' said Babs.

'Of course,' said Lydi as the bus pulled in.

They hugged again, and after boarding, Babs sat next to the window so she could wave to her friend till she was out of sight.

It was getting late, and Babs was surprised to see that Stan and Joy were still up when she walked into the kitchen. 'I'm sorry it's so late. I had a job getting a bus.'

'That's all right. We've had a bit of excitement ourselves.'

'Why? What's happened?'

'Well,' said Joy, settling herself down to tell her news. 'This evening we were sitting quietly listening to the wireless, when we heard this almighty scream from Mrs Bolton. Well, you know how thin these walls are. Stan rushed round to see if she was all right and there she was standing on the doorstop holding Terry. It seems he's come home and she was so shocked at the first sight of him she could only scream. Poor bloke must have wondered what had hit him.'

'Terry's home?'

Joy nodded.

'I bet Mrs Bolton is beside herself. I'm sure she's only kept going waiting for this day to arrive. What did he look like?'

'He's ever so thin and pasty-looking. I think he's had a rough time.'

'Poor bloke. Still, he's home now and I'm sure his mother will be fussing round him night and day.'

'That's what mothers are for,' said Joy.

'That's true. Well, I'm going on up. I've had a long day.'

'But was it a good day?' asked Stan.

'Yes. Yes, it was. Good night.'

'Good night,' they said together.

Chapter 20

FOR A LONG while Babs lay in bed listening to Ann's gentle breathing and thinking about her day. It had been lovely to see Lydi again, and when she'd talked about Gino and Demetrio, all the memories of these past years had come flooding back. Babs still felt very ashamed when she thought about how she had behaved when she'd first met them. They were decent blokes and never held a grudge, despite the fact that they had been taken from their homes and families. She had been sorry when they left. Poor Gino, he had nobody. How she would love to go somewhere like Italy. Gino had always made it sound wonderful. How much would it cost? she wondered. But that was all wishful thinking. People who lived in Rotherhithe didn't go to exotic places like that. Babs's mind was flitting from one thing to another. What about Frank coming back into Lydi's life? It would be wonderful if Lydi had finally found someone to love. By the look in her eyes when she talked about him, it could well be something serious.

Babs woke with a start to find Ann standing over her. The sun was streaming through the window. 'What time is it?' Ann moved so that Babs could see the clock. 'It's seven o'clock. What are you doing up?'

'You was crying, Auntie Babs. Are you very unhappy?'

'No. I must have been dreaming. I'm sorry. Did I wake you?'

Ann shook her head. 'No. But I was very worried when you kept calling out for Pete. That was the name of your boyfriend. Mummy told us he got killed.'

'I must have been dreaming about him.'

Ann sat on the bed. 'Was he very nice?'

'Yes, he was. Now I must get up and get ready for work.'

'I'll go and tell Mummy you're getting up.' Ann ran from the room, clutching the doll her father had brought her. She loved that doll and it was never out of her arms.

*

When Babs got home from work that evening, Joy was busy in the scullery, cooking tea.

'Had a good day?' asked Joy.

'No different from any other.'

'At least you've got a job.'

'I know. Have you been out?'

'Only for a bit of shopping. I was hoping to get some sausages for tea but the butcher ran out before I got to the front of the queue. That's why we've got corned beef. Seem to spend half me day now standing in a queue. Be glad when all this rationing ends and things get easier.'

'I think it'll be a long while before that day comes.'

'Stan went and signed on. He thinks it's about time he thought about a job.'

'Did he have any luck?'

'Not yet. He's got to go again next week.'

'It must be awful for blokes not being able to get back into their old jobs.'

'That's the trouble; he didn't have an old job. All I hope is that he don't go back to sea. I'd hate him to go away again. And so would the kids.'

'I'm sure something will turn up.'

'Yes, but will he stick at it?'

'Only time will tell.' Babs wanted to get off this subject as she could see that her sister was worried about it, so she casually asked, 'Seen anything of Terry?'

'Mrs Bolton popped in and asked if she could borrow some sugar. She said he was sleeping most of the time. I think he's had a bad time.'

'I'll just pop out to the lav before tea.' Babs looked over her sister's shoulder. 'The food smells good anyway.'

'Don't get too excited. As I said, we've only got corned beef and potato pie.'

'That suits me.'

Babs walked out to the lav just as Terry came out of his. Like the houses, the lavatories were back to back.

'Hello, Terry.'

'Hello, Babs,' he said, coming up to the bit of wire that divided the yards. 'Mum said you was living next door with Joy and Stan. Sorry to hear about yer mum and dad.'

'Thanks. How you managing?'

'Not bad. Having a few nightmares. Still, I don't suppose I'm the only one. They reckon those in the Jap camps are really badly off, poor bastards. Bloody Japs. I reckon it'll be a long while 'fore they finish them off.'

'Your mum's pleased to see you,' said Babs, wanting to get off all this usual talk about war.

'Yer. She's been ter see about getting me ration

book signed on at her shop. Can't wait to feed me up.'

Babs looked at the lav. She didn't want to tell him she was bursting. 'I'll talk to you later.'

'Yer. Yer, of course. Sorry.' He quickly moved away.

When she went back into the scullery, she said, 'Oh my God. That was embarrassing. I was dying for a pee when Terry came out of the lav and wanted to stand and talk. In the end I had to go.'

'I should hope so.' Joy laughed. 'I don't want to wash out your smelly drawers.'

'I wash me own out anyway.'

'I know. Anyway what did he have to say?'

'Not a lot, really. He seems taller than I remember, and better-looking, although he's very thin. He was ever so spotty in those days.'

'So come on. He must have said something.'

'No, just that he's having nightmares. Still, I bet a lot of people are.'

'Ann was saying that you did a bit of shouting in your sleep last night.'

'Yes. I'm sorry about that. It must have been seeing Lydi yesterday. All the old memories came back.'

'How's her fella?'

'Great. She also heard from Demetrio. He's hoping to go back to his hotel, but all this getting back and settling down is taking time. I just hope his wife and kids are waiting for him. He's going to take Gino on to work for him; they got on well together.'

'So almost as if nothing happened, they can just pick up their lives again. Not like Mum and Dad and some of the poor buggers who lost everything, including you.'

'We don't know that. Gino can't. Like us, his parents were killed.' Babs was surprised at Joy's outburst and at herself for sticking up for Gino. 'Lydi's given Demetrio this address, so he might write. Is that all right?'

'It's OK by me. What you do is your affair.'

Babs laughed. 'He's only gonner write. He ain't gonner come over here and whisk me away.'

'I hope not, otherwise he'll have me to answer to. We don't want no Eyeties in this family.'

Babs didn't reply. Joy's remark had made her realise how awful her own behaviour towards the two Italians had been.

On Sunday the fifth of August, Babs was once again on her way to see Lydi. This time she was going to stay the night, and tomorrow they were going to see Edna and Mr Johnson. Babs was really looking forward to that.

There were the usual kisses and hugs when

she got off the bus, and as they walked arm in arm, their laughter and chatter filled the quiet air.

'Frank's coming to tea tonight,' said Lydi out of the blue.

'That's great. He's not coming with us tomorrow, is he?'

Lydi looked at her friend. 'Do you mind?'

'No, course not.' But Babs did feel a bit put out; she wanted her friend to be there just for her. 'Is he staying with you?' She gave her friend a knowing wink.

Lydi laughed. 'Good heavens, no. In the spare room, not with me. My father would have a fit if he thought his only daughter wasn't going to walk up the aisle still a virgin.'

Babs stopped. 'You're getting married?'

'Yes. And we wanted you to be the first to know.'

'What about your mum and dad?'

'Frank's going to ask them tonight. Not that I need their permission; after all, I am over twenty-one.'

Babs was taken aback.

'You've gone very quiet. You do approve, don't you?'

Babs threw her arms round Lydi. 'Of course I approve. Just as long as he makes you happy.'

'He will. I know he will. By the way, have you heard from Demetrio or Gino?'

'No. I don't suppose they'll write. But it would have been nice to hear from them and know Gino had settled down.'

'You never know. He may get round to it one day.'

'I don't hold out any hopes.'

That afternoon, Babs and Lydi were sitting in the garden when Frank walked in. Lydi jumped up and held him tight, and Babs wanted to cry. She was remembering the last time they were together and Pete was alive.

'Hello there, Babs,' Frank said over Lydi's shoulder.

'Good to see you again, Frank.'

He freed himself from Lydi and, holding Babs close, whispered, 'I'm so sorry about Pete. He was a good mate.'

'Yes, he was,' said Babs.

'Now come on, you two, otherwise I'll get jealous.' Lydi was smiling.

'No need to worry about that,' said Frank as he put his arm round Lydi's slim waist. 'So how's life treating you, Babs? Lydi tells me you're back at Woolworths.'

'Yes, my life's just one long round of excitement.'

'So is mine,' said Lydi. 'Let's sit down.' She moved towards the garden chairs and they followed.

'What about you, Frank? You coming out of the RAF?' asked Babs, sitting next to Lydi.

'I hope to eventually, and when this lot is finally over, I'm applying to fly planes for a living.'

'That sounds exciting.'

'I hope so.'

'Not too dangerous, though,' said Lydi.

'No, it will be commercial flying. In Canada and America they fly all over the place, and so if I get in early enough, before all the others get demobbed, I stand a good chance of being one of the first.'

'But this is not America,' said Babs. 'I can't see us flying all over the place.'

'We will. Everybody will be flying one day.'

'Frank said that one of these days everybody will be able to fly anywhere in the world.' Lydi looked so happy.

Frank sat forward. 'They're building planes that will be bigger and go faster than ever before.'

'Don't know if I fancy flying,' said Babs.

'You will, I promise. There's nothing like it.'

Babs sat back and thought about what Frank had just said. That would be wonderful, flying anywhere in the world, but she knew that things like that didn't happen to the likes of her.

That evening after dinner they were all sitting in the drawing room chatting when Frank stood up.

He cleared his throat. 'Mr and Mrs Wells.'

They looked up.

'As a matter of courtesy I would like to ask your permission to marry Lydi.'

Mr Wells stood up. 'This doesn't come as any surprise to Lydi's mother or myself, and yes, young man, you have our blessing.'

Frank took a small black velvet box from his pocket and opened it. He took the ring whose three diamonds sparkled in the light, and, kneeling down, placed it on Lydi's finger.

Everybody was admiring the ring and seemed to be kissing everybody else. Babs thought how wonderful and old-fashioned this was. She was sad that nobody would be able to ask her parents for her hand, if the time ever came.

'This calls for a drink,' said Mr Wells.

Frank gave a slight cough. 'I hope you don't mind, sir, but I took it on myself to bring a bottle of champagne. It's in the car.'

'Bring it in, lad, and it can cool in a bucket of water. Lydi, fill a bucket.'

Lydi and Frank rushed from the room, leaving Babs alone with Mr and Mrs Wells.

Mrs Wells moved and sat next to Babs on the sofa. She took her hand. 'This must be very hard for you, my dear.'

'I'm very happy for Lydi and Frank. They deserve happiness.'

'Yes, they do. And so do you. I'm sure you'll find the right person for you one day. It won't be the same and you will never forget your young man. But time will lessen the hurt you feel.'

'I hope so,' said Babs, trying hard not to let her tears fall.

Frank and Lydi, whose eyes were shining, came back into the room.

Lydi took tall glasses from the cabinet and set them on the coffee table. Everything was done properly in this house.

'So have you any date in mind?' asked Mrs Wells.

'Not at the moment,' said Lydi.

'We thought we'd find out when I'll be out of the RAF, then we can make plans.'

'Very sensible,' said Mr Wells.

For the rest of the evening all the talk was about the forthcoming marriage. Babs sat and thought about Pete. They had only had one weekend together, and it was the happiest time of her life. She still loved him and wondered if anyone could ever take his place. At this moment, she didn't think so.

Chapter 21

THAT NIGHT AS Babs lay in the bed next to Lydi's, her thoughts were a jumble. She knew most of it was due to the champagne.

'I'm really looking forward to seeing Edna and Mr Johnson tomorrow,' said Lydi softly.

Babs mumbled, 'So am I.'

'It's going to bring back a lot of memories, some sad, but some very happy. I must remember to tell them I've heard from Demetrio.'

'Yes, you do that. Now please, go to sleep,' said Babs.

'I can't. I keep thinking of Frank just along the corridor.'

'Well go and jump into bed with him and let me sleep.'

'Believe me, I would if I thought I could get away with it. My mother would be out of bed in a flash if she heard any kind of movement. She can pick up sounds like a bat.'

'You should have gone away for a dirty weekend.'

'I know. I bet you'll never forget the weekend you had with Pete.'

'No, I won't. Now go to sleep and let me dream about him.' With that thought Babs fell into a deep sleep with a smile on her face.

Babs could hear a lot of chatter when she woke. This was unusual in the Wells household. They always respected people and their privacy.

As Lydi's bed was empty, Babs got up and put on her dressing gown. She opened the bedroom door to see Lydi on the landing, her face ashen.

'Lydi. What's happened?'

'I was just coming to tell you. The Americans have bombed Japan.'

'I'm not surprised. They've never got over Pearl Harbor.'

'Babs, they have dropped a terrible bomb. Thousands have been killed.'

Babs could see her friend was upset, but this was war. 'So now perhaps they'll end this awful war.'

'Come downstairs and listen to what Frank and Dad are saying about it.'

Babs wondered what could be so different about this bombing raid. Germany had bombed England and the Allies had done the same to them. Trust the Americans to make a big song and dance about something. She followed Lydi down the stairs into the dining room, where her parents and Frank were quietly listening to the wireless.

Babs could hear the announcer talking about a place called Hiroshima. He said that the smoke and dust rose to a height of five miles and that thousands of people were dead.

Frank let out a long, low whistle. 'All that with just one bomb. That must be one hell of a size.'

'What did he mean when he said it was an atom bomb?' asked Mrs Wells.

'Don't rightly know. It must be some sort of new weapon.'

'Well let's hope the Japs don't drop one on us,' she said.

'The Americans wouldn't have dropped it if they thought the Japs could do the same,' said Frank.

Mrs Wells walked to the door. 'I'm going to make breakfast. I managed to get some black-market eggs from the farmer down the road. Would a boiled egg and toast be all right for everybody?'

Lydi laughed and it eased the tension. 'I never thought I'd hear my mother admit to breaking the law.'

Babs smiled. 'As far as food's concerned, everybody breaks the law if they can get away with it.'

As they were driving to Sussex, the thought of the bombing in Japan was soon forgotten and they talked about seeing Edna and Mr Johnson again.

'Frank was telling me that when he went looking for me, he thought that Mr J didn't look too good.'

'It broke his heart to give up the farm. I wonder how he's doing staying with Norman and Iris,' said Lydi.

'At least he has the grandchildren to keep him amused.'

'Or they could be driving him nuts.'

'No. Not those kids,' said Babs.

They all talked nonstop about every subject, and Babs could see that her friend and Frank were so happy together.

'How about we stop at a pub for a drink and a sandwich?' said Frank. 'Keep your eyes out for the next one.'

'Will do,' said Babs.

'That sounds a very good idea,' said Lydi. 'But don't forget that they are expecting us, and I dare say they will be giving us something to eat.'

'I hope Edna has managed to make one of her wonderful cakes,' said Babs.

'But we mustn't take their rations,' said Frank.

'We know,' they both said together.

When they walked into the pub, the locals gave them a nod. Frank was still wearing his uniform, and the wings over his breast pocket always seemed to bring out the best in everybody. Pilots were held in very high regard.

'So, what d'yer think of this 'ere bomb they've dropped on Japan, then?' the landlord asked Frank as he served him.

'I think it might be the only way to stop the Japs,' Frank replied, taking the top off his beer before he handed Lydi and Babs their shandies. 'Let's sit over there,' he said, pointing to a table in the window. Sitting opposite them he whispered, 'They've only got fish-paste sandwiches. Will that do?'

Lydi screwed up her nose. 'Can't say I'm over fond of that, but if that's all he's got, it'll have to do.'

'I don't mind,' said Babs.

'He said he could put a bit of lettuce and tomato with it.'

'That's fine with me,' said Babs.

'What about you, Miss Fussy?'

Lydi laughed. 'I would have preferred smoked salmon, but then again, there is still a war on, even if it is a long way away.'

When they arrived at Norman's farm, everything looked the same. Frank parked the car and Lydi went round the back, calling for Iris.

Iris was standing at the kitchen door, and when she saw them, she screamed out their names and ran towards them. She hugged both the girls as Edna appeared in the doorway.

Edna held Babs then Lydi. 'It's so lovely to see you both again.' Then, looking over Lydi's shoulder, she said, 'We have met this handsome airman before.'

'Yes, I know, and I'll always be grateful to you for giving him my address,' said Lydi, just as the children ran towards them.

'Daddy said you were coming today.' Grace threw herself at Babs.

Robert stood back and smiled shyly. 'Dad said you were a pilot.' He was more interested in Frank than the girls.

'Yes, I still am.'

'Gosh. What planes do you fly?'

'Bombers mostly.'

'Gosh,' said Robert again.

'That's his favourite word at the moment,' said Iris.

'Dad said that a terrible bomb has just been dropped on Japan.'

'Yes, we heard the news.'

'Come inside and see Sidney,' said Edna.

'How is he?' asked Lydi as they all moved inside.

'Not too bad,' said Edna, adding, 'And I expect you'd all like a cup of tea?'

Babs hugged Edna again and laughed. 'I love to hear that you still know how to please us.'

Lydi and Babs were shocked when they saw Mr J sitting in the armchair and tried hard to hide their expressions. Frank was right behind them.

'Hope you don't mind me not getting up.' Mr Johnson's words were very slurred and slow. 'Me old leg plays me up a bit. Won't do what I want it to.'

Both Babs and Lydi rushed towards him and one after the other held him close.

Mr J grinned at Frank. 'See, it does pay. Never had a couple of pretty girls make a fuss of me like this when I could walk about.'

After the exchange of news, Lydi proudly showed off her engagement ring.

'So you see, I have a lot to thank you both for.' Her eyes were shining as she looked up at Frank.

'Both of you will be able to come to our wedding?' asked Frank.

'I would like that,' said Edna.

'I should hope so,' said Lydi. 'You will be our guests of honour.'

'What about me?' asked Babs, laughing.

'You're going to be my bridesmaid.'

Babs grinned. She'd been bridesmaid when her sister got married and had loved every minute of it. This wedding was going to be a very grand affair. No wedding breakfast in the front room for Lydi. This time they would be going to a very posh hotel.

All too soon it was time for them to go. There were a few unshed tears as they left, all the family waving them goodbye. Babs had to get back to Rotherhithe and Frank back to camp.

For a few miles they were silent, then Lydi said, 'I was really shocked to see Mr J.'

'So was I. I didn't realise how far downhill he'd gone,' said Babs.

'He tried to put on a brave face, but to see his arm and leg so helpless now was awful. He could at least walk a little with a stick when we were there,' said Lydi.

'I must admit, I did have a bit of a job to understand him,' said Frank.

'He is a lot worse than when we were there,' said Lydi.

'Can't anything be done for him?' asked Frank.

'Believe me, if anything was possible Edna would do all she could. They are such a devoted couple,' said Babs.

'He was such a strong man,' said Lydi.

'Now come on, girls, cheer up. I know you are both very upset about this, but we can come back another Sunday. I could see how he cheered up when you both walked in.'

'Thank you, Frank,' said Lydi, squeezing his arm.

Babs sat back. She was so envious of Lydi having someone as caring as Frank, but then again, if anyone deserved it, Lydi did.

It wasn't till the end of the following week and after another atom bomb had been dropped on Japan, that they finally surrendered.

It was Monday evening, and Babs and Joy had been to the pictures. They had sat in shocked silence as the newsreel showed pictures of

Hiroshima. It was then that the full horror of the bomb sunk in.

On the bus home, Joy said, 'What a terrible weapon. Please don't let us have another war.'

Babs gently patted her sister's hand. 'I don't think that can ever happen again. Every country would be too frightened.'

'I hope you're right,' said Joy. 'I was talking to Mrs Bolton this morning,' she added. 'She's worried about Terry. Seems he's very quiet and withdrawn.'

'I expect he is. It must have been very hard for him.'

'Babs, now don't take this the wrong way . . .'

Babs quickly turned and looked at her sister.

'Mrs Bolton was wondering if you would go out with him one evening.'

'I'm sure he'll find someone as soon as he settles down.'

'I hope you don't mind, but I said you would.'

'Oh, thanks. What if he don't want to go out with me?'

'I'm sure he will.'

'Come on, this is our stop.'

As they walked home, Babs said, 'I don't intend to stay with you for ever, you know.'

'I'm not trying to get you married off. I just thought it would be nice for both of you.'

'Thanks.' When they reached the front door, Babs stood to one side while Joy pulled the key through the letterbox.

'I'm sorry I said anything. But I didn't think it would do any harm.'

'Don't worry about it. I'll think about it.'

Joy grinned to herself as she pushed open the kitchen door. After all, she only had her sister's happiness at heart.

Chapter 22

THE FOLLOWING DAY Babs was miles away and daydreaming while standing at her counter. Her thoughts kept going over what Joy had said last night. Would it be so bad to go to the pictures with Terry? She would have to think about this and find out if Terry knew what his mother and her sister had talked about.

'Dreaming of a long-lost love?' asked Rene, who was on the haberdashery counter and sold ribbons and elastic; that was when there was some in stock.

'No, not really.' She hadn't told her workmates about Pete. 'It's just that me and me sister went to the pictures last night and saw that terrible bombing in Japan.'

'I know. Me dad said it's a good job it's all over

now. I wonder how long it'll be before things get back to normal.'

'Will they ever be normal again?'

'I hope so. Can't say I want all these shortages to go on for ever.'

'I think it's gonner take a while.' Babs knew that for some, things would never be normal again.

Rene laughed. 'They'd better hurry up and get some elastic, otherwise some of the old dears will be walking about without any drawers on. Look out, here comes the boss.'

Babs moved around some of the stock she had and tried to look busy.

As the evening was still warm, after tea Babs went and sat on the concrete coping that ran round the front-room bay window. Although Stan and Joy made her welcome, she always felt like an intruder. It wasn't long before Mrs Bolton came out, wiping her face with a towel.

''Allo, love. All right, then?'

'Yes thanks. It's a lovely evening.'

'Bit too warm fer me.' Mrs Bolton sat on her coping. 'I was telling Terry that he should get out more. Cooped up indoors all day. It ain't good for him.'

'I expect it'll take time.'

'Yer.' She began fiddling with the hem of her

overall. 'Babs, I was having a word with yer sister about Terry. Did she tell yer?'

'She did say something.'

Mrs Bolton moved closer to Babs and quickly looked around her as if making sure no one could hear. 'I was wondering if you'd mind taking him out one night.'

Babs wanted to laugh. This woman was talking about a grown man, not a little boy. 'D'you think he would like to come to the pictures?'

Mrs Bolton's face was wreathed in smiles. 'I'm sure 'e would. 'E's a bit shy and never was one for getting out and making friends.'

Babs thought that wasn't the Terry she once knew. Joy often told her that he used to like a drink with the lads and would come home three sheets to the wind. He would always slam the front gate and wake her, then she'd lie there waiting for the front door to slam. 'Just ask him what night would suit him.'

'Any night. You just say.'

'How about Thursday? They change the picture on Thursday.'

'I'll just pop in and ask 'im.'

Babs smiled. She'd never thought that a grown man would get his mother to set up a date. But then again, she didn't know what he'd been through.

Terry came out with his mother. 'Are you sure that's all right, Babs?'

'Yes, that'll be fine.'

Mrs Bolton went inside. She looked very pleased with herself.

Terry sat next to Babs for a while and they talked about many things: the bomb, and the end of the war in Japan. He wanted to know about her time in the Land Army. She tried to ask him what life was like when he was a prisoner, but he seemed reluctant to talk about it and shied away from the subject. She knew that he would tell her when he was ready.

After a while the front door opened and Ann came out in her nightie. 'Good night, Auntie Babs.' She came up to her and gave her a kiss.

'Good night, poppet. Tell Mummy I'll be in in a tick.'

'All right.' Ann looked shyly at Terry. 'Good night,' she said before running back inside.

'Sorry, I've been keeping you,' said Terry, standing up.

'No, that's fine. It's been nice talking to you.' Even though Babs knew it was her who had been doing most of the talking.

'Perhaps we could go for a drink one night.'

'I don't know.' She looked at him. He needed

a shave and his hair was long and matted. Going to the pictures wasn't so bad, at least it would be dark, but a drink?

He ran his hand over his face and smiled. 'Don't worry, I'll have a shave and get a haircut.' He suddenly seemed a lot happier.

'I suppose we could do.'

'What about Saturday?'

'OK.'

So that was it. She now had two dates with Terry.

The summer drifted into autumn, and Babs was going out with Terry on a regular basis. They really were just friends and she enjoyed his company. At least she was going out a couple of times a week now and not stuck with her nose in a book night after night. Terry had smartened himself up and was quite handsome in a rugged way, with his straight dark hair and deep-set dark eyes. When they said good night at the end of the evening, it was only a gentle peck on the cheek, which suited Babs; she didn't want this to go any further. She would always be comparing him with Pete. Terry wasn't the sort of man she could spend the rest of her life with. She didn't think any man could be as good as her first love.

Stan was now working on a building site, and as there was plenty of work for labourers, he had suggested that Terry join the same firm. Before the war Terry had worked in the office at a wholesaler's. He'd told Babs he didn't want to go back to working inside, even if there had been a job for him. Stan didn't work with Terry, as the boss thought Terry would be better suited in the office, but as it was a small firm and he was out and about round the site, he seemed happy enough. Joy and Mrs Bolton were always singing his praises, and Joy didn't understand why Babs was keeping him at arm's length. Joy told her sister that she was too fussy, but as Babs said, any commitment would be for life, and she didn't want that.

Just before Christmas, Babs took Terry to meet Lydi and Frank. On the way home he was very quiet, while Babs was excitedly talking about the dress she was going to wear for the wedding in June and the fact that Lydi and Frank were going to France for their honeymoon.

'I'm really looking forward to this wedding. What about you?'

'I ain't coming.'

'Why?'

'They ain't my sorta people. Too stuck up.'

Babs laughed. 'I can tell you, there's nothing stuck up about Lydi.'

'What about him? Just 'cos he was a pilot in the war.'

'Frank's not like that.'

'What about your bloke what got killed? I bet he was stuck up as well.'

'No,' Babs said softly. How dare anyone talk about her beloved Pete like that?

'All those RAF types are the same. Think they're the bee's knees.'

Babs didn't answer. If Terry didn't want to come to Lydi's wedding that was up to him. Nothing was going to stop her.

Although the war was over, the outlook for Christmas 1945 was still bleak, with many shortages. Everybody was fed up with the endless queues just for the basics. There was even talk about bread rationing.

Terry was very angry when he read in the papers that the Allies were feeding the Germans.

'They didn't bloody well feed us when we was prisoners, did they?' he shouted one Saturday evening when he and Babs were in a pub having a drink.

'Shh,' said Babs, looking round. 'Keep yer voice down.'

'Well it's true. Me old mum stands in queues

while the bloody Germans take the food out of our mouths.'

'I know, Terry, it's hard.'

Over the weeks Terry had told her about life in the prisoner-of-war camp and how they had to forage for food. They were forced to work and were often beaten. He had got really angry when she told him about Gino and Demetrio and how they lived on the farm.

'Must've lived like lords.'

'They had to work hard and it was to help feed us.' Babs knew there was anger in her voice.

Terry looked sheepish. 'I'm sorry, Babs, but I'm worried about Mum. Her feet are really bad and she won't go to the doctor; says she's got better things to spend her money on.'

'I know how she feels. Joy was saying that she wanted to take young John to get his ears syringed. In the end she managed to get some olive oil to put down them.'

But despite everything, there did seem to be some hope on the horizon, with new towns and airports being built. That meant that Stan, who had been made up to foreman, and Terry had plenty of work, though Stan would come home exhausted and unhappy.

Joy and Babs tried to make Christmas as

festive as they could. The children had made paper chains and covered some twigs with green paper to look like a Christmas tree, while Joy still had the baubles from previous years. She had scoured the shops for things to help the day go well; after all, this was the first Christmas they had all spent together. At the butcher's she had put her name down on a list and had managed to get a chicken.

Babs had been able to buy a few trinkets. There was a lipstick for Joy, a tie for Stan, a brush and comb for Ann and a tin car for John. She had got a lighter for Terry and a scarf for Mrs Bolton. Joy said that, to be neighbourly, she was inviting Terry and his mum in for the evening.

The day went well and everybody hoped that things would be better soon.

At the end of the week Babs received a Christmas card with a foreign stamp.

'Cor, look at that stamp,' said John when he saw the envelope. 'Can I have it?'

'Course.' Babs was thrilled to discover the card was from Gino. 'Fancy him sending me a Christmas card,' she said, grinning. 'I never thought I'd hear from him again.'

'I thought you said the other one wrote to your mate,' said Joy.

'He did.' Babs looked at the card. It was a view

of a lake and it looked very beautiful. 'But I didn't think Gino would bother about me.'

All through the winter life drifted on. One night after his tea, Stan was slumped in the chair, beginning to doze off, when Ann and John burst into the room, shouting and laughing.

Stan shot upright. 'Can't you two keep the bloody noise down?'

Ann and John stopped dead. Their father had never shouted at them before. Babs, who was reading a book, looked up. Joy came in from the scullery just as Ann began to cry. She rushed to her mother, who held her close, and buried her head in Joy's pinny.

'What the hell's wrong with you?' yelled Joy.

'I'm tired and don't need these two racing around like mad things.'

Babs wanted to get away but knew she didn't dare move.

'So you've had a bad day,' said Joy, hugging her children. 'Please don't take it out on the kids.'

Stan didn't answer. He picked up his paper and went outside. Joy and Babs knew he was going to sit in the lav and would be there a while.

'Go upstairs and get ready for bed,' Joy said to the children, then she sat at the table next to Babs. 'I can't seem to do anythink right. It ain't much fun queuing up, then getting in the shop only to find they've just sold out.' Tears trickled down her cheeks.

Babs held her sister's hand. 'Everybody's tired. Even though it's all over, all these shortages have been going on a long while and people just want things to get back to how they were.'

'I'm worried that Stan will go back to sea. He's so restless.'

'I don't think he will.'

'We can't go on like this.'

'Give it time.' But Babs too was worried that her brother-in-law would go away. Although he'd never said anything, was he fed up with her being in the house all the time? Was it time for her to move on?

Chapter 23

THE MONTHS FLEW by, and suddenly it was the week before Lydi's wedding. Babs had taken a few days off work to spend with her friend. As soon as they met up again, she felt all the time slip away and it was as if they'd never been apart. They hugged and laughed as they made their way to Lydi's car. How Babs wished they were still on the farm with Gino and Demetrio.

The following day they went shopping and had the final fittings for their dresses. Babs felt like a queen in her pale blue satin taffeta frock. Somehow Lydi had managed to get white sandals to go with it, and Babs was also going to wear a garland of flowers in her hair. She preened in the dressmaker's mirror.

'It's a pity Terry's not going to be here to see how lovely you look,' said Lydi, who was sitting on a padded chair watching her friend.

Babs smiled at her; Lydi looked so happy. 'Well, that was up to him. He had the invite.'

'I know. I wish you could find someone nice.'

'I did once.'

Lydi jumped up from the chair. 'I know.' She held her friend close.

'Don't make me cry, I'll drop tears all down me frock.'

'Well you'll be carrying a bouquet, so that'll hide it.' Lydi laughed.

'That's why we carry those flowers?'

'That's right. To hide a multitude of sins; you can even spill your wedding breakfast down it.'

Babs gently ran her hands down the front of her dress. 'I'll never do that. And I'll keep this for ever.'

It was Lydi's turn to smile.

Back at the house, the dresses were carried upstairs and carefully placed on hangers.

'I forgot to tell you with all the excitement that I've had another letter from Demetrio. He said to send you his fond regards and that Gino is finding it hard to settle down.'

'I know the feeling. I did tell you that Gino sent me a Christmas card, didn't I?'

'Yes. I can give you Demetrio's address if you

like and you could write to Gino, I'm sure he'd like that.'

'I don't know. The Christmas card didn't have any address, so perhaps he'd rather I didn't get in touch,' said Babs as she stood in front of the mirror and put her hair up. 'What d'you think, should I wear it up or down?'

'Try it with your headdress.'

Babs took the pretty garland of artificial flowers and plonked it on top of her head.

'Not sure,' said Lydi, laughing. 'I think it might need a bit of adjusting, like this.' She straightened the flowers and stood back. 'How does it feel?'

'Blooming marvellous. Oh Lydi, I'm so happy for you. But what d'you think, should it be up or down?'

'Sit here and we'll experiment.'

There was a lot of laughter and joy as Lydi tried different styles with Babs's short, dark hair.

'I thinks it looks best down and curly,' said Lydi.

So it was that Babs – with her hair down and curly – followed Lydi up the aisle on that sunny June day. She was finding it hard to keep back the tears when she saw Frank, who looked very handsome in his uniform, standing waiting for his bride. Lydi looked absolutely wonderful, her long white satin dress clinging to her slim figure. It was the same style as Babs's bridesmaid's dress, with its sweetheart neck, but had long sleeves that finished in a point over Lydi's hands. It was so elegant, and the long veil, held in place with a garland of artificial flowers, moved gently behind her as she walked down the aisle on her father's arm.

After the ceremony, back at the hotel, Frank said to Babs, 'So your young man didn't come after all.'

'No. He's a bit shy.' Babs thought to herself, Terry's not really my young man, and why am I making excuses for him?

'That's a pity. He would have seen what a smasher he's got. He should hang on to you. I've seen a couple of the lads from the camp giving you the eye.'

Babs grinned. 'I should hope so. I ain't standing here all done up for nothing. I can't wait for the music to start and the dancing to begin.'

'Well you're certainly not going to be lacking partners.' He looked over at Lydi. 'I'd better start to mingle, otherwise the wife might start nagging.'

Babs smiled as Frank made his way over to Lydi, who was laughing with some of the guests.

*

That night, when Babs was in bed back at Lydi's house, her head spinning with too much drink and excitement, she lay back and thought about the day. Frank had been right. She certainly hadn't lacked any partners when the dancing began. She'd danced every dance, from a waltz to the Lambeth Walk, and had laughed so much. It had been really wonderful. Lydi and Frank had gone to London, then tomorrow they were going to France for a few days. When they returned, they were going to live near Croydon airport, as that was where Frank was going to fly commercial planes. Before that, they would go into married quarters till Frank got demobbed. Lydi's life was now perfect and she would never want for anything again.

Babs took another peek at her bridesmaid's frock hanging on the wardrobe door. Perhaps she should be practical and think about getting it shortened. With that thought she fell into a deep sleep.

When Babs arrived home on Sunday, Joy handed her a letter. 'It looks like it's from that bloke in Italy again,' she said excitedly. 'Is it the one who sent you the Christmas card?'

'I would think so.'

'Auntie Babs, can I have the stamp? When I took the other one to show 'em at school, they all said you must've been a spy. I said you wasn't as you was in the Land Army,' said John.

'Course,' said Babs, grinning as she tore open the envelope and quickly scanned the one page. 'It is from Gino.' She gave the envelope to John and sat at the table to read the letter.

'Well,' said Joy. 'What's he got to say?'

'Don't be so nosy,' said Stan.

'It's all right,' said Babs looking up. 'He just wants to know if I mind him writing to me and if I am well. Here, have a read.' She passed the page to Joy.

'He's got lovely handwriting,' said Joy.

'His English is very good.'

'He says here that he misses England.'

'Whatever for?' said Stan. 'We ain't got a lot going for us over here.'

'I expect things are just as bad in Italy,' said Babs. She was very pleased that Gino had written to her and she had an address to reply to. After all, once she had got over her prejudices, he had been a real friend.

It was on August Bank Holiday Monday that Terry asked Babs to go with him and his mother to Ramsgate.

'Mum wants to go as she thinks the sea air might do her good.'

'Don't you and your mum just want to be together? Do you really want me dragging along?'

'No, she said to bring you.'

When Babs told her sister, Joy said, 'I reckon they've only asked you so you can take the old dear to the lav.'

'Thanks.'

'No, you go. It'll be a good day out.'

Babs wrinkled her nose. 'They're all right for a couple of hours, but all day?'

'Go on, it'll be a laugh.'

But Babs didn't think so.

When they boarded the train, it seemed the world and his wife had decided to do the same. After a lot of pushing and shoving, Terry managed to get his mother a seat. He and Babs had to stand.

When they got to the beach and were settled on deckchairs, Mrs Bolton said she wanted to go for a paddle.

'This'll do me feet the world of good,' she said, standing with her frock held up as the gentle ripples went over her feet.

'Mum, put yer frock down. Yer showing yer drawers.'

'I don't care, they're clean. Besides, look at those silly tarts over there splashing about, showing all they ain't got.'

Babs grinned as she too went for a paddle. Afterwards they had fish and chips for lunch and then a huge ice cream. The train wasn't so crowded when they came home, so they all sat back and enjoyed the journey.

Babs was sitting next to Terry, and her eyes began to close with the rhythm of the train. When it stopped at a station, the slamming doors woke her and she was surprised to find Terry's arm round her. She looked across at Mrs Bolton, who smiled widely.

Babs quickly sat up.

'You dropped orf and Terry was worried you might bang yer head on the winder.'

Babs smiled. 'Thanks, Terry.'

'It was my pleasure.' He slowly removed his arm.

Babs had to admit to Joy when she got home that she had enjoyed herself and it had been a lovely day.

'Well you've certainly caught the sun. Look at your face.'

'I know, and me arms.' Babs proudly showed off her red arms.

Later that evening, Terry knocked on the door and Joy answered.

'Hello, Terry, come in. I hear you had a good day today.'

He gave her one of his rare smiles. 'Did Babs say that?'

Joy nodded. 'Come on in.'

'I'd rather not, thanks all the same. Can I talk to her out here?'

'Course. I'll get her.' She went into the kitchen, where Babs was sitting at the table. 'Babs, Terry wants you. He won't come in.' As Babs passed her she whispered, 'He might wonner propose.'

'He'll be lucky,' said Babs.

As she walked up the passage she felt uneasy. 'Hello, Terry. Thanks for a smashing day.'

'Did you enjoy yourself?'

'Yes, I did. So, what can I do for you?'

'Can we go out next Sunday for the day again? We won't take Mum. I thought you might like to go to the zoo, and she couldn't do the walking. I've heard they're bringing all the animals back. What d'yer say?'

'That would be very nice, thank you.' Although Babs could think of better things to do, she was pleased that he was now trying to get his life back to normal.

On Sunday when Terry called, Babs was already waiting.

'I'm really pleased you wonner come out with

me,' he said as they walked to catch the bus.

Babs only smiled. Although she liked Terry, she felt he should look for someone who could give him the love he needed. 'How's your mum today?'

'Not too good. This warm weather really takes it out of her.'

'Still, it's cool indoors.'

Their conversation was very stilted and Babs was pleased when the bus came along. At least at the zoo they would have something to talk about.

After a surprisingly good day, they slowly made their way home. Terry had been more like his old self, the Terry Babs knew before the war. He had been laughing and making funny remarks about the animals all day, and as they walked along towards Packhurst Place, he stopped and turned to her.

'I can't thank you enough.'

'Whatever for?' asked Babs.

'Looking after me.'

Babs laughed. 'Me looking after you?'

'Yes. I was a wreck when I got back home, and if it hadn't been fer you and Mum I would have topped meself.'

'Terry, don't talk daft.'

'I ain't. I shall always be grateful, you know that, don't you?'

'I don't know what to say. I was only being neighbourly.'

'No. A lot of girls wouldn't have put up with me and the black moods I had when I got home, but you, you saved me and I will always be here if you need me.'

'Thank you. Now come on, Terry. Let's get home.' Babs was worried about how grateful he was. She was pleased that he had snapped out of his moods, but she only wanted to be friendly.

At the gate he gently kissed her cheek. 'Thank you,' he said again.

'And thank you. I really enjoyed myself today.'

His face lit up. 'Perhaps we can go somewhere next Sunday?'

'I'll see.' She turned and, walking to the front door, pulled the key through the letterbox. Looking back, she could see Terry still standing at the gate. Should she tell him to look for someone else, or should she wait just a little longer? As she thought about it, she began to get a bit annoyed with the situation. He was a grown man, with a good job; why did he need her? She gave him a wave as she stepped inside. She would give him a while longer, then tell him to find somebody else.

*

At the end of the week, Babs had another letter from Gino.

'Sounds like he's looking to come back over here,' said Stan when she told him the contents of the letter.

'I don't think so.'

'Well he does say the weather in Italy's a bit too warm and that he likes the English weather best.'

Babs laughed. 'He also says he likes working with Demetrio and his family. What sort of job would he find over here?'

'Well there's plenty of work for them that's willing to do a day's graft, and from what you've told us about him, he ain't afraid of hard work.'

'No, he's not.' Babs folded her letter and thought about the past. It would be rather nice if Gino did come here.

Chapter 24

On Saturday when Babs was coming home from work she could see a huddle of people standing around in Packhurst Place. In the middle was Joy. Babs hurried towards her.

'What's happened? What's wrong?'

'It's Mrs B. She fell down the stairs.'

'Oh no. Is she all right?'

'Terry's gone with her in the ambulance, they've taken her to the hospital.'

'Is she very bad?'

'When Terry was banging on me door I thought the war had started again. He was yelling, "It's me mum!" Me and Stan rushed in and she was on the floor in the passage. She looked terrible. We tried to stand her up but she just screamed out in pain, so Stan went and phoned for the ambulance.'

'Poor Terry.'

'He was pretty shook up.'

'He worships his mother.'

'I know. Look, come on in and have your tea. It's all ready for you.'

'Thanks, Joy.'

In the kitchen, Stan was sitting in his armchair. He looked up when the sisters walked in. 'Bit of a rum do next door.'

'So Joy was telling me.'

'The ambulance was ringing its bell when it came round the corner,' said John excitedly.

'All ambulances do that, silly,' said Ann, looking up from her drawing book.

'I know that, but we ain't had one down our street before.'

All evening Babs was waiting for Terry to knock and tell them how his mother was. When she went to the lav she looked at next door but it was all in darkness, and by the time they all went to bed there still wasn't a light showing.

On Sunday morning Babs asked Joy if she'd heard any noise from next door.

'No. I've been listening but I ain't heard a thing.'

'I think I'd better go and find out if Mrs B is all right.'

'Drink your tea first.'

When Babs had finished her tea, she went and knocked next door. There was no reply, so she knocked again, harder this time. She was just about to walk away when the front door opened and she was shocked at the sight of a bleary-eyed, unshaven Terry. His eyes were very red, as if he'd been crying, and his clothes were crumpled; it looked as if he'd slept in them.

'Terry, are you all right?'

He burst into tears.

Without thinking Babs went and hugged him. 'What is it?' She held on to him as he was shaking.

'It's Mum. She's broken her hip. I don't know what to do. I wanted to stay with her all night but they wouldn't let me and made me leave.' It all came out in a rush.

Babs gently pushed him into the house. 'Let's go inside.' As they made their way to the kitchen she asked, 'Have you had a cup of tea?'

He shook his head.

'I'll just put the kettle on.' She went into the scullery, and after putting the kettle on the gas stove, quickly returned to Terry, who was sitting with his head in his hands.

'Oh Terry, I'm so sorry. Look, have this cuppa and get yourself washed and shaved, and then we'll go to the hospital.'

He looked up. 'Will you come with me?'

'Yes.'

'Oh Babs. Thank you.'

She smiled and went and made the tea.

She sat with him for a while, then said, 'I'm going next door. While I'm gone, get yourself ready, then come and call for me. I've got to get changed and let Joy know what's happened.'

'All right.'

'Poor thing,' said Joy when Babs told them what had happened.

'I only hope Terry don't go to pieces again,' said Babs, peering in the mirror over the fireplace as she put on her lipstick. 'He's been doing well lately.' She pressed her lips together. 'That's better. I feel naked without it.'

'How long will the old dear be in hospital?' asked Stan.

'Dunno, don't know nothing about broken hips,' said Babs. She was straightening the seams of her stockings just as there was a knock on the door. 'Don't worry about dinner. I don't know what time I'll be back and we can always get something out.'

'OK.'

Joy watched her sister go, then turned to her husband and said, 'I hope she don't get too involved with him.'

'Why not? He's not a bad bloke.'

'I dunno. He's not as wild as he was before he was in the army. But it's taking him a long while to get over being a prisoner.'

'Well we don't know what he went through.'

'That's true.'

'Some of the blokes at work was saying that they know men who've gone orf their rocker since they've been home. So stop worrying about Babs, she knows what she's doing.'

But did she? Joy was worried about her sister. She would never find anybody all the while she was going out and about with Terry.

Babs smiled at Terry as they walked along to catch the bus. 'That's better. You look a bit more presentable now.'

'Didn't feel like doing anythink yesterday.'

'I know. But you mustn't let your mum see you looking so down.'

'Babs, you're like a tonic.'

'We'll get some flowers before we get to the hospital.'

He gave her a weak smile.

When they were ushered into a small room, it took all Babs's self-control not to gasp.

Mrs Bolton looked dreadful. Her long grey hair was all over the pillow and her face was ashen.

Terry bent and kissed his mother's cheek. 'Hello, Mum. It's me.'

Mrs Bolton didn't move.

Terry sat on the chair and held her hand. 'Mum, open yer eyes.'

Still no movement. Terry looked up at Babs, his own eyes full of tears.

'I'll go and see if I can find a doctor or someone to tell us how she is.' Babs left the room, pleased to get away from such sorrow. What would Terry do if his mother . . . She couldn't even begin to think of the consequences.

The nurse said she would get a doctor to talk to Mr Bolton.

Babs was in the room with Terry when the doctor came in.

'What's wrong with her?' asked Terry. 'Why won't she open her eyes?'

'She is very heavily sedated.'

'Why?' demanded Terry.

'She was in a lot of pain.' The doctor looked worried. 'She tried to get out of bed and had a fall, so we had to sedate her.'

Babs could see that Terry was getting agitated. 'How long before she will be able to talk to us?' she asked.

'I can't say. Your mother isn't in the best of health, so it will take time.'

Babs didn't explain to the doctor who she was.

'Why?' Terry asked.

'I'm afraid a lot of it is down to her limited diet.'

'But she always liked her food.'

'Was she alone during the war?'

Terry nodded.

'She may not have always been eating the right things. A lot of elderly people come here undernourished and worn out. Now I must go.'

'The bloody war again,' said Terry after the doctor had left. 'It left me a wreck, you lost yer bloke and now me mum's ill. I tell yer, Babs, if I ever set eyes on a German, I'll kill 'em with me own bare hands.'

'Look, why don't we go and find somewhere to eat?'

'I don't feel like eating.'

'Well I do.' She knew she had to get him away from here for a while. She picked up her handbag. 'Are you coming?'

He looked at his mother, then turned to Babs. 'Can we come back?'

'Course.'

Outside, Babs breathed in the fresh air. What was she doing? Why was she looking after Terry? But she knew he had no one else.

*

When they returned to the hospital, Mrs Bolton looked exactly the same.

'When will she wake up?' asked Terry.

'I don't know.' Babs could hear that his mother's breathing was hard and rasping.

'I'm gonner see if they'll let me stay all night.'

'I don't think they will.'

But Terry had made up his mind and quickly left the room.

Babs sat and looked at the poor woman. 'Please get well soon, for Terry's sake. He needs you to look after him.'

The door opened and Terry came in. 'They said I could stay if I don't get in the way.'

'Are you sure that's what you want to do?'

He nodded and gave her a faint smile. 'Do you mind taking yerself home?'

'No, course not.' Babs gathered up her handbag. 'Call in and let us know how she is, won't you?'

'Course.' He held her close and gently kissed her lips. 'Thanks, Babs. I don't know what I would do without you.'

'I'm sure you'd manage.'

'Mum getting you to come out with me was the best thing to happen to me.'

'I'd better be going.'

Outside, while Babs was waiting at the bus

stop, she thought about what Terry had said. How could she tell him she didn't want that sort of relationship? At the moment that would be too cruel.

'So how was Mrs Bolton?' asked Joy when Babs walked in.

'Not very good. She's still heavily sedated and they've let Terry stay the night.'

'That's not a very good sign.'

'That's what I thought.'

'Let's hope pneumonia don't set in. That can kill 'em.'

'Joy, I'm worried about Terry.'

'He's old enough to look after his self.'

'I know. But you should have seen him, he was like a small child.'

'If you ask me, you should keep your distance. Before you know it you'll be down the aisle and taking over where his mother left off.'

'She ain't dead yet.'

'I know, but be careful.'

'Yes, Mum.'

'I mean it, Babs. You always was a sucker for a sob story.'

Babs laughed. 'Not this time.'

As Babs walked away, Joy thought anxiously about the situation. She loved her sister and wanted to see her happy, but for some reason she couldn't put her finger on, she didn't think that Terry would be the right one for her.

Chapter 25

THERE WAS STILL no sign of life from next door when Babs left for work on Monday morning.

As she walked home that evening, she was tempted to go and see if Terry was in, but decided against it. She knew Joy would tell her if there was any news.

'There's a letter from your boyfriend,' said Joy when she walked into the kitchen.

'Boyfriend! I ain't got a boyfriend.'

'It's from Italy again,' said John eagerly.

Babs laughed.' And I suppose you want the stamp?'

He nodded.

'He's getting a bit keen, ain't he?' asked Joy.

'I've only had a few letters. I think he just needs someone to write to.' She turned to her nephew, who was waiting anxiously. 'I'll tell you what, John. When I write back, I'll ask him to send you some stamps.'

His face lit up. 'Cor, thanks. Everybody at school'll be jealous.'

'By the way, is Terry home?' Babs asked her sister.

'Not heard him,' said Joy. 'They was saying at the shop today that sometimes a broken hip can take months to heal, if ever.'

'Don't tell Terry that, he'll go mad.'

Babs sat at the table to read her letter. Now she was getting more than one page and Gino was beginning to sound a lot happier. She loved reading his letters. He would tell her about the wonderful views of the lake they had from the hotel, and about some of the people who stayed there. It was mostly Italians at the moment, but Demetrio was hoping that one day people from all over the world would come and stay. He thanked her and Lydi for being so kind when they were at the farm, which made her feel a little guilty, but he also told her not to worry about the past but to concentrate instead on the future. She folded the letter.

'You look sad,' said Joy. 'Anything wrong?'

Babs smiled. 'No. You can read it if you like.'

When Joy handed the letter back, she said, 'He sounds a nice bloke.'

'He is.'

'So why the sad face?'

'It's just that when I get a letter from him, I start to think about all that has happened.'

'You can't dwell on the past. You need to go out and find yourself a man.'

'Why? Here, you don't want to get rid of me, do you?'

'Don't be daft. You can stay here as long as you want to.'

'Thanks.'

'But honestly, Babs, I do think you should get out more and then you might find someone. After all, you're not bad-looking,' she joked.

'Thanks,' said Babs again.

'No, I reckon you could have any bloke you wanted.'

'I don't think so. Mr Right came along once; it can't happen again.'

Joy sat at the table next to her sister and touched her hand. 'There are plenty of women who lost their boyfriends and husbands in the war, so you must think about your future. You don't want to end up some miserable, cranky old maid.'

Babs laughed. 'I suppose I could always marry Terry.'

Joy looked shocked. 'You wouldn't, would you?'

'No, course not.'

'Thank Gawd for that. He don't want a wife, he wants a mother.'

'Poor old Terry. I wonder how Mrs B is.'

'He'll be in here soon enough to tell us his news. Now come on, clear the table. I want to dish up tea.'

Babs went upstairs clutching her letter. She sat on the bed and read it again. Italy sounded a lovely place. It would be wonderful if one day she could go and see Gino.

Joy called up the stairs. 'Babs, tea's ready.'

She went downstairs, but her thoughts were still on Gino.

It was later that evening that Terry knocked on the door.

When Babs opened it, she knew at once what had happened. Terry fell into her arms, sobbing uncontrollably.

After a while she asked, softly, 'Do you want to come in?'

He shook his head.

Joy came out of the kitchen. 'Is everything all . . .' She didn't finish the sentence when she saw Terry in Babs's arms.

Babs shook her head at her sister. 'I'm just going in with Terry.' She turned him round and together they made their way next door.

'Who was that?' asked Stan when Joy walked back into the room.

'Terry. He looked awful. Stan, I think his mum's dead. He was crying. I hate to see a grown man crying.'

'I'm sorry, but that's not gonner do him a lot of good.'

'Don't be so hard.'

'I'm not. It's Babs I'm worried about. He'll be leaning on her more than ever now.'

'That's what worries me too.'

'Mind you, this might be the making of him. He's got to pull himself together now there's no one to mollycoddle him. I reckon that's been a lot of his trouble: the old dear looked after him too bloody well.'

'I hope so. I hope you're right. I don't want Babs being a mother to him.'

'I shouldn't worry too much about her. She's got too much sense.'

'I hope so,' repeated Joy.

Next door, Babs gently pushed Terry into a chair. 'I'll put the kettle on. I expect you could do with a cuppa.'

He didn't answer.

Babs went into the scullery. As she waited for the kettle to boil, she looked out of the window into the yard. What would happen to Terry now? How would he cope? He was just beginning to get back to being his old self, laughing and looking happy. He had never told her or his mother how he'd been treated in the prisoner-of-war camp and he was still very bitter about it. She gave a soft sigh. There were so many victims of that terrible war. The kettle's lid bobbed up and down and Babs proceeded to make the tea.

When she returned to the kitchen, Terry looked up.

'Babs, what am I gonner do?'

She felt like shouting, 'Bloody well grow up. You ain't the first to lose your mum; remember, I lost me mum and dad *and* me boyfriend.' But she knew that wouldn't help him. 'I don't know. You'll have to go to the hospital, and to the undertaker's to make the arrangements for the funeral.'

'I don't know how to. I was only little when me dad died.'

'Don't worry, the undertaker will tell you what to do.'

'Babs, will you come with me?'

'I can't. I have to go to work.'

'Can't you take some time off?'

'No. I'm sorry, Terry, I can't afford to lose a day's pay.'

'What if I paid you?'

'No. I'm sorry, but you have to do this on your own.' She felt she was being hard, but he had to do things for himself from now on.

The following Monday, everyone in Packhurst Place came to their doors to watch the funeral of Mrs Bolton. Over the weekend, Joy had been round to every house to collect for a wreath. Only two sat on the coffin: the one from the neighbours and a huge cross of red roses from Terry. The Boltons didn't have any relations. All the front-room curtains had been drawn since the sad news became known. Londoners were very proud of showing their respects, and Mrs Bolton had been well liked.

Babs, who had taken the day off, helped Terry into the car and silently they went to the church.

As there was no one else to help out, Joy had said she would do a small lunch afterwards, but when they returned to Packhurst Place, Terry said he would rather go home. As Stan had to go back to work, Joy and Babs sat and ate the sandwiches and cake. All in all, it was a very sad affair.

'Do you think I should go in to him?' asked Babs as they sat around drinking tea.

'No. I don't mean to be hard, but he's a grown

man, and the more you run around after him, the worse he'll be.'

'But he ain't got no one and I'm worried he might go and do something stupid.'

The house was very quiet that afternoon as the children were now back at school. Joy was preparing the evening meal when suddenly noises from next door made them both jump. It sounded as if furniture was being thrown around.

Joy jumped up. 'What the bloody hell's going on?'

Babs was also on her feet. 'D'you think I'd better go in there?'

'No, I don't. It sounds as if he's gone raving mad.'

'Joy, please come with me. I'd feel awful if he's trying to . . .' She suddenly put her hand to her mouth. 'Oh my God. You don't think he's jumped off a chair.'

'Dunno, but let's be quick.'

They raced next door, where they knew the front-door key would be on a string hanging behind the letterbox.

They ran down the passage into the kitchen and threw open the door. Chairs were smashed and the table was turned over. Terry was standing with a glass in his hand, looking at them.

'What the bloody hell are you up to?' asked Babs.

'Just rearranging the furniture.' He grinned and was very unsteady.

'You're drunk,' said Joy.

'You, my dear lady, are very observant.' He pointed the glass at her.

'Your mother would be very proud of you,' said Babs as she picked up some pieces of chair.

'My mother ain't 'ere to see it, is she?'

'No, Terry, she isn't, and this kind of behaviour ain't gonner help you.'

'Oh yes, you know all about grief, don't yer. You're always telling me how you lost yer mum and dad and yer lover. Well now I've lorst me mum and dad but I ain't got a lover, so yer still one in front of me.'

'I can't believe you are talking like this,' said Joy.

'It ain't him talking, it's the drink,' said Babs.

'You shouldn't be defending him,' said Joy.

'I know. Come on, Terry, pull yourself together.'

He slumped into the armchair and cried like a baby.

Chapter 26

IT WAS BEGINNING TO get dark and Babs was still sitting with Terry. All evening he had been talking about his mum and the things she had told him about his father. Babs gathered that his mother had loved her husband very much, and after he'd died had showered all her affections on to her son.

He sat nursing the cup of tea Babs had made him. 'Sometimes, especially when I was growing up, I wished I'd had a brother or sister, then perhaps Mum would have had someone else to worry about. I did go off the rails a few times, but I always knew where me bread was buttered and she always forgave me. I think me being a prisoner made me realise what a worry I was to her when I was young.'

Babs sat quietly listening.

Earlier on Joy had brought them in some soup, and now she came back to collect the dirty crocks as an excuse to talk to Babs. While they were in the scullery she said, 'Look, if you want to come back home, Stan said he'd come and sit with him.' She kept her voice very low. 'But if you ask me, he should be looking after himself.'

'I know.' Babs gently pulled the door to the kitchen to. 'You can see what a state he's in. I can't just leave him.'

'Now you listen to me. He's got to take control of himself. You're not his keeper. What would he do if you wasn't around?'

'I know what you're saying's right, but . . .'

The door opened and Terry stood looking at them. 'It's all right, Babs. You go on home, I'll be fine.'

'Are you sure?'

'As yer sister said, I've got ter start looking after meself.'

Babs smiled. 'OK, but only if you're sure.'

'I'll be all right.'

'Come on, Babs,' said Joy, gathering up the crocks. 'Bye, Terry, see you tomorrow. I'll pop in and see if there's anything you want.'

'Thanks, Joy. Bye, Babs.' He kissed her cheek.

Outside, Babs hesitated. 'I wonder why he suddenly perked up.'

'Dunno.'

Slowly Babs followed her sister. 'You don't think . . .'

'Babs, fer Christ's sake, stop worrying about him.'

'I can't help it.'

'If you're that worried about him then I reckon you ought to marry him. That way you can keep your eye on him all the time.'

'Thanks.'

All the next day Babs worried about Terry. He had seemed so sad and vulnerable. Why was she so concerned? Did she have feelings for him that she wouldn't admit to herself?

For the rest of the week Babs sat with Terry every evening. He talked about his mum and what he'd hoped to provide her with. He talked about taking her on holiday.

It was Friday and they were sitting listening to the wireless.

'Babs, d'yer fancy coming to the pictures termorrer?'

'Yes, I do.'

'Right, that's settled. D'you want me ter pick you up from work? That way we can go for something to eat first.'

'That will be great. Terry, I'm so pleased to see

you taking an interest in things again.'

'Well, I've gotter pull me socks up. Gotter get back ter work. Can't sit around here moping for ever. If me mum was here, she'd give me a clip round the ear.'

Babs smiled.

When Babs went back home, she told her sister what Terry had said.

Stan looked up from his paper. 'Thank Gawd for that. Now perhaps we can all start to get on with our lives again.'

Babs looked at Joy, who just shrugged.

On the way back from the pictures, Terry suggested they went for a drink, and as Babs didn't have to get up for work the following morning she agreed.

Babs was pleased Terry was now like his old self again, and they sat in the pub laughing and drinking till closing time. It wasn't till Babs stood up that she felt a little drunk.

'What you been putting in me drink?' she asked.

'Nothing. Don't forget, you didn't eat much.'

'I know, I just wasn't hungry.'

Slowly they made their way back to Packhurst Place, with Babs giggling all the way home.

'You'd better come into my place and have a

cup of tea or something. Joy and Stan won't be that pleased if you go in there and wake the kids up.'

'D'you know, I think you're right, I'll have me tea first, then when I go back I'll be ever so quiet and take me shoes off.'

Terry held on to Babs as he pulled the key through the letterbox.

In the kitchen she slumped into the armchair and Terry went into the scullery.

When he returned she was asleep. She had a smile on her face, and as he stood over her watching her steady breathing, he knew he loved her, but did he stand a chance? She was the reason he'd suddenly bucked up his ideas: he knew that if he wanted her to be with him, he had to make her see that he was fine.

The following morning Babs woke and, looking about her, began to panic. She wasn't in her own bed in Joy's house; she was in Terry's house, and was this his bed? She quickly sat up and her head started spinning. What had happened? She pushed the bedclothes back and could see she only had her undies on. Fear filled her. Had he . . . She couldn't even begin to think that he would take advantage of her. Where was he?

The bedroom door opened and Terry stood

there holding a tray. 'Good morning. Here's a nice cuppa. I bet your mouth feels likes a drain. I'll do breakfast when you're ready.' He went and opened the curtains.

Babs winced against the bright sunlight. 'What time is it?'

'Nine o'clock.' He sat on the bed. 'I hope you didn't mind but I took yer frock off. I didn't want it to get all creased up as it's really pretty.'

She edged away from him. 'You've got a bloody cheek.'

'What?'

'I said you've got a bloody cheek undressing me. Is this your bed?'

'Yes. And before you go storming off, I slept downstairs.'

'I bet. Was that before or after you took advantage of me?'

'Babs, I swear I didn't touch you. Not that I didn't want to.'

'How can I believe you?'

'You can't, not if you can't remember.'

Babs lay back down again. Did she believe him? 'What am I gonner tell Joy?' she asked in a sad voice.

'The truth. You were too drunk to go home, so you stayed here for the night, and I slept downstairs.'

'She's not gonner believe that.'

'Does it matter?'

'It matters to me.'

'Babs, I know this isn't the right time, but I wonner tell you how grateful I am that you've pulled me through all me ups and downs.'

'I ain't done nothing.'

'You was there when I first got back and you went out with me, and now you've been here after Mum . . .' He stopped and looked at her. Her dark hair was tousled, and although she looked angry, there was still something lovely about her. He desperately wanted to tell her that he loved her, but he knew he would have to tread very carefully.

'Give me me frock. I feel very uncomfortable lying here in me undies.'

He passed her her dress and she quickly slipped it over her head. Then she sat up and swung her legs over the side of the bed away from Terry. She stood up and tried not to show she was having difficulty. How much had she drunk last night?

'Are you all right?'

'Yes thank you.'

'Babs. I wouldn't do anything to hurt you. You know that, don't you?'

She looked at him. Although she was almost

sure he was telling the truth, she still had niggling doubts.

He went to touch her and she jumped back. 'I should have knocked Joy and Stan up and let them take care of you.' He walked away.

'I'm sorry, Terry.' She carefully followed him down the stairs.

'I only did what I thought was right.'

When Babs walked in next door she was ready for questions.

'So where have you been?' asked her sister.

'Only next door.'

'Well I gathered that.'

'Where's the kids and Stan?'

'He's taken 'em to the swings; he thought it best they wasn't here when you showed up. Ann's been asking where you was.'

'What did you tell her?'

'That you was staying with a friend.'

'Thanks.'

'Well?'

'Well what?'

'Did you two get it together?'

Babs sat at the table. 'What d'you mean?'

'You know full well what I mean. Did you let him have his wicked way?'

'I don't know.'

'What?' It was more of an explosion than a question.

'I was very drunk.'

'I thought you went to the pictures. How did you get in that state?'

'We went for a drink afterwards and I guess I had too much.'

'So you slept together?'

'Not that I know of. I was in Terry's bed and he said he slept downstairs.'

Joy gave a false laugh. 'I bet he did. Do you believe him?'

'I don't know.'

'Well you'll find out soon enough.'

'What d'you mean?'

'Babs. What if you finish up the duff?'

Babs looked shocked. 'You don't think . . .'

'Don't know. Wouldn't like to say. By the way, there's a letter for you.'

'Thanks.' Babs looked at the writing. 'It's from Lydi. I hope she's settled now and got an address I can write to.' She sat at the table and began to read the letter. Suddenly tears ran down her cheeks.

'What is it?'

She looked up at her sister. 'It's Mr Johnson, he's dead. He was like a father to me.' She read on. Lydi had heard the news from Iris. Apparently the funeral had been well attended. Lydi knew that Babs wouldn't know about it in time to attend. She was really sorry.

Babs put the letter down and dashed outside. When she reached the lav, she was sick. As the tears streamed down her face, she realised she had never felt so lonely.

Chapter 27

ALTHOUGH BABS CONTINUED to go out with Terry, she still wasn't sure what had happened that night, and at the end of the month she was relieved when she had the curse. This was something she hated and it always made her miserable, but this month she was overjoyed. She wasn't pregnant.

'You look pleased with yourself,' said Joy when she came in from the lav.

'I am.'

'Everything all right?' asked her sister.

'Yes. It is now.'

'So you still think he might have . . . you know?'

'I don't know. He said he didn't.'

'And you believed him?'

'Well anyway, I'm not up the duff so that's got to be good news.'

'Remember not to knock 'em back like lemonade in future. I've seen you, and you can be very silly when you've had a few.'

'Yes, Mum.'

'You look happy,' said Terry as they waited at the bus stop for a bus to take them to the pictures.

'I am.' She shivered. 'Mind you, I don't like the thought of the nights drawing in and the winter coming.'

'How did you get on when you was on the farm? You must have been frozen at times.'

'It wasn't too bad when we was milking, being in the cowshed with the cows; they are very warm. The job that Lydi and me hated was picking sprouts. We were very artful. We used to try and get out of it and let Gino and Demetrio do it.'

'Well, they had to do what they was told. They were prisoners. Do you still write to him?'

Babs's face lit up. 'Yes, I had a letter from him last week. Italy sounds wonderful. I'd love to go there one day.'

'Not me. I've done enough travelling ter last me a lifetime.'

'Yes, but being in the army was different. Like Gino, you had to do as you were told.'

'I know, but we didn't have it so cushy as

them.' He looked down and shuffled his feet. 'Where's that bloody bus?'

Babs put her arm through his. 'It'll be along soon.' This was the first time Terry had seemed interested in her job or Gino, so she decided to add a bit more. 'I had a letter from Lydi. She's very happy and Frank hopes to be flying passenger planes soon.'

Terry didn't answer. Babs smiled to herself; she knew he thought Lydi was stuck up, but she didn't care.

It was a dark night and the stars were very bright as they walked home. Suddenly a shooting star raced across the sky.

'You've got to make a wish,' said Babs excitedly, standing very still with her eyes closed.

'What did you wish for?' asked Terry.

'I can't tell you that, otherwise it won't come true.'

He stood in front of her. 'Shall I tell you what I wished for?'

She looked at him. He looked very serious. 'No, as I said . . .'

'I wished that you would be my girl,' he blurted out.

'I suppose I am in a way.'

'No, really my girl. Engaged and all that.'

'Terry, I don't think I could make you happy. You know how I felt about Pete, and I don't think anyone could ever replace him.'

'I don't wonner replace him. I just want you to be here with me.'

'I don't think so.'

He grabbed her arms. 'Please, Babs, I need you and I love you. I'll do anythink for you.'

Babs struggled to get away. 'Terry. I'm sorry.'

'Say you'll think about it.'

She gave him a slight nod and continued walking. She didn't know what to say, but knew she had to let him down gently. 'We'll talk about this some other time.'

'Great.' He fell into step beside her.

It was always a quick kiss on the cheek when they said good night, and tonight Babs wasn't going to hang around talking just in case Terry had other ideas.

When she walked into Joy's kitchen, her sister looked up from her knitting and asked almost automatically, 'Had a good time?'

'Not bad. Just seen a shooting star.'

'That's lucky. Did you make a wish?'

'Yes.'

'Bet I know what you wished for,' said Stan, folding his newspaper and turning down the wireless.

'Now what would she wish for?' asked Joy. 'I

would have thought she's got everything here that she wants.'

'Money to go and see that bloke in Italy,' said Stan with a grin.

Babs laughed. 'I don't think so.' She wasn't going to tell them that that was just what she had wished for. She wanted to get away to start a new life, and according to Gino, Italy sounded just wonderful.

'Anyway, d'you want a cup of cocoa? I'm just gonner make one,' said Joy.

'Why not.' Babs followed her into the scullery.

'Joy.'

Joy stopped what she was doing and quickly turned round. Her sister's voice sounded serious. 'Is something wrong?'

Babs shook her head. 'Not really. It's just that . . .' She stopped and began stirring the cocoa in the cup. 'Joy, Terry wants us to get engaged.'

'What? And what did you say?'

'I told him no.'

'I should think so an' all.'

'Don't you like him?'

'He's all right, but I think if you marry him it'll be for the wrong reasons. You'll be just like a mother.'

'He's got a lot better lately, suggesting places we can go to and films to see.'

'But would he be any good as a husband?'

Babs shrugged.

'Here, you're not thinking of accepting his proposal, are you?'

'I can't live with you for ever and I might as well move in next door. After all, he knows how I feel about Pete.'

'But Babs, that will be for life.'

'I know.'

'I think you should wait.'

'I intend to do that, but I will give it a bit of thought. I won't tell Terry that, though. Don't wonner build his hopes up.'

'No, don't do that. Come on, I'd better take this in to Stan; he might think I've run off somewhere.'

'As if you would.' Babs held open the scullery door for her sister.

That night when they were in bed, Joy told Stan what Babs had said.

'So, do you think she might marry him?' Stan asked.

'Dunno.'

'Joy, I've been thinking . . .'

'Oh yes, wise one, and what little gem have you come up with?'

Stan levered himself up and switched on the

bedside light. 'You know you can't look after your sister for ever.'

'I know. Come on, lie down.'

'No. I've got something to tell you, and it might help Babs to make up her mind when you hear what I've got ter say.'

Joy quickly sat up. Fear ran through her. What was Stan going to tell her? 'What is it?'

'You know how fed up you are with all this queuing, the coal shortage and trying to make the rations go round?'

She nodded.

'Well, I've been finding out about going to Australia or Canada.'

'What?'

'Shh, you'll wake the kids.'

'You must be out of your mind.'

'We can go to Australia for ten pounds. Their government wants us Brits.'

'Well they can have other people, not me. I was born here and this is where I'll die.' Joy got out of bed and moved to the window. 'I would have thought that after all your traipsing around the world you would have been happy enough to settle down with me and the kids.'

'I am, but there's a lot better places out there than Rotherhithe.'

'It's always been good enough for me and me family.'

'I know.' Stan could see that Joy was beginning to get angry. He sat right up and leant back against the headboard. 'Are you really happy here? Do you mind that our kids play in the rubble of bombed-out buildings? What if, God forbid, they found an unexploded bomb and was blown to bits, would you ever forgive yourself?'

'Don't say things like that, Stan.'

'We read about that sort of thing happening all the time now.'

'Don't try to frighten me.'

'I'm not, love. I just want the best for you and the kids. Canada's so clean and the kids would love it, and as for Australia, with kangaroos and plenty of space, it would be great for them and us. And think of all that sunshine and no more queuing for grub.'

'How long have you been thinking about this?'

'Ever since I came back to this sad country. It's gonner take years to get back to how it was, that's if it ever does.'

Joy shuddered.

'Come on, love, get back inter bed. You'll freeze out there.'

Joy slowly returned to the bed.

'You're like a block of ice. Come here and let me cuddle you.'

Joy snuggled against him.

'You wouldn't have to worry about being cold in Australia.'

'No, Stan. I'm not going anywhere. You can get that idea right out of your head.'

But as Stan held on to his wife, he knew that this idea wasn't going to go away.

The following day, as Joy wandered round the few stalls that were out in the Blue Anchor market, she knew she would have to go to the shops and queue up for something for dinner. She felt miserable and her thoughts were still on what Stan had said last night. On this cold, wet, rotten morning she couldn't help thinking about sunshine. Everybody always looked happier when the sun shone, despite all the problems they had to deal with. No. She mustn't even think about that. What about Babs? Would she be able to go too?

''Allo love,' said Norah, the woman who had the haberdashery stall. The few wares she had laid out looked really pathetic. 'You look like you've lorst 'alf a crown and found a tanner.'

'I feel a bit like that this morning, trying to think of what to get my lot for dinner.'

The old lady looked about her and moved closer to Joy. 'I did 'ear they 'ad sausages round at the butcher's. That's if you're registered with that one.'

'Yes, I am.'

'Might be all bread, but you look like you could do with a bit o' cheering up, and if yer got somefink ter put in front of yer old man, well, anyfink could happen.' Norah laughed, showing her gums.

'Thanks. I *could* do with a bit of cheering up.'

''Urry up then, and if it works you can name it after me.' Her cackle followed Joy all through the market.

When Joy turned the corner she could see the queue from the butcher's stretching down the road. Should she bother to wait? Would there be any sausages left by the time she reached the door? How many would he let her have? All these questions filled her mind as she stood behind a woman who looked as miserable as Joy felt.

The thought of living somewhere with no queues and endless sunshine at this moment was certainly very appealing.

Chapter 28

That evening, Joy was deep in thought as she cooked the four sausages the butcher had let her have. All day her thoughts had been going over what Stan had said. When he was in the merchant navy, she had always known from his letters and picture postcards that he loved all the wonderful places he visited, but she had hoped he would settle down once he was home.

'Something smells good,' said Stan as he walked into the scullery. He put his arms round her waist and kissed the back of her neck.

'It's only sausages, and they've split open – got more bread in 'em than meat – but I managed to get an onion and we can have that with a bit of mash, and I got a tin of peas.'

'Wow, sounds like a real feast.'

Later that evening, as Joy and Babs were washing up, Babs said, 'You don't look very happy tonight. Is everything all right?'

Joy felt very tempted to tell her sister what Stan had said last night. Although she had been adamantly against it, she knew Stan might get the kids to wear her down. 'No, I'm fine, just a bit fed up with the weather and the thought of Christmas creeping up on us.' Fear filled her. What if this was the last Christmas they were here? What about Babs? Where would she go? She couldn't leave her sister; she was all the family she had.

'I know,' said Babs, interrupting her thoughts. 'I've been racking me brains trying to think what to get the kids and Stan and Terry. Joy, I was wondering, do you think Terry could have his Christmas dinner here with us? I don't like the idea of him being on his own.'

'Don't see why not.'

'Thanks. I'll get him to give you his ration book so he won't feel he's sponging off you.'

'OK.' Joy wasn't going to tell her sister what was really on her mind.

Babs put the plates in the cupboard. 'D'you think he'd like a pair of gloves?' she asked.

'Who?'

'Terry.'

'Dunno. Does he wear them?'

'He might when it gets really cold. What about Stan?'

'Can't see him wearing gloves.' How could Joy tell her sister that this might be the last Christmas they spent together?

That night, as soon as they were in the bedroom, Joy decided to tackle Stan and find out more. 'Why did you tell me about Canada and Australia last night?' she asked as she sat in front of the mirror, brushing her hair. The mirror was a bit spotted; it was a second-hand one she'd managed to get, as the old one had been broken in the bombing.

'I'd been reading about it in the papers and it sounded a good idea.'

'Is that all?'

'Why? You interested?'

'No, just curious, that's all.'

Stan, who was already in bed, sat up. 'Honestly, Joy, it would be wonderful for the kids. Australia is my choice. Just think of all that sunshine, and the sheep. We could live on lamb.' He sounded so enthusiastic.

Joy listened to the rain beating on the window.

'D'you know, we could go for ten pounds? Just think, the other side of the world for ten pounds.'

Joy got into bed. 'But what about Babs?'

'I expect she could come as well, and she don't mind travelling. Besides, what's she got to keep her here?'

'Nothing, I suppose.'

'Well that's settled, then.'

'Wait a minute. Don't go rushing into it. I ain't said yes yet.'

'No, but I know you're thinking about it.'

Joy didn't answer and snuggled down beside him. She had to admit it did sound wonderful. No more queuing, and all that sunshine. Stan ran his hand under her nightie and she turned towards him. She would wait till the weekend to tell her sister what they had talked about. She closed her eyes as Stan kissed her passionately and then, in his usual expert way, made love to her. Afterwards, Joy fell into a deep sleep with a smile on her face.

Terry came and spent Christmas Day with them. As he was leaving to go back home, he hugged Joy and thanked her for such a lovely day. 'I ain't had such a smashing Christmas since I was a kid. Your two know how ter keep us busy with all them games. Thanks.'

'It was our pleasure, Terry. Good night.'

At the door he took Babs in his arms and

kissed her long and hard. 'I do love you, Babs, and I want us to get engaged, but you keep turning me down.'

'Terry, I do like you, but . . .'

'There's always that *but*.'

'I'm sorry.'

He tried to kiss her again but she turned her head.

He laughed. 'I will get you to change your mind one day. You wait and see.'

'Good night, Terry.' Babs gently pushed him out of the door.

It was now 1947, and Joy still hadn't had the courage to tell her sister of Stan's plan. In some ways she was hoping he would forget it, though he said he was waiting for more information.

January was cold and wet, and the road transport strike, rationing and coal shortages were making everybody miserable. When both the children had rotten colds and looked pale and sad, even Joy began warming to the idea of emigrating, but decided to wait till Stan had more to tell her before she said anything to her sister.

'Hello, love,' said Stan one afternoon as he walked into the kitchen.

'You're early,' said Joy, holding up her cheek for a kiss.

'Can't lay bricks in this weather. If the cement freezes, the lot will come tumbling down come the thaw. Besides, I've been ter see about us emigrating.'

Joy was pleased they were on their own.

Stan took a lot of papers from his jacket pocket and sat at the table, and Joy sat next to him. 'It seems they want tradesmen, and me being a brickie fits the bill.'

'Good job you decided to do that when you left the navy.'

He smiled. 'They want young and healthy people.'

'Don't feel very healthy at the moment,' said Joy.

'We have ter have examinations just ter make sure we ain't got TB or something like that. Then we go and see a film show and talk to people and then we can make up our minds after that.' Stan jumped up and hugged Joy. 'Oh love, I'm sure this is the best thing we can do for us and the kids.'

'What if we don't like it?'

'We have ter pay our own fare back.'

'We ain't got that sort of money.'

'But we will like it. We'll be together, and

Joy, we'll have a wonderful life.'

Joy began looking at the booklets Stan had brought home. It did look very interesting and exciting. 'When have we gotter go to this film show?'

'I just have to go and tell them and they'll book us in. It seems hundreds of people are thinking of going.'

'Don't say anything to the kids or Babs just yet. Let's be really sure before we make up our minds.'

'But what about yer sister? What if she wants ter come with us.'

'I'll sound her out. Give me that leaflet, I'll leave it lying around.'

'I'm so pleased you've decided to see things my way.'

'I think what really made me think about it was you saying the kids could be blown up. I'd go mad if anythink happened to them.'

Stan kissed her cheek. 'So would I. Now, what we got for tea?'

'Spam fritters.'

'Nice,' he said, screwing up his nose.

When the children came home from school, John as usual went into the scullery looking for something to eat.

'You can have some bread and jam to stop you

from starving to death,' said Joy as she spread the butter and jam thinly on a slice of bread.

'What's this, Mum?' asked Ann, picking up the leaflet Joy had left on the table.

'Just somethink someone put in me basket when I was out shopping this morning.'

'Cor, look, John. It's all about Australia. We've been learning about that at school.'

'It looks a smashing place,' said John. 'And they've got great big kangaroos and those lovely little bears; they're all cuddly and sleep all day.'

'Well, you two have certainly been listening to what your teachers have been telling you,' said Stan, giving Joy a quick glance.

'I'd like to go there,' said John. 'When I'm grown up I'm gonner be a sailor like you, Dad, and go all round the world.'

'You'd soon get homesick,' said Ann.

'No I won't.'

'Right, now stop it, you two. Ann, lay the table.'

'Oh Mum. Why is it always me?'

'John will help. And no arguing.'

They both went into the scullery to get the knives and forks.

'Seems like we could have those two on our side,' said Stan, picking up the newspaper. 'Now we only want Babs to agree and then it'll all be down to those in charge.'

Joy didn't say anything as she took the tablecloth from the dresser drawer just as her sister walked in.

Babs stood in front of the fire, warming her hands. 'It's freezing out there. I had a job to walk along; I was worried I might slip over.'

Stan was reading his newspaper. 'I see they're gonner start bringing the troops in ter move the foodstuffs.'

'About time too,' said Joy. 'Been queuing all day.'

'So what did you manage to get for tea?' asked Babs.

'Spam fritters,' said Stan.

'Oh, nice,' Babs replied.

'There wasn't a lot of veg about today, because of the transport strike and the bad weather,' said Joy.

'I can understand that. There's nothing worse than freezing in a field picking up potatoes. I must've been pretty tough then; couldn't do it now.'

'You would if you had to,' said Joy.

'Never thought I'd say it, but even standing behind a counter in Woolworths is better than working in a cold, wet and windy field.'

'Auntie Babs, look what Mum got today. It's a thing about Australia.' John shoved the leaflet at Babs.

'Who's going to go there?'

'No one, it's just something that was put in me basket.'

'All that sunshine,' said Stan. 'That bucks you up no end.'

'That's why in many ways I envy Gino. He's always telling me how good the weather is in Italy.'

'Would you like to live there, Auntie Babs?' asked Ann.

'Where?'

'Italy?'

'It would be rather nice.'

'What about Australia?' asked Stan, sitting up and folding his newspaper.

'Dunno about that. It's a long way away and I'd never see you lot again.'

'We could all go,' said Ann.

'Oh yes, and who would pay for all of us to go flitting off to the other side of the world?'

Joy looked at Stan. 'It does say here we could all go for ten pounds.'

'Ten pounds!' Babs looked from one to the other. 'Is that true?'

'Yes,' said Stan. 'Would you be interested?'

'Dunno.'

Joy put the plates on the table. 'Don't let these get cold, not after the time it took me to get 'em.'

Babs looked at her sister and brother-in-law. Joy looked guilty. What were they planning?

Chapter 29

AFTER THEY'D FINISHED their meal of Spam and chips, Babs was in the scullery helping her sister with the washing-up. 'Joy, have you and Stan been talking about this?' She put the leaflet Ann had showed her under her sister's nose.

'We just talked about it, that's all.'

'So would you?'

'Dunno. It's a big step.'

Babs carried on drying the cutlery and putting it in the drawer. 'You ain't answered my question.'

'Don't start getting shirty with me.' Joy crossed her fingers under the washing-up water. 'I don't know what Stan's got in mind, do I?'

'Well you should do, you are married to him.'

'I know that.'

'Will you let me know if you're gonner up sticks and bugger off?'

'Babs, don't get upset. You could come with us.'

'So you are going?'

'No. As I said, we've just been talking about it, that's all.'

'Well it would've been nice to be included, that's if you wanted me to go with you.'

Joy wiped her wet hands down the front of her pinny. 'Babs, don't get upset.' She went and hugged her sister, who stood stiff and unbending. 'Honestly, Babs, we would want you with us.'

'So why keep it to yourselves?'

Joy knew her sister was angry. 'At the moment it is just an idea and we were going to talk about it with you. So, what about it? Would you come with us if we decide to go?'

'Dunno. It ain't something I'd ever thought about.'

'You're always saying you'd like to go to Italy.'

'I know, but only for a holiday. Besides, Italy ain't the other side of the world, and it wouldn't be for good.'

'What you got to keep you here?'

'Dunno. It's where we was born, and besides, Mum and Dad are still here.'

'No they're not. They've gone, and do you honestly think they'd want us to stay and not make a better life for Ann and John?'

Babs looked at Joy. 'So you really have thought this thing out, then.'

'No, not really, but I'm fed up with this weather and the strikes and all this queuing for any small morsel the government will allow us. You'd never think that we'd won the war.'

Babs walked away. She knew what her sister was saying was right. They were all fed up.

'Everythink OK, Babs?' asked Stan.

'No it bloody well ain't.'

He looked over his paper. 'It says here this is the coldest winter on record, and we're gonner have more power cuts. What with that and the food shortages, no wonder some folk want to up and leave.'

'You'd know all about that, wouldn't you?' said Babs. With that she left the kitchen and went to see Terry.

'So you're saying that Stan and Joy are going to emigrate?'

'Looks like it.'

'You thinking of going with 'em?'

'Dunno.'

'Babs, please don't go.'

'Honestly, Terry, I dunno what to do.'

'Well if you ask me, they should have told you when they first thought about it, not wait till it was nearly settled.'

'It ain't settled yet, but I know what you mean. That's what I thought. I feel really upset that they didn't include me when they first started talking about it.'

'Babs, I know I shouldn't say this, but do you think they really want you with 'em?'

She looked at Terry and tears rolled down her cheeks. 'That's what's upset me. I don't think they do.'

He held her close. 'I want you. You could marry me, and that way you'll feel wanted and loved. I really do love you, Babs.'

Babs smiled through her tears. 'It's very kind of you, Terry, but let's wait and see what's gonner happen.' The last thing on her mind was marrying him.

'But will things ever be the same between you and Joy now?'

She shrugged.

'Look. Let's have a drink.'

'No thanks.'

'Come on, it will help you relax.' He went to the dresser and brought out a bottle of whisky.

'Where did you get that from?' asked Babs in

amazement. 'Whisky's nearly as hard to get hold of as meat these days.'

He touched his nose and grinned. 'I do get around, you know.'

Babs was surprised at how Terry had changed. No longer was he the sad man who was always whining. He was now standing on his own two feet. He had a good job in the office of the building firm, and by the looks of things he was beginning to take control of his life. So did he need her? She suddenly felt all alone and unwanted.

'Here, drink up.' Terry handed her a large whisky.

'I can't drink all this.'

'I'm sure you can.' He smiled at her and sat next to her on the small sofa. 'Now. Have you decided what you might do?'

She shook her head. 'No.'

'Australia is supposed to be very nice.'

'That's what they told me.'

'So who or what will keep you here?'

'Dunno.'

'I was hoping you might have said me.'

Babs held her glass with both hands and sipped the golden liquid, which warmed her through. 'I do like you, but . . .'

Terry laughed. 'There is always that *but*. I hope

you're not going to grow into a miserable, lonely old maid.'

'So do I.'

The glow from the fire and the effect of the whisky was making Babs feel very melancholy. 'I might try and get to see Lydi; she might help me make up my mind.'

Terry put his arm round Babs and she snuggled closer. 'You wouldn't come to Australia with me, would you?' She looked up at him and giggled; the whisky and his warm, comforting arms made her feel relaxed.

Terry kissed her lips and she didn't push him away, so he kissed her again with much more passion, and this time she responded. Soon they were kissing passionately and Terry put his hand on her breast and she didn't push him away. Then he pulled up her skirt and found the parts that he never thought in his wildest dreams he would be exploring.

Babs moaned. Her sister had rejected her and all she wanted out of life was to be loved and wanted.

Terry kissed her neck and whispered, 'Babs, I want you so much.'

Her thoughts went to Pete and she lay back with her eyes closed and let Terry remove her knickers.

He wanted to carry her upstairs but he worried that the moment might be lost if he did, so he took her there on the floor in front of the fire.

Afterwards they lay silently together.

It was a while before Babs pulled on her knickers and sat back on the sofa. She fluffed up the back of her hair. 'That floor's hard.'

'I would have liked to have taken you upstairs, but . . .'

'I'm sorry, Terry, I shouldn't have led you on.'

'No, it's me who should be sorry. I took advantage of you. You was very down and the whisky lowered your resistance. But I hope you don't mind if I tell you that I did enjoy it.'

Babs didn't answer. She wanted to tell him that for the first time in years she felt wanted and like a woman again.

'Do you forgive me?' he asked.

'It takes two,' was all she was prepared to say on the matter. 'Now I must get back, otherwise Joy might think I've left home.'

'Remember, there is always a place for you here.'

'I will.' She pulled on her coat and made her way down the passage. She stood at the open front door. 'Terry, remember, this was a one-off. It won't happen again.'

'I know.' He kissed her cheek and watched her go next door.

When he got back into the kitchen, he sat on the sofa and smiled. 'Mum,' he said out loud. 'You would have forty fits if you knew I'd just had Babs on the rag rug you made all those years ago. At least now she knows I'm all man.'

Babs was pleased that Joy and Stan were in bed when she got back. She didn't want any more arguments. She sat in the armchair. She shouldn't have let Terry have his way, but to be fair, it wasn't all his fault. She'd needed to be loved. Tears ran down her face. Once again her thoughts went to Pete. Would she ever get over him? To be fair to her sister, she too felt she needed to get away, but where could she go? Australia was such a long way away. Could she save enough money to go to Italy? It would be warm, and Gino would be happy to see her and would make her very welcome.

She began reflecting on what would happen if Joy and Stan did decide to go to Australia. She could understand them wanting to leave the country for somewhere warm. Britain was a sad place at the moment. The roads were treacherous, and getting to work was a nightmare. When you got there, you had to work by candlelight because of the power cuts.

Stan couldn't work because of the weather and the strikes, and poor Joy was always trying to find something appetising for them to eat. After all these years of war, things were worse now than ever before.

Babs slowly made her way up the stairs. Next week was the beginning of March, and hopefully spring was just around the corner. With that thought she went to bed.

Chapter 30

THROUGHOUT FEBRUARY, THE main topic of conversation in every household had been the weather, the food shortages and the strikes, but now that they were in March and the cold spell had begun to ease at last, it was stories of floods that filled the papers and newsreels.

For the past couple of weeks, Babs had been seriously thinking about going to Australia, but she kept it to herself till Stan and Joy had been to see the film and had discussions with the people who were going to answer their questions and give them all the information they needed. That way, hopefully, they would be certain that this was what they wanted to do.

It was the middle of March, and one evening Terry had met Babs from work and they had gone to the cinema. When she got home, she realised that Joy and Stan had been to the meeting and seen the film on emigration. They were sitting at the table, busy looking through all the papers and information they had collected.

'I'm gonner make some cocoa; d'you two want a cup?' Babs wanted to interrupt and ask how they'd got on. She could see from her sister's flushed cheeks that she was happy and would tell her in good time.

'Yes please,' said Joy.

'Kids in bed?' asked Babs.

'Went ages ago, don't know if they'll sleep, though. Good film, was it?'

Babs screwed up her nose. 'Not bad. News was more interesting.' She couldn't wait any longer; she was dying to know how they'd got on. 'I bet your film show was better.'

'It was wonderful. We had to wait for ages, there were so many people wanting to go in.'

Images of people leaving Britain and ships sinking quickly flitted through Babs's mind.

'Oh Babs, you wait till you see it,' continued her sister. 'The scenery took my breath away and the people all seem to be happy and there is so much space.'

'And they said there was plenty of jobs for men *and* women,' said Stan, sitting back in his chair with a satisfied look on his face. 'I might not be getting as much as I am now, that's when I can work, but there seems to be plenty of scope to get on and no bad weather to worry about. So what d'yer say, Babs? Come with us.'

'Looks like you've made up your minds then.'

Joy looked at Stan and said, 'Yes we have, and we want you to come with us.'

'We've got the forms, and when we've filled 'em in, we have to have medicals and X-rays. It'll take a while but at least our names will be on the list, and if you change your mind, that's all right.'

'Mind you, we've gotter pass the medical first,' said Joy.

'That's after we've got through this lot.' Stan held up a bunch of papers.

'So what d'you say, Babs?' asked her sister.

Babs looked at all the brochures and leaflets that were strewn about the table. She hadn't told anybody that she had already decided that she was going with them.

'I'll have to tell Terry.'

'Oh Babs.' Joy jumped up and hugged her. 'I'm so happy. When did you make up your mind?'

'I didn't tell you, but a few weeks ago I slipped over on the snow. I didn't hurt meself but I thought, that's it, I've had enough of this weather. I want some sunshine.' She hugged her sister back. 'Besides. I can't let Ann and John grow up without me around, now can I?'

'I'm really chuffed, Babs,' said Stan. 'So it's look out, Oz, here we come.'

'I'd better go and make that cocoa,' said Babs, smiling as she went into the scullery. She knew she had done the right thing. Now all she had to do was tell Terry, and that wasn't going to be easy.

On Friday evening, Babs was sitting in a pub with Terry as usual. This seemed to be how their lives were going – pictures on Saturday and the pub on Fridays. It was almost as if they had settled down together. Needless to say, he wasn't happy when he heard about Babs's decision.

'I don't know why you wonner go all that way.'

'For a new life. It looks wonderful, and besides, I need something in my life. You know, Terry, you could do the same. It sounds wonderful. Is there any chance you might come as well?'

'Do yer want me to?'

'That's up to you. I ain't your keeper, you can do what you like.'

'I'd like to be with you, so would you marry me if I decided to go?'

'I don't know.'

'What if we wasn't married and we got over there and then you found yourself another bloke. Where would that leave me?'

'You might leave me for an Aussie girl.'

'I'd never do that.'

'Well think about it.'

'Sounds like you've made up yer mind.'

'I think so.'

'Always said I'd never go abroad again.'

'I know, but this time it will be what you want to do.'

'But is it?'

For the rest of the evening the conversation was stilled and difficult. Did she want Terry with her? Would he be happy over there? What if she did find someone? There were so many things to talk over and for her to get straight.

That night she was still pondering about Australia. Did she really want to go? She was quite happy about it but not so full of enthusiasm as Joy and Stan, and Terry had tried to put a damper on everything she said. She turned over. Well, that was his problem, not hers.

The next morning she had a lovely letter from Gino. Dear Gino, he sounded so content and his friendly letters always cheered her up. Italy sounded just as nice as Australia but not so far away. How much would it cost to go there?

As she waited for the bus, she decided that tonight she would write to Lydi and see if she had any ideas. She hadn't heard from Lydi for a while. She and Frank were now living near Croydon and their lives seemed to be full, but Babs would love to see her friend again and ask her advice.

'You all right?' asked Joy that evening after they'd finished their meal. 'You look a bit pale. I know the dinner ain't up to much, but corned beef ain't that bad, not when it's got potatoes and onion mixed in with it.'

'It was very nice. You do wonders for us and I'm fine.'

'Don't you go getting the lurgy or something. Don't want you going down with some terrible disease.' Joy laughed. 'You know they don't want you in Australia if you've got something wrong with you.'

Babs gave her a weak smile and went outside to the lav.

Two days later, Babs had a letter from Lydi telling her all about where they now lived and asking her if she could come down for Easter. Babs decided that it would be a wonderful opportunity to see Lydi again.

*

On Sunday the sixth of April, Babs caught the train to see her friend.

When she arrived at the station, Lydi and Frank swept her off her feet.

'You look wonderful,' said Lydi, holding her at arm's length.

'So do you two. And being a civilian certainly seems to suit you, Frank.'

'Can't grumble. It's great to see you again, Babs.' He took her arm and pulled it through his. 'Come on, the car's just outside.'

'So what's all this about the family going to Australia? Are you going with them?' asked Lydi after they had settled in the car.

'I'll tell you all about it after we get to your place.'

'Do you fancy stopping for a drink first?' asked Frank, quickly looking behind.

'No thanks.'

'I can't believe we've caught up at last,' said Lydi. 'I know we've been moving about, but now that Frank seems to be settled, we can stay here till he's too old to fly planes. And it's so good to see you again.'

'And it's good to see you. Are you working, Lydi?' asked Babs.

'Not with Frank travelling all over the place and working all hours. I like to be here when he's at home.' Lydi squeezed his arm.

'Do you like going to these different places, Frank?' Babs asked.

'Don't get much chance to see them from the ground, but they look good from the air. I've got to go to France tomorrow, so you two can chatter away all you like without me overhearing about your love life, Babs.'

'*Is* there any love life?' asked Lydi, raising one eyebrow.

'I'll tell you tomorrow.' Babs was pleased that Frank would be away. She would keep till then all she had to tell Lydi.

'I must say, that sounds very interesting and I can't wait.'

'So. No babies yet?' said Babs to steer the subject away from her.

'No,' said Frank. 'And it's not through not trying.' He laughed.

'Now whose love life we discussing?'

'Take no notice,' said Lydi.

'Just as long as you two are happy.'

'We are,' said Lydi, who was thinking about Pete and if only . . .

Babs sat back in the car. This morning she was feeling sick, and as her period was late, she had started to get very worried. She had sat in the lav and pondered the possibilities. Stupidly, up to now she hadn't even considered that that evening she'd needed to be cheered up might lead to a baby. What if she was pregnant? The disgrace. Joy would never forgive her. All her own plans for going to Australia would have to be shelved, and what about Terry? Would she have to marry him? What could she do?

'Are you sure you're feeling all right?' asked Lydi, interrupting her thoughts and looking at her quizzically.

'I'm fine.' Babs sat up. 'It looks very nice round here,' she said, watching the countryside go past. 'D'you know, I'm really looking forward to these couple of days.'

Lydi patted the back of her hand. 'And so am I. It's going to be great talking about old times.'

Chapter 31

'YOU DIDN'T HAVE to bring any food,' said Lydi as Babs placed on the deal kitchen table a small amount of butter and a twist of tea and sugar.

'You know Joy. She would hate to think that I wouldn't be sharing me rations.'

'I'll let you into a little secret: every time Frank goes abroad, he just about manages to get to some shops and bring back a few goodies.'

'But I would have thought that all of Europe would be short.'

Frank shook his head. 'Not if you know the right people. I've got a lovely wine for tonight.'

'I ain't tasted wine since your wedding.'

'Well there's a bottle or two we can work on this evening. Come on, I'll show you your room and give you a tour. It's not a very big house, but we love it.' Lydi looked so happy.

'How did you manage to get such a lovely home together, with everythink being so short or on dockets?' asked Babs after she had done the grand tour.

'Most of it is second-hand. A lot of Frank's parents' friends and mine helped out. As you know, mine aren't short of a bob or two, and money talks if you know the right people. Right, now let's have lunch.'

For the rest of the day they talked and laughed together and the memories came flooding back.

'I was sad when you wrote and told me Mr Johnson had died. I feel that part of our lives is now slipping away,' said Babs as they settled down for the evening in the comfortable room. It had a lovely beige three-piece suite and an oak coffee table that matched the sideboard. There was a warm fire blazing. To Babs, this was pure luxury. She would have plenty to tell Joy when she got home.

'Yes, it was sad. If only I'd been able to tell you in time for you to make it to the funeral, Babs. It would be great if everyone had telephones. I feel guilty that we haven't been to see Edna since we moved here, as we're not that far away, but I don't know where the time goes, and the bad weather doesn't make you want to go out if you don't have to.'

'That weather was terrible,' said Frank. 'Didn't fly for weeks, as the runways were frozen and dangerous.'

'Do you worry about him, Lydi?'

'Not really. Now, how about we try to go and see Edna sometime?'

'I told Lydi we can go in the better weather,' said Frank. 'It would be nice if you could come with us before you finish up the other side of the world.'

'I'd like that.'

'So Gino still writes to you?' said Lydi.

'Yes. His letters are lovely and his handwriting is much better than mine. I'm surprised he can read it.'

'Drink, Babs?' asked Frank.

'Please.'

'Red or white wine?'

She giggled. 'Dunno.'

'Well you'd better have both. Start with white and then you can go on to the red.'

'If you say so. D'you still hear from Demetrio?' Babs asked Lydi.

'No. I think he's too busy with his hotel and family.'

'Italy sounds wonderful.'

'Better than Australia?'

'I don't know. Not been anywhere that's exotic.'

'France was wonderful.'

'So it should be, you was on your honeymoon.'

'So what about Terry? Is he going with you?'

'I don't know.' Babs looked into her glass.

'Are you two going out together?'

'We go out together but in a friendly way. We go to the pictures and a drink, and some Sundays he has dinner with us. But that's about all.'

'Sounds as if you're a couple,' said Frank.

'But he's not going to Australia with you?' added Lydi.

'Dunno. That's up to him.'

'He hasn't got anything to keep him here, has he?' asked Frank.

'No. Well, nobody else came to his mother's funeral.'

'He'd be a damn fool to throw away an opportunity like this.'

'That's up to him.'

The conversation continued about mundane things. Babs had so much she wanted to tell Lydi, but after a few glasses of wine her eyes began to close.

'I think it's time we went up,' said Frank. 'I do

have to get up early. I'll try not to wake you.'

'I'm sorry,' said Babs. 'That was very rude of me, but I was so comfy and warm and I don't think the wine helped.'

Lydi laughed. 'I've put a hot water bottle in your bed so you've got something to cuddle up to.' She wanted to tell Babs to find a husband, as that was even better, but knew that wasn't the right thing to say to her friend. As they made their way up the stairs, Lydi wondered if Terry was right for Babs. All she knew about him was what Babs had told her, and after meeting him she didn't think he was the right one. Perhaps Babs would be a little more forthcoming when they were on their own tomorrow.

Frank had gone off to work, and as Lydi lay in bed she could hear Babs being sick. Was it the drink, or had she eaten something that didn't agree with her?

'Are you all right?' asked Lydi, looking at her friend's ashen face when she walked into the kitchen.

Babs sat at the table.

'Would you like an egg for breakfast?'

Babs shook her head and let her tears fall.

Lydi rushed over. 'What is it? What's wrong? Don't you feel well?'

Babs looked up at her. 'Lydi, I think I'm going to have a baby.'

Lydi plonked herself on the chair next to her.

'Don't look at me like that.'

'Are you sure it's not just the drink last night that's making you feel ill?'

Babs shook her head.

'So who's the father? I'm sorry, I shouldn't have asked that. I presume it's Terry's.'

'Yes.'

'But I didn't think you thought of him like that.'

'I don't.'

'So how . . .'

'I was in his house one evening and I was feeling very low, as Joy and Stan had been talking about going to Australia but hadn't said anything about including me.' She stopped to take a deep breath.

Lydi went and got her a glass of water.

After taking a sip, she continued. 'Well, to cut a long story short, I had a glass of whisky, and when he started kissing me I just let him. I needed to be loved and wanted.'

'And then it happened?'

'Yes, right there on the floor.' She let a smile lift her sad face.

'Does Joy know?'

Babs shook her head. 'I felt a bit queasy

yesterday, but I wasn't sure meself till just now, when I was sick.'

'But it could have been the drink.'

'I don't think so. I am late.'

'What are you going to do?'

'I don't know.'

Lydi looked sad. 'I wish it was me.'

'Why?'

'We have been trying ever since we got married, but it doesn't seem to happen.'

'I wish it was you as well.'

'What about Terry? Will you marry him?'

'I don't know.'

'So is this goodbye to the Australian dream?'

'Looks like it.'

Lydi hugged her friend. The thought that was filling her head was, 'It would be wonderful if you could give this baby to me.'

Soon Babs was over her morning sickness and they spent the rest of the time they had left laughing and talking.

Later that afternoon they stood at the station for a while, holding each other close.

'Now you know where we're living, you must try and come to see us more often.'

'I will.'

'And don't worry about you know what. I'm sure everything will work out fine.'

Babs just smiled back.

As she sat on the train, she thought over what Lydi had just said. How could this work out just fine? Her whole life would now be turned upside down. Did she want Terry's baby? Should she marry him? And what about when Joy and Stan found out? Would they still go to Australia?

She looked at her reflection in the window, and as the tears rolled gently down her cheeks, she thought what a mess she had made of her life.

As soon as Frank got back that evening, Lydi was full of what Babs had told her about the forthcoming baby.

'I can't believe that she would have been so silly,' said Frank when finally Lydi finished. 'Is she going to marry him?'

'I don't know.'

'I can't say I'm that keen on the man, but that's Babs's choice.'

'I don't think she wants to marry him; she doesn't love him.'

'So what's she going to do?'

'I don't know.'

'Poor Babs.'

'She's worried about what her sister will say about this.'

'Will they still go to Australia?'

'I don't know. Frank?'

Lydi's expression made Frank look at her quizzically. This was her tone when she asked for something.

'Could we adopt Babs's baby?'

'What!'

'Well, we don't seem to be having any luck, and she could come here and I'd look after her, and when the baby's born we could adopt it.'

Frank sat looking at his wife. 'How long have you been thinking about this?'

'All day. Ever since she told me.'

'You haven't said anything to Babs, have you?'

'No, of course not. I wanted to see what you said first.'

'I can't think of anything to say, I'm too stunned. I went off to work this morning, and when I get home my wife is talking about adopting her best friend's baby.'

'Yes, I must admit it does sound a bit bizarre, but it would solve a lot of problems.'

'Would it?'

Chapter 32

THE FOLLOWING MORNING, Babs lay in bed, dreading moving. Thank goodness Ann was still fast asleep, as she knew she might be sick as soon as she got out of bed. Very slowly she put her feet to the floor and then carefully made her way downstairs.

'Hello, you're up early,' said Joy, who was busy buttering some bread. 'There's a cuppa in the pot. I'm just doing a few jam sandwiches for Stan. It's all wrong that a man has to have just a jam sandwich to take with him for his lunch. In his job he needs something more substantial. A nice piece of ham or a doorstep with cheese would be really lovely, but there you are, it's no good dreaming.'

Babs didn't want to talk, as she was doing her best not to be sick. Slowly and cautiously she made her way outside. She was terrified of moving fast. Thank goodness nobody was in the lav, and as soon as she got inside she was sick. While sitting in that gloomy place recovering, the thought that was filling her mind was, 'How am I going to tell Joy?'

'Auntie Babs, hurry up, I'm bursting,' shouted John from the other side of the door.

'Just a moment.' Babs wiped her mouth and went out. 'Sorry about that, love.'

John didn't stop to talk as he dashed inside.

'You sure you're all right?' asked Joy. 'You don't look at all well. If I was you I wouldn't go into work today.'

'I think I will stay home.'

'It must have been all that food you ate yesterday.'

Babs had told her sister about the food and wine she'd had at Lydi and Frank's.

'Our stomachs just ain't used to it. But not to worry. Look, why don't you go on up to bed? I'll bring you a cuppa when they've all gone off.'

'Thanks.'

'Don't you feel very well, Auntie Babs?' asked Ann, who was getting dressed and watching Babs as she crawled back into bed.

'No, love.'

'I hope you're better soon,' said Ann as she left the room.

'Thank you.' But Babs knew that this would never be better.

She woke with a start to find her sister standing over her holding a cup of tea. 'Sorry, didn't mean to wake you. D'you feel any better?'

'Yes, I do.' She sat up slowly and took the cup and saucer from Joy.

'What d'you think's upset you?'

'I know what it is, and Joy, I think you'd better sit down.'

Joy looked worried as she sat on the bed.

'I'm finding this very hard to say, but I'd better get it over and done with . . .'

Joy held up her hand. 'You're gonner have a baby?'

Babs nodded. 'How did you guess?'

'I've had two, remember. So when did the dirty deed take place?'

'When all the talk was about you going to Australia and I thought you didn't want me with you. I was feeling very low and all alone, so I had some whisky at Terry's and . . . well, it just happened.'

'I bet it did. You are a silly cow, Babs, and no mistake. So what's gonner happen now?'

'I don't know.'

'You gonner marry him?'

'I don't know.'

'Have you thought about it?'

'That's all that's been on me mind these last few days.'

'Did you tell Lydi?'

'Yes.'

'And what did she have to say?'

'Not a lot, really.'

'I'm surprised at you, Babs. I would have thought you'd have had more sense.'

'Please don't nag.' Again Babs's tears began to fall.

Joy held her sister close. 'I'm sorry. It's just that I don't like anything like this happening to you. I'll kill Terry.'

'No, Joy, remember it takes two.'

'I know, but to take advantage of you when you was low. That wasn't very gentlemanly of him. You wait till I see him.'

'Please don't say anything till I've told him.'

'You should have said something when we was talking about Australia. You might have known that I would never leave you all alone, now would I?'

'If I marry him, that's one thing you won't have to worry about any more.'

'Babs, please don't marry him if you don't think it's the right decision.'

'What other option do I have?' Babs lay back. What had she done?

'I don't know. This is something we have to talk about.'

'I expect Stan will be angry with me.'

'I'll tell him when we're alone. Kids have ears and they're always flapping, and we don't want this to get out.'

'I'll get up now.'

Later that morning the sisters went shopping and spent most of the time queuing for anything that was on offer. Babs stood waiting in the butcher's for some liver, while Joy went round the market for veg.

At home, Babs made herself useful round the house and the baby wasn't mentioned again.

The children were home from school first, and Babs helped them with a puzzle.

'It's very hard,' said John. 'All these blue bits.'

'Are you feeling better?' asked Ann. She was a very caring girl.

'Yes thank you.'

'I hope I don't catch it.'

Babs looked at her sister and gave a half-smile. 'I don't think there's any fear of that, love.'

When they'd finished their meal and washed up, Babs said she was going next door.

'Will you be all right?' enquired Joy. 'D'you want me to come with you?'

'No, I'll be fine.'

Stan looked up from his newspaper. 'I don't think yer sister needs you to hold her hand.'

Joy didn't reply. She would tell him once the children were in bed.

''Allo, Babs,' said Terry as he opened the door. He leaned forward to kiss her cheek but she stood back. 'Everythink all right?'

'I'll tell you when we're inside.'

He stood to one side to let her pass. 'Sounds a bit mysterious,' he said as they made their way down the passage. 'Did you have a nice weekend with yer friends?'

'Yes thank you.'

'When they reached the kitchen, Babs shivered. 'It's cold in here.'

'Yer. I ain't bothered to light the fire. Too much messing about clearing out the ashes and then setting it for when I get in. It ain't worth the trouble for the short time I'm home. So I just sit in front of the oven before I go to bed. Fancy a cuppa?'

'Yes please.' She would have liked something stronger to settle her nerves, but decided against that, remembering what happened the last time she was in here drinking whisky.

'I'll just pop up and get a blanket to put round yer shoulders.'

'Thanks.'

He was back in a flash, and as he draped the blanket over her he said, 'You all right? You don't look very well.'

'I didn't go to work today.'

'Why's that?'

'I've got something to tell you.'

'You're not ill, are you?' He was moving about all the while she was trying to talk to him.

'No, not really.'

'I'll just make the tea first.' He went off to the scullery.

In a short while he popped his head round the door. 'I ain't got any biscuits.'

'No, don't worry. Tea will be fine.'

He put the tray on the table and sat next to her. 'Now, what's the problem?'

'Terry, I'm gonner have a baby.'

He was speechless. He just stared at her.

'Did you hear what I said?'

'Yes, I did.' He grinned. 'So we'll have to get married. Can't have you being talked about, can we?'

'Is that all you've got to say?'

'What else should I say?'

'That you're sorry. That we shouldn't have done it.'

'I must admit that it's a bit of a shock, but I'm not sorry.'

'Well I am. This could mean any dream I had of going to Australia has gone.'

'We can be just as happy here, Babs. Me and you and the baby.'

Babs looked at him. 'Just tell me that you didn't plan this.'

'No. Honestly. But you know I want to marry you. It can't be a big white wedding now, can it? But then again, I wasn't the first, was I?'

She wanted to slap his face and walk out, but knew she couldn't do that. She had given this a lot of thought and still hadn't come up with the right answer, but she knew that if she kept the baby and went to Australia with Joy and Stan, who would look after her? If she stayed here, she would still have to go to work to keep herself and the baby and she couldn't afford to stay on next door on her own. Terry wouldn't like it if she moved away, so what option did she have but to marry him? 'If we did get married, would we still be able to go with Joy and Stan?'

'Dunno.'

'Is that all you can say?'

'I don't want my kid to be born in Australia.

No, I'm sorry, but he's gotter be born here.'

'Perhaps he, it, will be born here and we can go afterwards.'

'We'll have to wait and see about that. Now, what about a date? We could get married in a couple of weeks if I got a special licence.'

Babs wanted to cry. This wasn't what she wanted.

'I suppose you've told Joy?'

Babs nodded.

'What she have to say about it?'

'Not a lot.'

'What about Stan?'

'Joy's telling him when the kids have gone to bed.'

'So I can expect him to be banging on me door any minute, then?'

'I don't think so.'

Terry sat back in the armchair with a big grin on his face. 'Fancy me gonner be a dad. I'm dead chuffed about that. Me old mum would have been that proud of me. She always reckoned I didn't have lead in me pencil. Well, I've proved her wrong. I forgot to ask, when is it due?'

'November sometime. I'm not sure. I've got to see a doctor.'

'That'll be nice. Just think of the Christmases we can have.'

Babs was close to tears. She felt so low and miserable.

'By the way, love, when you move in, you can shift things around a bit, but don't go chucking stuff out. Don't want too much of Mum's stuff to finish up in the dustbin. She worked hard for this lot.'

He was getting everything under control. She wanted to scream, 'I don't want to live in this dreary place. Everything is old and decrepit.' But she kept her silence.

'You going ter work termorrer?'

'I hope so. I don't know how long this morning sickness will last.'

'Look, if you want, you can give up work and live here till we get wed.'

'No, thanks all the same but I'll stay next door.'

'Not after we're married, I hope.' He grinned. 'You know, Babs, I'm really glad we're gonner get married. It'll be nice having you here all the time looking after me.'

'Is this what this is all about, you need a housekeeper?'

'No. I didn't mean that. I know I don't always say the right things, but I do love you.' He took her hand and kissed it.

She didn't know what to say. She was trapped.

Chapter 33

TERRY WALKED BABS to her door and bent to kiss her lips, but she turned her head away.

'Oh come on, Babs, don't be like this. We'll be married in a few weeks. Yer not gonner push me aside then, are you?'

'I'm sorry, Terry. Me mind's in a whirl.'

'Don't worry, love. I'll look after yer.'

She shivered.

'Go on, you'd better go in, don't want you to catch cold. And if Stan gives you any trouble, just come back to me and I'll sort him out.'

'No. I'm sure everything will be all right.' She pulled the key through the letterbox and, going inside, closed the door behind her.

She took a deep breath before she pushed open the kitchen door. Stan was dozing in his armchair. His newspaper had slid down his legs and was a crumpled heap on the floor.

Joy was sitting at the table, sewing. She looked up and smiled when the door opened. 'Hello, love. Everythink all right?'

'Yes thanks.'

Stan made a few grunting noises and, sitting up, picked up his paper. 'So you're back, then?'

Silently Babs took off her coat.

'Well?' asked Joy. 'What did he say?'

'He wants us to get married soon by special licence.'

'And what do you want to do?'

Babs sat next to her sister. 'Not got a lot of choice, have I?'

'No, suppose not.'

'What did he say about Australia?' asked Stan.

'He don't wonner go.'

'And what about you?' he asked.

She shrugged. 'If I'm married to him, then I ain't got a lot of say in the matter, have I?'

'What did he say about the baby?' asked Joy.

'He seemed pleased.'

'Just as long as he's not looking for a cheap housekeeper. You know what a wimp he used to be.'

'Don't say that, Joy.' Babs had to put on a front although she had more or less said the same thing herself earlier. 'Besides, I don't come cheap.'

'So that's it, then,' said Stan. 'I must say I'm surprised at you, Babs. Always thought you had a bit more sense.' With that he settled back down in his chair and carried on with reading his newspaper.

'If you're getting married, I'll have to find out where you go to get the extra ration allowance for a wedding. D'you think Lydi will come?' asked Joy.

Babs couldn't believe that the arrangements were being talked about already. She really didn't want to marry Terry, but she had to think of the baby.

Over the following week, Babs felt she was being swept along, and all too soon the date was set. Saturday the third of May would be her wedding day.

Ann's face was a picture when she was told that her auntie was going to be married.

'I love weddings,' she said enthusiastically. 'What colour frock am I gonner have?'

'Dunno yet,' said her mother.

'I want a pink one, and can I have flowers in me hair and carry a lovely basket? When I walk down the aisle behind you, Auntie Babs, I'll be ever so careful not to tread on your veil. Will it be a very long one that goes all the way to the floor?'

'I'm sorry, Ann,' said Babs, 'but I'm not getting married in a church.'

'Why not? Everybody gets married in a church.'

'No, some people get married in a registry office.'

'What you getting married in an office for? It won't be a proper wedding.'

'It will in the eyes of the law.'

'It ain't fair,' whined Ann. 'I wonner be a bridesmaid.'

Babs bent down and hugged her niece. 'I'm sorry.'

'I think you're being very mean. You was me mum's bridesmaid.'

'Ann, that's enough,' said her mother.

'You promised me a pink frock.'

'I will try and get you a pink one. We'll go to Brick Lane and see if we can find you a really pretty one.'

'I bet you don't.' Ann ran from the room in tears.

Babs sat at the table. 'I'm sorry. I should have thought about that.'

'Well you can't change it now.'

'I know.'

'So what about you? Have you thought about what you'll be wearing?' Joy asked.

'No.'

'Have you got any clothing coupons?'

'Not that many.'

'I can scrape a few together if that'll help.'

'I could ask Terry. I shouldn't think he uses his.'

'I'll come with you when you've got it sorted.'

'Thanks.'

Joy felt sorry for her sister. She could see that her heart wasn't in it.

On Saturday morning Babs had a letter from Lydi. As she read it she let out a sad 'Oh no.'

Joy, who was in the kitchen with her, looked up. 'What is it?'

Babs passed the letter to her sister.

My very dear Babs,

I hope you are feeling well and that dreadful morning sickness is getting better. Please don't be upset or offended at what I'm going to say, but Frank and I have been giving this a lot of thought and have had long and serious talks about you and your situation.

You see, we don't think we can have children, and we were wondering if you could come and live with us during your pregnancy and then when the baby is born we would like to adopt it.

I know this will come as a shock, but please don't be angry with us, and give it some thought. Please, please come and see us as soon as you can and we can talk about it.

You know I have always looked on you as a sister as well as my best friend, and I would hate to see you unhappy, so if we can help we will.

Love you lots,

Lydi XXXXX

Joy threw the letter on to the table. 'How dare she make such a suggestion? Don't be offended indeed. Who does she think she is, with you getting married in a couple of weeks?'

'She didn't know that when she wrote the letter. She should be getting her wedding invitation about now,' said Babs with tears in her eyes.

'If you ask me, I think she's got a bloody cheek. I know that type always get what they want and bugger everyone else.'

Babs hadn't heard her sister go off like this for years. 'Lydi's not like that. She always thinks of other people.'

'So, what? You're willing to give your baby away?'

'I didn't want it in the first place.'

'I know, but it's on its way now.'

'I wish I could turn the clock back.'

'I bet a lot of people wish that. So, what you gonner do?'

'I don't know.'

'You can still cancel the wedding if that's what you want.' There was anger in Joy's tone.

'I said I don't know.'

'You've still got a couple of weeks to think about it.'

'It would solve all me problems, and Lydi would make a wonderful mother. And I'd be well looked after till it was born.'

Joy sat at the table. 'Well I don't know about that. You would have to think about Terry. I'm sure he'd have something to say; after all, it's his baby as well.'

'I don't know what to think at the moment. You must admit it's a very tempting offer.'

'Is it? Would you be willing to give your baby away?'

'If I went to Australia, I would never see it again.'

'Well, that could be a good thing.'

'I've really got to think long and hard about this.'

'Why don't you go up the road and phone

her? That way you can tell her about how you feel.'

Babs looked at the clock on the mantelpiece. 'Look at the time. I must go to work. They're not very happy about me having the week off after I get married as it is.' She collected the letter and her hat and picked up her handbag. At the kitchen door she said, 'I'll ring her on me way home.'

'Good luck.'

Babs left, and Joy sat looking at the dirty crocks on the table. That was a right turn-up for the books. How could anyone even think about giving a baby away? What should she advise her sister to do? And what about Terry? What would he have to say about it? Babs's life was such a mess. Had Terry planned this baby hoping to keep her here? And what about this poor little mite? Its mother didn't really want it. In many ways it would be the best thing that could happen to it if Lydi took it. A good life in a nice home and a doting mother. For all she had said about her a few minutes ago, Joy knew from what Babs had told her that Lydi would be a wonderful mother. She also knew that Frank was a nice man, as he often sent pictures of planes to John. Should she give her blessing to this?

Chapter 34

ALL DAY LONG Babs seemed to be working on autopilot. She didn't remember serving anyone. Her mind was on Lydi's letter. What should she do? Deep down in her heart of hearts she would love to give her baby to Lydi, but . . . There was always a but. This was a person and you didn't just give people away. After all, Terry was its father and he was going to marry her, so the baby would have a home and parents. She was also worried that Stan and Joy would give up their dream of going to Australia if she decided not to marry Terry. What a mess she'd made of her life.

She was pleased when it was time to leave work and she quickly made her way to the nearest phone box. She dialled Lydi's number and let it ring, but there was no reply.

Slowly she made her way back home. Was this an omen? Deep down she knew she should keep this baby.

'I could see by the look on your face that you didn't manage to get hold of Lydi,' said Joy when they were alone in the scullery.

'No. What should I do?'

'That's up to you. How d'you think Terry will feel if you decide to take up Lydi's offer?'

'I don't know.'

'Just remember it's his baby as well as yours and you'd never see it again if you went to Australia.'

'I know.'

'And Terry's not a bad bloke.'

But Babs didn't want him as a husband.

The rat-tat-tat of the knocker sent Ann hurrying to the door. 'It's Mr Bolton,' she called out, coming back into the kitchen with Terry walking behind her.

He was beaming. 'You'll have to call me Uncle Terry from now on.'

'Why won't you marry my Auntie Babs in a church?'

'Well some people don't like a lot of fuss.'

Stan, who had come in from the lav, put his newspaper on the table and said, 'I suppose I should congratulate you. I'm sorry, but I don't feel like it.'

Terry looked stunned.

Joy said to Stan, 'Where's your manners?' Turning to her daughter she said, 'And as for you, young lady, I think you should be getting ready for bed.'

'I wanted to be a bridesmaid,' said Ann crossly as she stood at the door.

'I said bed.' Joy was also looking angry.

'It looks like I've caused a bit of a storm.'

'Don't worry about it,' said Joy, smiling politely. 'I'm sure it will all work out.'

'And how are you, my dear?' Terry asked Babs, kissing her cheek.

'I'm fine.'

'I've just popped in to tell you I've booked us into a hotel for our wedding night. Got to do things properly. And we will be having the wedding breakfast there as well.'

Babs was just about to speak when he held up his hand. 'The young lady was telling me that they can't ice cakes now because of the shortages so they use a cardboard cover. She showed me and it looks very authentic.'

'I was going to do something here,' said Joy.

'Thanks all the same, Joy, but it's all been taken care of.'

'But I've been to get the coupons for some extra food.'

'Don't worry about it. I'm sure you can make good use of them.'

Babs couldn't believe this was being talked about as though she wasn't there.

'Now, Babs, are you coming in with me to sort out a few details?'

She took her coat from behind the door and followed him.

Stan was on his feet as the door closed. 'That bloke makes my blood boil. He comes in here and tells us what he's done without so much as a by your leave. And I can't believe that Babs is taking it all so calmly.' Stan looked very angry.

'He has changed,' said Joy. 'And like you, I never thought our Babs would just sit there and not say a word.'

'D'you think she's frightened of him?'

'No.'

'So why's she marrying him?'

'That baby's got to have a father.'

'But not a bloke like that.'

'Now sit down, Stan, and I'll tell you something, but don't interrupt.'

He plonked himself in the armchair and remained silent till Joy had finished telling him about Lydi's offer.

'What's she gonner do?' he asked quietly.

'I don't know.'

'She can't give her baby away. It's wrong.'

'I know.'

'I know she's fond of Lydi, but to do that . . .'

'She's also worried that we won't go to Australia if she's on her own.'

'Well we can't go and leave her in the lurch, can we?'

'I think that's why she's going to marry Terry.'

'Joy, love, we can't run your sister's life for her, can we?'

'No, I know. But I want her to be happy.'

Stan sat back in his chair. 'I'm sure everything will work out fine. After all, she has got a home to go to; that's more than some poor buggers have got.'

Joy didn't answer. She was still too worried about her sister. If only Babs would show some enthusiasm about getting married.

Next door, Terry was fussing round Babs. 'Sit yourself down and I'll make you a cuppa. Is everything all right? You look very worried.'

'It's just that everything is happening so fast.'

'I think it needs to. After all, we can't have you waddling to your wedding, can we? Babs, I'm so happy. I promise you I'll look after you and our baby.'

Should she tell him about Lydi's offer?

'I'll just get the tea.'

While he was in the scullery, she thought hard about Lydi's letter. She felt trapped. What if she just upped and left and went and lived with Lydi and Frank? They would make her very welcome, especially if she agreed to what they'd asked. But that wouldn't be fair to Terry, and she knew he would come looking for her.

'You do know I love you,' he said, putting the tray on the table. He'd made it look very nice, with a flower, and a few biscuits set out on a pretty floral plate. 'Me mum's best,' he said, smiling. 'Wanted to make a bit of an effort just to show you how much I care for you.'

It was then that she decided she would fall in with his plans and marry him. 'Terry, I'd like something nice to wear, but I ain't got any coupons.'

'I'll get you some. I've got plenty, though I'll have to buy a new suit. Babs, I still can't believe you're gonner marry me.'

'And I can't believe I'm getting married in a couple of weeks.'

John hurried to the door when he heard the postman.

'It's from Italy,' he said, waving the letter. 'Auntie Babs, did you tell him all me mates thought those stamps were smashing?'

'Yes, I did, John.' She took the envelope from him. She was always pleased to get letters from Gino; they were happy and bright, telling her about his life. She had to write and tell him that she was getting married, but not to stop writing, as she regarded him as a very dear friend and loved to hear how he and Demetrio were doing.

'I'm gonner write an' tell him about Australia when we get there,' said John.

'That's nice.'

'And I'm gonner write to Frank and tell him as well.'

'That's nice,' repeated Babs, not really taking notice of what John was saying.

'I did thank him for all them smashing pictures he sent me of planes. The kids at school think you're ever so lucky, knowing all these people.'

'Was that another letter from Gino?' asked Joy.

'Yes, it was. Letters from him always make me think of the best time of my life.'

'I know, but as I said, you have to look forward now, not back.'

Babs only smiled. As John had said, she was lucky knowing people like Gino and Lydi.

The following week Lydi sent them a lovely card with a letter saying she was sorry but she and Frank couldn't come to the wedding, as he was flying and she had promised her mother, who was poorly, a visit.

When Babs received the letter she was very upset.

'If you ask me, I reckon she's worried that you might have told Terry about her offer,' Joy said.

'I told her I hadn't. I begged her not to break our friendship. She'll be the only friend I have here when you go.'

As they held each other close, Joy felt her sister's tears on her shoulder. 'Babs, please don't cry.'

'I can't help it. What a mess I've made of my life. Just one silly mistake.'

'That's all in the past. You've got to think of your future.'

Babs wiped her eyes. 'I know. And I will, for this little one's sake.' She gently patted her stomach.

At eleven o'clock on Saturday the third of May 1947, Babs, who was wearing a pale blue suit, was given away by Stan and became Mrs Terry Bolton.

The small wedding party, consisting of Joy, Stan, Ann and John, caught the bus with the bride and groom and accompanied them to the hotel for the wedding breakfast.

It was a very quiet meal. Stan did say a few words about how he thought the world of Babs, and looking at Terry, said he hoped they would be happy together. Then it was all over, and Joy and family left for home.

During the afternoon Terry had had quite a few drinks, and when they were going up to their room he decided to take a bottle of beer with him. 'Not paying any more of their fancy prices,' he said. He poured it into a glass and, raising it, said, 'To you, Mrs Bolton.' He took a big swallow and wiped his mouth with the back of his hand. 'Only wish me mum could have been here. That would have made the day just perfect.'

Babs, who was sitting on the bed, said softly, 'I know what you mean.' She looked at Terry and felt very apprehensive. Turning the gold ring on the third finger of her left hand, she knew now that she really was Mrs Bolton. What did the future hold for her?

Chapter 35

After Babs had got over her morning sickness, her pregnancy was progressing well, although she was still very unhappy. It was now August, and as she sat on the coping outside the house, trying to get a bit of fresh air in the stifling heat, she reflected on these past three months.

Since they'd got married, Terry had changed. He was miserable and snappy in the same way he'd been after he'd returned from the prison camp and after his mother died. Babs could do no right in her husband's eyes, and whenever anything went wrong, it was always her fault. She knew that she'd never wanted to marry him, but it was for the baby's sake and she knew she should try a little harder to make it work. After all, marriage was for life, and as Joy had pointed out many times, Babs wasn't the only one who had been forced to get married because of a baby. But Terry was always comparing her with his mother. Any attempt she had made to move things around in the house was met with horror and a lot of shouting, and that worried her. Did he really love her, or had it all been an act? When she wanted a new bed, she had collected the dockets they needed but he'd refused to buy one, saying their bed had been good enough for his mother. She told him it was making her back ache and went and bought a single bed, which she put in the second bedroom, saying she was going in there to sleep. He was so angry that she was afraid of what he would do, but he did get them a new bed in the end.

'All right then, love?' asked Joy when she came out of her house. 'Bit warm today.' She was holding a letter.

'That for me?' asked Babs whose letters were still delivered next door.

''Fraid not.' Babs still cringed when she recalled how it had come about that she had had to tell Gino and Lydi to still send their letters to Joy's house. Just after they were married she had had words with Terry, who hadn't been very happy about her getting letters from her friends. At first she had stood her ground, but one day he was home when the postman called, and he walked into the kitchen with a letter from Gino.

'I thought I told you to stop writing to this bloody Eyetie.'

'Why? There's no harm in it.'

'You're me wife, and I don't want yer writing to him or that stuck-up cow. D'yer hear?'

He took the letter and threw it on to the fire.

She was so angry. 'How dare you?'

'You're me wife and this is my house and you should do as you're told.'

'Why did you bother to marry me if I can't do anythink right?'

'For me son's sake.'

What Joy had said before she married Terry often came back to Babs. She was treated like an unpaid housekeeper. As she didn't want to lose her friends, she told them she had moved back in with her sister, at least until the baby was born.

They both wrote back very concerned but she told them not to worry and that it was because Terry was away a lot. She felt very guilty at telling lies, but their friendship meant so much to her.

Joy came and sat next to her.

'Well, what is it?' asked Babs.

'We've got a date for when we sail.'

Babs looked shocked, although she'd known that this day would soon come. A month ago they had had their medical examinations and were all given a clean bill of health. 'When?' she asked.

Joy looked at her and took a deep breath. 'November the thirteenth.'

'Oh no.'

Joy took her hand. 'Don't worry, we might still be here when the baby's born. After all, you've never been sure of the date.'

'But what if you're not? I want you here with me.'

Joy looked at her sister's face. She knew she wasn't happy. She also knew that she should never have let her marry Terry. But it was too late now. 'I'm sorry, Babs.'

'Not as sorry as I am. What am I gonner do without you?'

'You'll be fine.'

'Will I?'

Joy couldn't answer that. She knew things weren't too good between Terry and her sister.

'Where are you sailing from?'

'Tilbury. You must come and see us off.'

'I will if I'm still around.'

'You reckon the baby's not due till the end of the month, and we go on the thirteenth.'

'That's only a couple of weeks before.'

'I know. Most babies have a habit of coming late.'

'Knowing my luck, this one will be early.'

'In that case we'll be able to see it before we go. Come on, Babs, for once look on the bright side.'

'I'm sorry, but I don't want you to go. I'll never see you again.' Tears streamed down her face.

Joy put her arms round her sister and whispered, 'You never know what's round the corner.'

Babs was still tearful when Terry walked in.

He put his coat on the nail behind the door. 'It's been bloody hot today.' He took the newspaper from his pocket and sat at the table, then looked at Babs's red eyes and tear-stained face. 'What you got to snivel about today?'

'Joy. They're going in November.'

'About bloody time an' all, if you ask me. I'm fed up with Stan saying where they're going and what they're gonner be doing, I reckon give 'em a year or so and they'll be back. And I daresay he'll be wanting his old job back and she'll be wanting to move in next door again. Well they'll come unstuck there, with places being snapped up as fast as they come empty.' He opened his newspaper. 'What we got for dinner?'

'I thought I'd do a corned beef salad.'

'Is that all you can come up with? My old mum could make some delicious meals out o' nothing, but you, you're useless.'

'You didn't have to marry me.'

He put the newspaper on the table. 'We gonner come up with that old chestnut again, are we? And I told you before, I married you because of me son.'

'What if you don't get a son?'

'We'll worry about that if an' when it happens.'

Babs made her way into the scullery. She was fed up with hearing about his dear old mum. She looked at the food on the plates. Food that she'd spent all morning queuing for. If only she had the nerve to chuck it at him. This wasn't the sort of life she wanted. And now that Joy was going, what would her life be like? If only she could stand up to Terry, but she knew she couldn't, not all the while she was pregnant.

There were times she almost hated this baby and the way she had been trapped. Then she felt guilty. It wasn't the baby's fault; it hadn't asked to be conceived. She sometimes thought that perhaps she should have taken up Lydi's offer. But that too would have been very wrong.

Babs sat on her sister's bed, watching her pack.

'I only hope that when we stop we'll be able to buy some summer clothes, as it'll be hot when we get to Sydney. Sorry, I've already told you it's their summer.'

Babs nodded. 'I still can't believe you're going to the other side of the world.' She was very upset about her sister going away. They had always been close, and even more so since their parents were killed.

'Now don't forget, you've got the key to this place till the landlord rents it out again, so come in and take whatever you want. There'll be all our bed linen, not that any of it is in great shape. Most of the sheets I've had to put sides to middles, but you might find a use for 'em. The same with the pillows: you can always make a couple of new ones with the feathers.'

'Thanks, but you've given me loads of stuff already.'

'Only things I can't take. The rag-and-bone man said he would take the rest of the furniture, so you've got nothing to worry about. You should get a few bob for what's left.'

'Thanks,' said Babs again.

For weeks now pots, pans, glassware and all sorts had been coming in from Joy's house, much to Terry's annoyance.

'What do we want with all their old rubbish?'

Babs was angry. 'It ain't rubbish,' she shouted. 'This is my sister's home and some of the stuff belonged to my parents, so you of all people should shut up about that. After all, I have to put up with all your mother's old bits and pieces cluttering up the place.'

His face was red with anger, but she didn't care.

After the evening meal, Terry went for a drink and Babs popped in next door.

'Auntie Babs, I got this for your new baby.' Ann handed her a teddy bear.

'But Ann,' said Babs. 'This is yours.'

'I know. But Daddy said I can only take so many toys and I want the new baby to have this. Will you tell it that it's from me, Ann, its cousin who lives far away?'

Babs hugged Ann and the teddy bear. 'Of course I will, and I'll tell it all about you and what a pretty girl you are.'

'Can I give you this?' asked John, not to be outdone. He handed Babs a book about trains. 'Look, I've put inside that it's a present from your cousin John.'

'Oh John. What can I say?' Babs hugged him, all the while tears rolling down her cheeks.

Joy went into the scullery to hide her tears. All she and Babs seemed to be doing lately was crying. Sometimes she was sorry they were going so far away, but she had to think of her own children and their future.

*

Babs was waiting with Joy and the family for the bus that would start them on their way to Tilbury.

'I'm so glad you're coming to see us off,' said Joy.

'So am I. Mind you, I feel like a side of a house next to you.'

'Yes, but you'll lose it after the baby's born.'

When the bus arrived, they all sat downstairs as Babs couldn't manage the narrow stairs.

'Blimey,' said the bus conductor, looking at all the bags and parcels. 'Where're you lot off to?'

'Australia,' chorused John and Ann.

'Well I think you've got on the wrong bus,' he said, grinning. 'This one don't go to Australia.'

'We know that. We're going on a big boat,' said John.

'Well that's all right, then. Good luck.'

'Thanks,' Joy and Stan said together.

Babs also smiled, but she was worried as she'd had another twinge. She thought she'd had one earlier but hadn't taken much notice, but this one was a lot stronger. Please God, she said to herself. Don't come today of all days. Let me get home first.

'You all right?' asked Joy. 'You've gone very pale.'

Babs smiled. 'Must be all the excitement.'

But Joy was looking at her very suspiciously.

As they got off the bus, Babs doubled over.

'Oh no,' said Stan.

Joy dropped her bags and went to her sister and held her tight.

'Kids, pick up yer mum's bags,' said Stan.

Ann and John, who both looked bewildered, did as they were told.

'Can you manage to get inter that shop?'

Babs nodded, and with Joy's help slowly made her way along the pavement.

'I'll go ahead and get the shop to phone for an ambulance,' said Stan, taking control of the situation.

'I'll go with her to the hospital,' said Joy.

'You can't,' yelled Stan. 'We've gotter be on the boat by twelve o'clock.'

'But I can't leave her.'

'She'll be all right when she gets to the hospital.'

'Joy, please go. It might only be a false alarm.'

'I can't.'

'Please, Joy,' pleaded Babs as she struggled to the shop. Once again tears were streaming down her face.

'I'll wait with you for the ambulance.'

By now a small crowd had gathered, and Ann and John looked on completely baffled.

'What's wrong with Auntie Babs?' asked Ann.

'She's not feeling very well.'

'She's not gonner die, is she?' asked John.

'No, of course not. Don't talk such utter rot,' said Joy, holding on to Babs's arm as they made their way into the shop.

'Right, ambulance is on its way,' said Stan.

'What about Terry? He'll have to know,' said Babs.

'Wait till you get to the hospital and see what they say,' said Stan. 'After all, they must be used to this sort of thing happening.'

Joy stood and watched the ambulance take Babs away. More tears fell as she realised that this might be the last time she saw her sister.

Chapter 36

ON THE EVENING OF the thirteenth of November, Babs gave birth to a six pound one ounce very noisy baby girl and, as she held her close, she felt a love like no other. Terry had arrived at the hospital in the late afternoon, after he had been informed by the police that his wife was in hospital, and after Babs and his daughter had been cleaned up, he was finally allowed into the ward.

'Isn't she lovely?' said Babs, who was still cuddling the baby. She pulled the blanket down so he could see his daughter.

'I don't think so. She looks more like a monkey. And will she always keep crying like that?'

'No, course not.' But Babs was worried. She remembered reading somewhere that an unhappy pregnancy made for an unhappy baby.

'So how long you gonner be in here?'

'Nine days.'

'Nine days!' he repeated. 'Thought you'd by out by the weekend.'

'Sorry, but that's what the doctors say.'

'Good job you're not in the jungle. Those poor cows have to get up as soon as they've dropped it behind a bush.'

'This is Britain and we are a civilised country.'

'So they say.' He'd started to get fidgety.

'Don't you want to know how I got here?'

'The copper said you'd gone to hospital 'cos you was in labour.'

'Stan phoned for the ambulance as we was all on the bus when I started.'

Terry didn't say anything.

'I hope they got off all right,' said Babs.

'Don't see why not. Look, I'm gonner go. Not much point in hanging about here. Besides, I ain't had me dinner yet. I didn't see anythink ready.'

'No, I'm sorry. I didn't do the dinner before I left.'

'Well I expect I'll manage to find something.' He stood up.

Babs noted that other husbands were holding their wives' hands and looking lovingly at their babies. 'Will I see you tomorrow?'

'Dunno.'

'Could you bring me the suitcase I'd got ready to come in with?'

'Where is it?'

'In the bedroom.'

'I'll try.' He moved towards the bottom of the bed.

'Are you gonner kiss me goodbye?'

'Course.' He leant over her and quickly kissed her cheek, then walked down the ward and out of the door without turning to wave.

Babs settled down. She couldn't believe how different things were between them. For the first few weeks after they were married, she was reasonably happy. Then, as the weeks went on, Terry had changed. When she'd asked him why, he'd said he wasn't ready for marriage.

'But you was always asking me to marry you.'

'I know. But I didn't know then you'd give up work and I'd have ter support yer.'

'That's what most men do when their wives are expecting.'

'Me mum went cleaning after she got married.'

'Well I ain't going cleaning.'

And so the rot had set in.

'Mrs Bolton.' A nurse calling her name pulled the curtains round the bed and took the baby from her. 'Hello, my pretty one,' she said as she gently placed her in the cot next to Babs's bed. 'Have you and your husband settled on a name for her yet?'

'No, not really.'

'You know you have to register her?'

Babs could only nod, as the nurse had put a thermometer in her mouth and was taking her pulse. After a while she began writing something on the form that hung on the bottom of the bed. 'I noticed your husband didn't stay very long. Is everything all right?'

Babs put on her biggest smile. 'Everything's fine.'

Although Terry came in to see Babs most nights, he never stayed very long, saying he didn't know what to talk about. Everybody else was talking about the royal wedding. Papers were brought in so the mothers could see pictures of the beautiful bride, Princess Elizabeth, and her handsome husband, Prince Philip.

But it was her wedding dress that was the talk of the ward.

'Ain't she lucky getting all those clothing coupons given to her?' said Sadie in the bed opposite Babs. 'I had ter borrow me mum's frock.'

'And what about the size of that cake that was

given to 'em an all?' Jenny was holding her baby boy. 'I'd like a lump of that; very fond of a bit of fruit cake I am, and I ain't had icing fer years. My cake had a cardboard top.' The talk went on, with many of the young women reliving their wedding days, but Babs didn't join in that conversation.

Babs was waiting for a bus to take her home. As it was a Saturday she had been hoping Terry would come to meet her, but he'd told her the night before that he had to go to work. If only Joy were here, she thought. What would it be like not being able to go next door for a chat or advice? She still had Joy's key in her bag, and as soon as she had got the baby settled she would go in next door and see if there were any letters. There had been a few quiet words in the hospital when Babs told Terry that she was going to name their daughter Shirley. He'd insisted that she be called Nell after his mother. So it was Shirley Nell Bolton who arrived in Packhurst Place.

Babs placed her daughter in her cot and decided to make herself a cup of tea. She was shocked at the state of the scullery. The sink was full of dirty plates and dishes; Terry obviously hadn't washed up at all in the past nine days.

After she'd rinsed out a few cups, Babs took

her tea into the kitchen. Gazing down at her daughter, who was sleeping peacefully, she remembered what she'd heard people say about a mother's love. She knew she would love this tiny baby for ever. 'If only your daddy had been Pete,' she whispered. But she knew that couldn't be and she had to make the most of what life had given her.

The banging on the front door startled her. She hurried down the passage and was surprised to see a young man standing there.

'You Mrs Bolton?'

'Yes. Who wants to know?'

'Me and me missus. The landlord said you'd got the key to next door.'

'Yes, I have.'

'We're gonner move in there as soon as we can. Bin waiting fer you to come back from the hospital. The woman over the road said you was having a baby.'

'Yes, that's right.' Trust the neighbours to know everything, she thought. She looked at the young woman standing at the gate and smiled. The woman gave her a quick smile back.

'Can we go and have a look?'

'I'll get the key.'

'You don't have ter come with us, we can look round on our own.'

'I'd rather, if you don't mind. I think there's some of me sister's stuff I need to pick up.'

'Please yerself.'

Babs wasn't sure she liked the gruff attitude of this young man. She picked up Shirley and put Joy's key in her coat pocket.

When they pushed open the front door, Babs was pleased to see there were two letters on the floor and she quickly put them in her pocket. They made their way round the house, and Babs wanted to cry when she saw propped up on the mantelpiece a pretty postcard of a thatched cottage from Joy and the family. 'It's from me sister, they've gone to Australia.'

'That's a long way away,' said the young woman.

'Yes, it is, and I shall miss them. Do you have any children?' she asked.

The girl shook her head.

'Well I reckon this'll do us,' said the man. 'By the way, me name's Fred, Fred Dobbs, and this 'ere is Rosie.'

Babs held out her hand. 'Pleased to meet you. I'm Babs, Babs Bolton, and me husband's Terry, and this little 'un is Shirley.' Proudly she pulled back the cover, and Shirley wriggled and made snuffling noises.

'What's gonner happen to all the stuff that's left?'

'I shall be taking some of it, but the rag-and-bone man will be round to buy the rest.'

'Look, we ain't got much, so if yer like we can take some of it off yer hands. Anythink we don't want we'll let the rag-and-bone man have. We can't give yer much, though. Will that suit?'

'I think so. When do you want to move in?'

'Rosie can get the rent book and key next week, so it could be next Sat'day.'

'That'll be fine. It'll give me time to take me bits and bobs.'

Babs waved them goodbye and hurried back home to read her precious letters. The thought that flashed through her mind was, how would she be able to pick them up now? She would have a word with Mrs Dobbs on Saturday and tell her the arrangement, just as long as her husband didn't tell Terry. She sat at the table to read the letters and the card from Joy, who wrote that she had left it for Babs as she couldn't put into words how she felt about leaving her and that she hoped that one day they would meet again.

Babs cried. It hadn't really sunk in till now. Her sister, Stan and the twins were out of her life. It was almost as if they had died.

When she felt better she got round to reading

her letters. As usual, the years disappeared and she was reminded of the good times she'd had on the farm. The one from Lydi was an answer to the one Babs had written to her friend when she was in hospital. Lydi was thrilled to hear that Babs had had a baby girl and she wanted to come and see the new baby. Babs wasn't too sure about that, as Lydi had never been to her home. It was so drab and dingy. This was something she would have to think about. She looked at the other envelope and smiled. John always loved the stamps Gino sent him. She carefully opened it and read its contents.

My very dear Babs,

You may have had your baby by now. I hope it's what you want, and if it's a girl I expect she will be as lovely as you.

Lydi has written to us and said that you and Terry are very happy and that your sister and her family are going to Australia. I've been told that it is a very nice country.

Don't forget we would always make you and your family very welcome if you ever decide to come to Italy. I often think of our time together. I was very happy then.

Love, Gino

Babs sat and looked at Shirley in the cot. 'Somehow I'll have to get you down to see your Auntie Lydi. I know she's gonner love you to bits.'

Chapter 37

After the Dobbses moved in next door, Babs made herself known to Rosie, but as she worked in the local shirt factory, it was only at weekends that she managed to see her. Babs told her about some letters that might be sent to their house, as she hadn't had time to tell her friends about her new address.

Rosie did look at her a bit suspiciously when Babs said not to bring the letters in when Terry was around.

Terry wasn't interested in his daughter at all. The only thing he wanted was to start another baby, but Babs, who had moved into the other bedroom to be with her daughter, made the excuse that after all the stitches she'd had, the doctors had told her to wait. Terry wasn't happy about that.

Shirley was a delight, and Babs spent so much time pouring her love on to her daughter.

'Can't you stop that stupid noise? I'm trying ter listen ter the wireless,' Terry growled. Babs was holding her daughter and cooing softly.

'Sorry.'

'You think more of her than me.'

Babs would have liked to say that Shirley showed more affection than he did, but knew that wasn't wise.

'I had a card from Joy today.' Babs was pleased she had sent the card here. 'They stopped off at Lisbon.'

'Good for them.'

'Don't you wonner read it?'

'No.'

'Please yourself. I'm just gonner give Shirley her ten o'clock feed.'

'So when do I get me cocoa?'

'When I've finished.' She didn't like feeding Shirley in front of him, as he seemed to glare at her, and it was warmer in the scullery, with the oven door open.

Babs wasn't looking forward to Christmas without Joy and her family, and was thinking how miserable it would be without the children around. So at the beginning of December she decided to make some paper chains to cheer herself up. She had bought the packets and was busy sitting at the table sticking them with flour-and-water paste when Terry came in.

'What the bloody hell's this mess all about?'

'I'm making paper chains.'

'I can see that. Suppose this is fer her?'

Babs smiled and nodded. 'It is Christmas.' She was remembering how grateful he was last year when he spent Christmas Day with Joy and the family. Where in the world would they be now, and what sort of Christmas would they be having?

On Saturday afternoon, Terry was home from work and Babs was in the bedroom. She hadn't seen Rosie from next door since last Sunday and was thinking of popping in just to make sure she was all right. To Babs, Rosie always seemed very quiet and fragile and they only exchanged a few words whenever they met. She hesitated, however, as she didn't want to appear to be a nosy neighbour. There was a knock on the front door. Babs stood at the top of the stairs and watched Terry answer it. It was Fred. She hurried down the stairs in case there was something wrong with Rosie, then thought she would die when Fred held out an envelope.

'This come to our place. It's fer you, Mrs B,' he said.

'Thanks, Fred.'

'It's from Italy.'

Terry took the letter and closed the door as Fred moved away.

Babs felt her knees buckle and she held on to the banister.

'What's that bloody Eyetie doing sending letters next door?'

'I did tell him not to write any more. He don't know Joy don't live there any more.'

'Well it seems the bloke can't take no for an answer. Let's see what he's got ter say for himself, shall we?' He tore open the envelope.

Babs breathed a sigh of relief when she saw it was a Christmas card.

Terry threw it on the floor and walked away.

She picked it up and read the message. 'Hope you have a very Merry Christmas. Love Gino and Demetrio' was all it said. She went defiantly into the kitchen and put it on the mantelpiece.

That evening when she'd finished the washing-up and returned to the kitchen, she noticed straight away that Gino's Christmas card had gone. She looked at the fire and could see paper burning. She became very angry. 'What's wrong with you?' she yelled.

'Now what have I done?'

'You've burnt Gino's card.'

'It's only a card.'

'And it's probably the only one we'll get as well.'

'I ain't interested in Christmas.'

'Well I am. And what about your daughter?'

'What about her? She don't know nothink, all she's worried about is yelling for her food.'

Babs couldn't answer that. She left the room and went to bed.

Babs woke with a start. Terry was in her bed and was trying to get on top of her. Her nightie was being pushed up and his hands were all over her and his mouth was on hers. She wanted to scream, but was frightened she would wake Shirley. She tried hitting him and pushing him off, but he was too heavy for her and he smelt of drink.

'Go away,' she said in a loud whisper.

'I ain't going anywhere till I get me rights.'

Babs kicked and punched and squirmed under him as he tried to enter her. His arm was across her face, so she bit down hard. Releasing his hold, he yelled out, waking Shirley, who began to cry. Babs pushed him off the bed and jumped out of his way. The hatred she felt for this man surprised her.

'Come here, you.' He went to grab her, but she

was too quick for him. Just as she was about to lift Shirley out of her cot, he hit her on the back of the head. Babs dropped Shirley back into the cot and fell to the floor.

She didn't know how long she'd been lying on the cold lino. Her nightdress was round her waist and she was freezing cold, and Shirley was crying. She went to move, but her head hurt. She touched the back of her head and her fingers were wet and sticky. She felt sick and sat up carefully. The bedside light was on the floor beside her. The tops of her legs hurt. Her husband had raped her. She stood up slowly and, picking Shirley up out of her cot, took her into her bed.

As she lay comforting her daughter, Babs knew she had to get away from Terry. He was dangerous and she feared for both their lives. In the cold, dark night she tried to think of a plan.

Sunday morning Babs couldn't bring herself to talk to her husband, and Terry didn't seem to think anything was wrong as he went about his day as usual. First he went to the shop and bought his cigarettes and newspaper, then when he came back he sat in his chair and had his breakfast. Babs had made some scrambled egg with dried egg powder. Normally he would have moaned about it, but this morning he just sat and ate it without a word. Was he sorry for what he'd done?

Babs went upstairs to feed Shirley. She carefully looked over her daughter but didn't think her father would hurt her. Then again, she'd heard of some dreadful stories of men who'd had a few drinks and done something terrible. Why had Terry done this? Had he always had a violent streak but was clever enough to wait till Stan and Joy had gone? Babs looked at the tops of her own legs and arms. There was a lot of bruising – she knew she must have put up quite a struggle – and when she went to comb her hair she winced. She would have to remember to be careful doing that.

All day they moved around each other and hardly a word was said till the evening, when Terry announced that he was going to the pub.

That night when she went to bed, Babs carefully put the chair under the door handle. She wasn't going to have that happen again. She cuddled her stone hot water bottle and knew this was the end. She didn't have to put up with this life; she had to get away.

On Monday morning, Babs waited till Terry had left for work and then she packed as many things as she could take for Shirley and herself. Then, taking her Post Office book, which had a few pounds in, both their ration books and their identity cards, she left the house. She was never going to come back here ever again.

She decided she would go and stay with Lydi till she sorted her life out. She didn't have to worry about food for her daughter, as she was still breast-feeding, so she made her way to the bus full of hope.

The bus and train seemed to take for ever to get her away from London. At long last, when the train arrived at their destination, Babs went to the nearest phone box to phone Lydi.

She let it ring for a long while and felt full of despair when there wasn't any reply. Where could she go? Her arm ached holding her daughter and her bags, so she walked back into the station and sat on a seat in the waiting room.

'You all right, love?' asked the stationmaster, who had been watching her.

Babs shook her head; she couldn't speak as she was afraid the tears might fall.

'You waiting for someone?'

Babs let her tears trickle down her cheeks.

'There, there, love. It can't be as bad as that.' He sat next to her. 'You've got a good 'un there. Boy or girl?'

'Girl,' sniffed Babs.

'So where you off to?'

'I was hoping to go and see me friend, but she ain't in.'

'Was she expecting you?'

Babs shook her head.

'Look, why don't you go and have a cuppa? Leave your bags here, I'll put 'em in me office. Then after that you can give her another ring and she might be home by then.' He gave a nervous little cough. 'You know you can always go in the ladies-only waiting room if the little 'un wants her lunch.'

'Thank you. I'll do that first.'

He took her bags and she made her way to the ladies' waiting room to feed Shirley.

After she had finished feeding and changing her, Babs came out and asked her way to the nearest café.

'Don't worry about that. I've got the kettle on and it'll be nice to have a bit of company. Milk and sugar?'

Babs nodded. 'Thank you.'

'Looking forward to Christmas?' he asked.

'Not really.' Babs had noticed the paper chains in his office.

'I love it. Only wish I didn't have to work.'

'Don't you get time off?'

'Some years, depends on me shifts.'

'That must be hard for your family.' Babs hugged her warming cup.

'It is, but the kids are grown up now. You wait, give it a year or two till the little 'un can take notice, I can tell you, that's the best time, seeing their little faces on Christmas morning, there's nothing like it. So can I ask where you want to go?'

'To my friend Lydi Brook. Her husband's a pilot at Croydon.'

'I know them. Smashing-looking couple.'

'Yes, they are.'

'Have you checked the car park to see if their car's there?'

'No.'

'Well finish your tea while I pop out and have a look. If it's there, that means they've both gone off for the day. Sometimes the young lady drops her husband off.'

Babs smiled for the first time that day. 'Do you know all your regulars?'

'Only the nice ones.'

With that he left Babs full of hope.

Babs sipped her tea. She prayed that Lydi's car was there and that they'd be here soon.

Chapter 38

IT WAS GETTING DARK when Babs saw Lydi and Frank get off the train. She rushed towards them.

'Babs, what are you doing here?' yelled Lydi when she caught sight of her friend clutching her baby.

Babs couldn't speak and just burst into tears.

Lydi put her arm round Babs's shoulders and then took hold of Shirley while Frank took the bags and, holding her arm, guided Babs to the car.

They were on their way before Babs could take control of herself and allow her tears to subside. Lydi and Frank sat in silence while she told them what had happened.

'He raped you?' said Lydi in disgust.

Babs could only nod.

'Bastard,' said Frank.

Lydi was silent. When Babs finished talking, they were outside their home, and Shirley was fast asleep in Lydi's arms.

'I didn't know who else to turn to. Do you mind me coming here?'

'Do we mind?' asked Frank. 'That's a silly question. Now come on, let's get inside. It's starting to rain.'

In the warmth of their house and after the trauma of the day, Babs collapsed on a chair, exhausted.

'I'll put the kettle on,' said Frank. 'And Lydi, perhaps you could sit with Babs for a while and we can sort her room out later. I expect you're dying for a cup of tea, Babs, or would you like something stronger?'

'Tea will be fine, thanks. The stationmaster has been very good, he made me tea.'

'He's a nice bloke. How long had you been waiting for us?'

'Since this morning.'

'I'm so sorry,' said Lydi, who was sitting next to Babs and still holding Shirley.

'It wasn't your fault, you didn't know.'

'She is lovely. You must be very proud.'

Babs let a smile lift her sad face. 'I am. Oh Lydi, why is my life in such a mess?'

'I'm afraid that's the way things go. Some people are lucky and some . . . Well, I'm sure this will all work out in the end.'

'Are we likely to see anything of this husband of yours?' asked Frank.

'I don't think so. He don't know your address.'

'Well I'll tell you now that if he does show his face round here when I'm around, I won't be responsible for my actions.'

'He's got to get past me first,' said Lydi.

'By the way,' said Frank, hoping to lighten the mood, 'we've had a Christmas card from your sister.'

'I didn't know she knew your address.'

'Well, John wrote to Frank before they left, thanking him for the pictures of planes he'd sent him.'

'That was good of him. Mind you, I expect Joy had to nag him.'

'But at least when they get settled they'll be able to get in touch,' said Lydi.

'I do hope they've done the right thing,' said Babs wistfully.

'Are you sorry you didn't go with them?'

'In some ways. But then again, I might not have kept Shirley. She's my life now.'

After a while, Babs felt very tired. 'Would you mind if I went to bed?'

'Of course not. You've had a long, exhausting day. Frank has taken out one of his drawers for Shirley to sleep in, till we get something more permanent. I'll come up and give you a hand.'

'Thanks.'

'Tomorrow you and I can go shopping. We'll get Shirley some clothes and a cot. What else do you need?' asked Lydi as she fussed around them.

'That will do for now. Thank you both.'

'I'll make sure Lydi's got enough money,' said Frank.

'I have a few pounds in my Post Office book. I need to get that out first.'

'D'you know, this sounds exciting. I wish I was coming with you,' said Frank.

'We can manage perfectly well on our own, thank you,' said Lydi, grinning. Turning to Babs she said, 'I'm so happy with you being here.'

'Not as happy as me,' said Babs, knowing then that she had done the right thing.

When Babs woke, she sat up and gazed out of the window at the white frost on the trees. She couldn't believe she was safe here in the country with Lydi and Frank. She looked over at her daughter, who was wide awake and waving her arms. 'Young lady, you smell.'

After breakfast, Frank went off for the day. He kissed Lydi and then hugged Babs. 'I'm so pleased you came to us.'

'Thank you.'

'Right, as soon as we're ready we can go off to Croydon.'

'Wrap up well,' said Frank. 'Won't be back till late tonight, so don't wait for me to eat.'

'He's so thoughtful,' said Babs as he left. 'You are so very lucky.'

'I know.'

They were having lunch in a café and Babs said she couldn't remember having such a lovely day. They bought so many things for Shirley, including a second-hand cot and pram; they were going to be delivered the next day. The shops were trying hard to look Christmassy despite the shortage of goods. The atmosphere made Babs want to join in with the carol singers standing on the corner and sing out loud with them. How could things be so different in such a short time?

'She's so good,' said Lydi, who insisted on holding Shirley.

'I don't want you spoiling her,' said Babs.

As Lydi looked down at Shirley she said, 'You can't spoil anyone with love.'

Babs swallowed hard as she looked at her friend's happy face. She would make a wonderful mother. She hoped it would happen one day.

They arrived home exhausted but happy.

Since she'd left home, Babs had been trying to remember if there were any letters or anything with Lydi's address on it. She desperately hoped not. Terry was the last person she wanted to see.

On Christmas morning, the presents under the tree were opened. There was so much laughter at some of them. Babs gave Frank a pair of bright red socks and Lydi had a black feather boa.

'Where did you get these from?' asked Lydi, sashaying round the room, throwing her boa over her shoulder. 'I love it.'

'That morning I wandered down into the village there was a jumble sale on, and I thought these would come in handy.'

'It can get quite cold waiting around to get the plane de-iced, so yes, these will be great.'

'I thought you'd just managed to get some covers for the pram,' said Lydi.

'That's the good thing about having a pram, you can hide things. Right, you two, sit down, I'm gonner see to breakfast. You've only got dried egg on toast, so I don't want any complaints.'

'Would you like a sherry first?' asked Frank.

'No thank you. I need a clear head. Besides,

Shirley might get to like it, then I shall end up having a drunken daughter.' As soon as she'd said that, she thought of Terry. 'I'll go and see to breakfast.'

In the kitchen, she wondered how Terry was managing. He wouldn't be having a very merry Christmas. Was he eating? For all his faults, she couldn't help herself thinking about him. After all, he was still her husband and her daughter's father.

That evening they sat playing cards and listening to the wireless. Then, all too soon, Christmas Day was over.

In bed, Babs was wondering how she could ever pay back her friends' kindness. The food had been wonderful, and the gifts they had bought Shirley were beautiful. They included a lovely pram cover, a pretty frock for the summer and as many toys as they could find. Yes, she was truly blessed. Her thoughts often went to her sister and the family. How had they enjoyed Christmas? She missed the children and wondered if she would ever see them again. But she knew that all Christmases from now on would be better, now she had her daughter. After all, Christmas was for children.

Before New Year's Eve, Lydi had told Babs they

had to go to a dinner dance at the airport. 'I'm sorry, do you mind? Only it was arranged months ago and Frank has worked his shifts round it.'

'Don't talk daft. Course I don't. And please don't let me stop you from doing anything you would normally do if I wasn't here,' Babs reassured her.

'Thanks. We'll be home as soon as we've seen the New Year in, then we can celebrate it with you,' said Frank.

'You don't have to hurry home on my account. I'll probably be asleep anyway.'

They stood ready to go. Lydi looked positively gorgeous in a pale green fitted evening frock, with a lacy gold stole around her bare shoulders.

'Lydi, you look wonderful,' said Babs.

'What about me?' said Frank, twirling round. He was wearing an evening suit and did indeed look very handsome.

'And you look wonderful as well. Now be off with you and have a really lovely time.'

'If you are in bed we'll try not to wake you when we come home,' said Frank gently, putting Lydi's fur coat round her shoulders.

'You just go off and enjoy yourselves.' She kissed them both and waved them off. She shuddered as she closed the front door. It was a bitterly cold night.

Babs turned on the wireless. What could she do with herself? She would have liked to write to Joy and the family, but that would have to wait till they were settled. What wonderful things had they seen? She wouldn't be getting any more cards till she could write and tell them where she was. At least they had Lydi's address. She got out her last letter from Gino and decided to write to him and tell him that she had a new address for the time being. But she felt distracted and couldn't help thinking about where she would finish up. She couldn't stay here for ever; she had to find work, but what?

As she sat listening to the wireless and dozing in the chair, something made her jump. It sounded like a plant pot had fallen off the windowsill, but it wasn't windy. Terrified, she went to the window and peeped through the curtain. She went cold. Trembling, she sat on the chair. It was Terry. How could he have found her? She had been so careful not to leave Lydi's address anywhere before she left. She wanted to cry. What did he want?

'Babs. Open up. I know you're in there.' He began banging on the window.

She pulled back the curtain and shouted, 'Go away!'

'I'm not going till I've got me daughter.'

'You're not having her.'

'Let me in.'

'No.'

'I'll break this bloody window if you don't open the door.'

In the cold night air, Babs could see his breath forming clouds. 'Go away, Frank will be after you.'

'I know they're out, so open the door.' He moved away.

Babs could see he was looking round the garden and she guessed it was for something to break the glass with. 'All right. I'll open the door.' She hurried to the front door, and as she passed the stairs she looked up and prayed her daughter wouldn't wake.

As she opened the door, Terry pushed past her. 'About time too. It's bloody freezing out there. Got any whisky in the house?'

'Come through to the kitchen.' Babs didn't want him standing on the doorstep causing a scene.

He followed her and in the kitchen sat at the table. 'Nice place yer mate's got,' he said, looking around.

Babs didn't answer.

'Where's the whisky?'

'I don't know.'

'Don't give me that.' He stood up and began looking in the cupboards.

'Stop that. And go away.'

'I ain't going anywhere without a drink. After all, it's New Year's Eve and we ought to have a toast to our future.'

'I ain't got no future with you.'

'That's what you think. Where's he keep his whisky?' He carried on looking in the cupboards and slamming the doors. 'I'm bloody freezing. Standing out there fer ages waiting for 'em to go. Then I went to the pub for a quick one.' He was still searching through the cupboards.

'I'll make you a cup of tea. Then you have to go.'

He came up close to her and put his face next to hers; his breath smelt of drink. 'I ain't going nowhere till I've got me daughter.'

'Why? You wasn't interested in her before.'

'Well I am now. Where is she, upstairs?'

He moved towards the door but Babs beat him to it and barred his way.

'Get out me way.'

'Over my dead body.'

'That can be arranged.'

He smacked her across the face, making her teeth chatter and tears come to her eyes.

'Do you honestly think I'd let you anywhere

near my daughter?' Babs shouted. 'You're nothing but a bully and a drunk. Anyway, how did you get this address?'

He grinned and touched the side of his nose. 'I ain't as daft as you might think. I thought you might do a runner one day so when I saw a letter from yer mate, I copied the address down, just in case it might come in handy one day. See, it did pay off. So now 'ere I am.' He threw his arms open and laughed.

Babs was trembling. What if he knocked her out? She wouldn't be able to protect her daughter. 'Look, if I find you a drink, will you go after that?'

'Dunno. Let's have the drink, then I'll let yer know.'

She looked at the clock. It was only eleven o'clock. It would be hours before Lydi and Frank came home, and getting rid of him was the only thing she could think of as they made their way into the front room.

After a few drinks Babs knew he wouldn't go, so she quickly refilled his tumbler with whisky every time he sat back and relaxed. Gradually he began to close his eyes and she prayed that soon he would drop off to sleep. Then when Frank came home he could throw him out. As she sat watching him slowly get drunk, she wondered what good that would do now he had this address. She had to get away from him for ever. But where could she go? In time she could follow her sister. What a mess she had made of her life. She thought of her daughter upstairs and knew that she came before anything else.

'You're still up,' said Lydi on opening the front-room door. 'Oh my God!'

Babs jumped to her feet and Terry stirred. 'Shh. Don't wake him.'

'What's he doing here?'

Babs ushered her friend into the hall. 'He came for Shirley.'

'What? How did he get this address?'

'Apparently he copied it down a long while ago, just in case I might go off.' Tears began to spill down Babs's cheeks.

'And what have you done to your face?

Babs looked in the hall mirror and touched her check. There was an ugly bruise. 'Where's Frank?'

'Putting the car away. Did Terry hit you?'

Babs couldn't deny it.

'I don't fancy his chances when Frank comes in.'

'Please, Lydi. I don't want Frank to get hurt.'

Lydi grinned. 'I don't think there's any fear of

that, seeing the state Terry's in.' She nodded towards the door just as Frank came in from outside.

'It's freezing out there. What's wrong with you two? You look like you've just seen a ghost, Babs.'

'She has in a way.' Lydi went on to tell him what had happened.

'I hope you don't mind, but I've been giving him your whisky,' said Babs.

Frank held her close. 'That's the least of my concerns. It's you and Shirley I'm worried about.'

The front-room door burst open. 'Thought I heard voices.' Terry staggered forward. 'This looks very cosy, I must say. You cuddling me wife. Is this what goes on down here in the country? Everything shared. In that case, I'll have you, darling.' He went to grab Lydi, but Frank was too quick for him and punched him in the face.

Terry was flailing his arms about but none of the blows connected. Instead, it was Frank who floored Terry. He lay on the floor unconscious, with blood pouring from his nose.

Shirley began to cry and Babs quickly ran upstairs to collect her.

As she came back down the stairs holding her daughter, she turned to Frank, who was rubbing his knuckles. 'I'm so sorry. What are you going to do with him?'

'Throw him in the car and take him to the police station. I'll tell them he's an intruder who broke in and tried to kidnap a baby and rape my wife. That should do for starters.'

Babs sat down at the bottom of the stairs. 'But won't the police say he's got a right to see his daughter?'

'Not when I tell them what he's been up to. He's not fit to look after a child. Don't worry, we'll sort it out.' He kissed Shirley's cheek and then Babs. 'A happy New Year to you both.'

Babs sat cuddling her baby as tears streamed down her face, while Frank dragged Terry out to his car.

'What a start to 1948,' said Lydi.

'Let's just hope it'll get better,' said Babs.

Chapter 39

AT THE END OF January, Lydi came into Babs's bedroom just as Babs was feeding Shirley.

'There's a letter here for you from Gino. I've got one as well. I'm pleased you wrote and told him where you're now living.'

Babs could see the letters were in different envelopes. 'He should have put them in the same envelope, that would have saved him money.'

Lydi sat on the bed. 'Always the practical one who looks after the pennies.'

'I have to.'

Lydi pretended to yawn and tapped at her mouth. 'Don't let's start on that again.'

'You know how I feel about staying here and not contributing.'

'I know. Now read your letter.'

Gino was very concerned at Babs leaving her

husband and was worried about how she was managing. His letters were always warm and caring. He was such a nice man.

'What on earth did you say to the poor fellow?' asked Lydi when she'd finished reading her letter.

'I dunno.'

'Well it must have been pretty heart-rending.'

'I wrote on New Year's Eve. I was feeling very low and miserable.'

'So I gather.'

'That was before Terry arrived and . . . well, you know the rest.'

'Yes, but that's all in the past now. He won't show his face here again.'

'I hope not.'

'I'm pleased you and Gino have kept in touch.'

'So am I. He's a very good friend, and ain't that what friends are for, to listen to problems?'

'Suppose so. But it's a bit unfair to bother him when he's so far away, and he does sound very concerned about you.'

'I know.' Babs felt very guilty at pouring out her troubles to Gino. 'I'd better answer this right away to put his mind at rest.'

'That's a very good idea.'

Lydi was about to do the same. Gino was a

kind, sensitive man and Lydi knew he was very fond of Babs.

After the incident with Terry, Babs had a long chat with Frank and Lydi, and between them they had decided not to press charges as it would drag on and be more upsetting for her now she had decided to divorce him. Frank had gone to see the sergeant at the police station, and Terry had been let off with a caution and told not to bother them again.

Although Babs was beginning to feel more relaxed, she also felt that she was in the way. Although neither Lydi nor Frank had said anything, she felt awkward and knew she had to find something to do to bring in some money as her Post Office book was now empty. But what? The only skill she had was farming, and so she decided to go to the labour exchange and see if there was something she could do. She might even be able to find a job and live in. That way she would be independent again.

On Wednesday morning Lydi looked very smart and told Babs they were going to lunch to meet one of Frank's fellow pilots and his wife.

'I'm really looking forward to today,' said Lydi.

Babs knew this would be her opportunity to go to Croydon and the labour exchange.

'Now you will be all right?' asked Lydi as she pulled on her black kid gloves.

'I'm not gonner run away.'

'I didn't mean that.'

'Sorry.' Babs was trying to keep her excitement under control. Hopefully by the end of the day she would have a job and somewhere to live.

After she waved them goodbye she wrapped Shirley up against the bitter March wind and made her way to Croydon.

There were many people sitting around the labour exchange and it was a while before she was called over.

She had filled out the card and listed her skills. The woman on the other side of the desk looked at her, then at her card.

'Would you be taking the baby with you?'

'Yes.'

'What about your husband?'

Babs was wearing gloves so the woman couldn't see she wasn't wearing her wedding ring. 'I've left him.'

'I see.' The woman raised her eyebrows. 'This is not a good time of the year for work on the land.'

'I know that, but I can milk cows and do anythink on a farm. I just want a job and somewhere to live.'

'So where are you living now?'

'With a friend.'

'I see.' She raised her eyebrows again.

'She's a friend I worked in the Land Army with,' Babs wasn't going to let this woman think that she slept around.

'I'm afraid there is nothing in that line at the moment. The only thing I might be able to offer you with accommodation is a chambermaid. But I don't think they would want you to bring your baby.'

Babs felt dejected. 'Could I go and see them?'

'No, that's not possible. If you like, I could give them a ring.'

'Would you?'

'I still think the answer would be no.' She smiled. 'But I can see how much you want to work, so I'll try.'

'Thank you.' Babs crossed her fingers and waited for the woman to dial a number. From the conversation that followed, she knew that the answer was going to be no.

'I'm sorry.'

Babs stood up. 'Thanks for trying.'

'Come back again when the weather picks up, and who knows, you may be lucky.'

Babs walked away. She knew that luck had never been her bedfellow.

As she was sitting on the bus, a thought popped into her head. Should she go and see Norman, Mr Johnson's son? He knew what a good worker she was. She suddenly felt better. She would discuss this with Frank and Lydi tonight.

Babs was pleased that she was home before Lydi and Frank. After seeing to Shirley and putting her to bed, she began to start the tea. She was singing along with the wireless when she heard the front door close and voices filled the house. Babs opened the kitchen door and looked out into the passageway. She stood holding on to the door in shock. Then suddenly, without thinking, she ran and threw her arms round Gino's neck.

'How? What?' was all she could say.

'Just a moment.' Gino was smiling as he untangled Babs's arms from round his neck.

'What are you doing here in England?' She couldn't believe her eyes.

'Demetrio and myself were very worried when we received your sad letter.'

Babs looked down. 'Oh no. You haven't come all this way just to cheer me up? I'm so very sorry about that. I shouldn't have written to you when I was feeling so low.'

He touched her hand. 'That's what friends are for.'

Babs felt tears well up. She grabbed his face and kissed his suntanned cheek. 'What can I say?'

'You could offer us a cup of tea,' said Frank, who had been standing watching this scene.

'I'll see to it,' said Lydi, who was grinning fit to burst. 'Look, you two, go into the front room and I'll bring the tea in.'

'First, can I see this beautiful *bambino*?' Gino asked.

'Of course. She's upstairs and should be sleeping.'

Gino followed her upstairs, and in the bedroom she watched the tender smile he gave her daughter as he looked in the cot.

He kissed his fingers and gently touched Shirley's cheek, then turned to Babs and whispered, 'She is beautiful, beautiful, just like her mother.'

'I always liked the way you talked.'

'Babs, I was so very sorry to hear what your husband did to you.'

'Did Lydi write and tell you that?'

He nodded. 'Don't be angry with her.'

'She shouldn't have told you. That's my business.'

'She is very worried about you.'

'So why are you here?'

'Demetrio would like you to come and work in his hotel.'

'What?'

Shirley snuffled.

'Shh, you'll wake the *bambino*.'

'I can't go to Italy to work.'

'Why not?'

'This is ridiculous. Let's go and have this tea.'

When they walked into the front room, Frank stood up.

'Lydi, did you ask Demetrio for a job for me?'

'Not in so many words, but I thought it would be lovely for you to go to Italy, and so good for Shirley.'

'Thank you. Look, if you're fed up with us being around, I'll leave, but it won't be to go to Italy. I don't want you running my life.'

'Babs, I wouldn't do a thing like that. You know you can stay here as long as you like, but I know you want to be on your own.'

'So you thought you'd pack me off to Italy.'

'Babs, please sit down,' said Frank. 'Lydi didn't mean to hurt you.'

'Why is it that everybody wants to help me before they say anything to me? First it was my sister and Stan. That's how I finished up expecting; I was upset and felt unloved and that I was being pushed out. Now it's happening again.

Lydi, why didn't you say anything to me? I'm not a child.' Tears were streaming down her face.

Gino looked bewildered. 'Babs, I'm so sorry my being here has upset you. We only want you to be happy.'

'It's not your fault, Gino,' she sniffed.

'Please, Babs, sit down and listen to what Gino has to say.' Lydi was obviously upset at Babs's reaction.

'Demetrio wrote to Lydi a long while ago asking if she knew of a nice young lady who would come and work at the hotel. He needs an English lady to work for him as he's going to expand and wants English people to come to us. More so now some people have started flying to Italy.'

Babs knew this was true, as Frank had told her how they were now flying to many places in Europe and even beyond.

'So when Lydi wrote and told us about you and how unhappy you'd been, I thought I would come over and see if I could persuade you to come back with me.'

'Thanks all the same, but no thanks.'

'Why don't you look at the photographs of the hotel first before you make up your mind?' said Lydi.

'As I said, no thanks. I want my daughter to be

brought up in England. Tea's ready,' she said, going into the kitchen.

They finished their evening meal with several items that Gino had brought with him.

'That wine was delicious,' said Frank, sitting back and savouring every last drop. 'And as for the cheese . . .'

Gino laughed. 'I will have to come here more often.'

Babs looked at him, with his dark eyes and lightly tanned skin; he was now even more handsome than she remembered. But although they sat around talking about all sorts of things, including Demetrio and his family, the atmosphere was very tense, and Babs knew it was her fault. She liked Gino very much, but she couldn't help feeling uncomfortable. She gave a sigh of relief when she heard Shirley crying for her supper.

'I'll be going up now,' she said, leaving the room. 'See you all in the morning. When are you going back, Gino?'

'Probably at the weekend.'

'Good night.' As she climbed the stairs, her thoughts were racing.

Would it be such a bad thing to go to Italy with him? After all, she would have a job and a home for her and Shirley, so why was she so against it? She knew why: it was just like her sister not telling her about Australia or even discussing it with her. But these people loved her and were only trying to look after her, so why was she being so stubborn?

All night Babs tossed and turned. What should she do? She had to admit if only to herself that the thought of living in Italy and working in Demetrio's hotel with Gino did appeal to her. She was so very fond of them, and a job like that was something she could never have here in England. Plus she would never have to set foot in Rotherhithe again.

At the same time, Gino was also thinking about Babs. How thin she was, and her once bright eyes were now dull. He knew he could make her happy. The way she'd lit up when she'd first seen him convinced him that things could work out for them in Italy. He would get her on her own and try to make her see that he loved her and wanted her to be with him.

The following morning was crisp and bright.

'Babs, could you go along to the village and get some bread?' asked Lydi. She knew that Gino wanted time alone with Babs.

'I would like to come, if that's all right with you?' said Gino.

'That's fine.'

As they walked along the lane, Babs pointed out things in the hedgerows that he would remember from his time in England. They laughed at some of their memories: things like the time the cows got out, haymaking, and other things they had once shared. They also became serious when Gino said how sorry he was to hear about Mr Johnson.

'He was a very good and fair man.'

'Yes, he was,' said Babs. 'I was thinking of going to ask Norman, his son, if he would give me a job and somewhere to live.'

'Why? You don't want to be planting potatoes and picking sprouts again, do you?'

'Not really, but I don't have any other skills or a home. Lydi and Frank have been more than kind, but I do have to stand on my own two feet.'

He stopped and looked at her. 'They are not your feet?'

Babs laughed. 'Your English might be perfect, but sometimes you take things too literally.'

Gino held her shoulders. 'You could come to Italy and teach me.'

'No Gino. England is my home.'

'But you have no home. Babs, I love you and always have.'

She went to speak, but he put his finger on her lips.

'Let me finish. I have waited a long while to say this to you. When Pete came along and I saw how happy you were, well, that was the end of my dreaming about you, and we left before I could tell you my feelings.'

'Gino, what can I say? I am still legally married.'

'I know. But do you love your husband?'

'No, I always felt sorry for him.'

'So what have you got to lose?'

She couldn't answer him.

'Please, Babs, come to Italy with me. I have so much to offer you and Shirley.'

Babs knew she was weakening. 'Let's get this bread.'

They started to walk on.

Babs was deep in thought. Gino loved her. Why had she been so blind before? She remembered all the tender letters he'd written to her. He was a good, kind man who she knew would make her very happy. And what about her daughter? She had seen the way Gino had looked at Shirley. She was in turmoil.

'You all right?' Lydi asked Babs when they returned. Her friend had a glow about her. It might be the sharp weather that had put some colour in her cheeks, but today Babs looked happier than Lydi had seen her look for a very long time.

'I am very well, thank you.'

Gino was also grinning.

'You two look like a couple of cats who got the cream.'

'Pardon?'

'Don't confuse him, Lydi. I'll just take Shirley's hat and coat upstairs. Can you hold her, Gino?'

Gino took the little girl and sat at the table with her.

'You look so at home with her.'

He didn't answer.

'I'll make some coffee.' Lydi filled the kettle. She was dying to ask what had gone on.

When Babs returned, she sat at the table next to Gino. 'I suppose we'd better tell you before I burst.'

Gino looked at her, puzzled. 'Why will you burst?'

'I can see I shall have my work cut out teaching you. Lydi, I am going to Italy.' She felt a thrill when Gino squeezed her hand. 'I know I'm still married, but that doesn't matter. I know I have made the right decision for the first time in my life. I have just realised how much I love Gino.'

'But you can't marry him. You're not divorced.'

'Not yet, and he doesn't care.'

Lydi held her friend close. 'I'm so happy for you.'

'Now comes all the work. I need a passport and there's so much to sort out for Shirley.'

Meanwhile, Gino sat looking at Babs, feeling like the luckiest man alive. Babs had told him she loved him and that this time it would be for keeps.

Babs couldn't believe how happy she was. Although she would be getting a home and a job, that wasn't the reason why she had decided to go to Italy. It had been when Gino had kissed her. She'd realised that she loved him and had done so for a long, long while. She was still thinking of that incredible kiss as she started packing. She knew there would be plenty more. After all, Gino was Italian.

All That Jazz

Dee Williams

Step into the colourful world of the Jazz Age . . .

1921. When the influenza epidemic sweeping the nation claims the life of their mother, Daisy Cooper and her sister are left all alone in their squalid rooms in Rotherhithe. Working long hours to keep a roof over their heads, Daisy hates leaving little Mary alone so often, but what else can she do?

The arrival of moving pictures offers the sisters a glimpse of a magical world, and Daisy dreams of joining the beautiful dancing girls on the stage. When a chance meeting leads to an audition for the chorus line, Daisy wonders if this will be the door to a brighter future for her and Mary. But just as Daisy embarks on the glamorous path to fame, tragedy strikes . . .

Sunday Times bestseller Dee Williams' novels have been warmly acclaimed:

'An inspiring tale' *Woman's Weekly*

'Harsh times, brave hearts and always a hint of hope' *Northern Echo*

'Another wonderfully warm-hearted winner from Dee Williams . . . Her readers will be queuing up for this one' Gilda O'Neill

978 0 7553 3956 3

headline